10/13

THE
SÉANCE
SOCIETY

THE SÉANCE SOCIETY

Michael Nethercott

MINOTAUR BOOKS

A THOMAS DUNNE BOOK

NEW YORK

A THOMAS DUNNE BOOK FOR MINOTAUR BOOKS.
An imprint of St. Martin's Publishing Group.

THE SÉANCE SOCIETY. Copyright © 2013 by Michael Nethercott.
All rights reserved. Printed in the United States of America.
For information, address St. Martin's Press,
175 Fifth Avenue, New York, N.Y. 10010.

www.thomasdunnebooks.com
www.minotaurbooks.com

BOOK DESIGN BY NICOLA FERGUSON

Library of Congress Cataloging-in-Publication Data

Nethercott, Michael.
    The Séance Society : a mystery / Michael Nethercott—First edition.
        p. cm
    ISBN 978-1-250-01739-0 (hardcover)
    ISBN 978-1-250-02835-8 (e-book)
    1. Private investigators—Fiction. 2. Murder—Investigation—
Fiction. 3. Séances—Fiction. I. Title.
    PS3614.E523S23 2013
    813'.6—dc23

                                                    2013024710

Minotaur books may be purchased for educational, business, or promotional use. For information on bulk purchases, please contact Macmillan Corporate and Premium Sales Department at 1-800-221-7945, extension 5442, or write specialmarkets@macmillan.com.

First Edition: October 2013

10 9 8 7 6 5 4 3 2 1

This book is dedicated to Helen, my wife,
and to GennaRose, my daughter,
and to Rustin, my son,
...my special people...

And to the memory of my parents

ACKNOWLEDGMENTS

To Linda Landrigan, esteemed editor of *Alfred Hitchcock Mystery Magazine,* for her early recognition of Mr. O'Nelligan and Lee Plunkett. Likewise to the women and men of the Wolfe Pack. To the organizers of the Crime Bake mystery conference for providing a creative playground for authors and aficionados. To David Wilson, erudite owner of the Mystery on Main Street bookstore in Brattleboro, Vermont, for his assistance in countless ways. (And, yes, I've tried to count 'em.)

To the comrades of my youth, with a special nod to Peter Selgin, one of the finest writers I know, for being my go-to guy whenever I have a literary question. To Noree Ennis, Cynthia Atwood, Janet Reid, and, as always, my wife, Helen Schepartz, who all read and supported this novel in its fledgling form. To my family, at hand and extended: brother, offspring, in-laws, cousins, aunts, and uncles—and there are a zillion of you.

To my literary agent, Susan Gleason, who with true and steady aim guided this book to its destination. To the good people of St. Martin's Press, most notably India Cooper and her clever green pencil. A very special thanks to my talented editor Kat Brzozowski, and also to Kat's mom, who stocked their home with a bounty of Agatha Christie novels, thus infusing her daughter with the love of a lively whodunit.

I am thy father's spirit,
Doom'd for a certain term to walk the night,
And for the day confin'd to fast in fires,
Till the foul crimes done in my days of nature
Are burnt and purg'd away.

—The Ghost, *Hamlet,* Act 1, Scene 5

Truth is like the sun.
You can shut it out for a time, but it ain't goin' away.

—Elvis

THE
SÉANCE
SOCIETY

PROLOGUE

Otherworld

R. O'NELLIGAN ONCE TOLD me in his rolling brogue, "Heed well the dead, Lee, for they hover at our ears."

It wasn't the afterlife that was being discussed here, but, rather, the investigation of a murder. Now, I'll level with you, I've never fully understood the clockworks of the O'Nelligan brain, but I think what he meant was this: The slain can reveal a good deal by how they lived. And how they died. While, as I say, my friend was alluding to the physical realms, a case did fall into our laps near the end of 1956 in which "heeding the dead" referred not just to facts, but to phantoms.

Our involvement came with a prelude of sorts. On the first November evening of that year, Audrey, my perpetual fiancée, cajoled Mr. O'Nelligan and me into attending the Otherworld's Fair in White Plains, New York. This was roughly a month before those events that would eventually inspire a rash of seedy tabloid headlines. On this night, however, the focus remained on the supernatural, not the homicidal. Audrey had heard that the evening's theme was based on an old Irish myth, and, since Mr. O'Nelligan was somewhat of an old Irish myth himself, she insisted he join us.

To avoid raising any false expectations, I'll say right up front that nothing really happened on that particular night. Maybe something would have, were it not for that overzealous octogenarian who nearly poked my eye out—but I'll get to that in a moment. The drive down from Connecticut took about an hour, and we arrived at the large rented hall just as things were getting under way. The decor proved to be fairly hokey: strings of blue lights and a pair of bulky machines belching makeshift fog. This was the second evening of the four-day event, which had begun, fittingly, on Halloween. While the organizers had grandiosely named it after the World's Fair of '39, it was, without question, a much humbler affair. Still, close to three hundred people had crammed into the space this night in anticipation of spirited high jinks. Or, as in Audrey's case, hoping for a genuine otherworldly experience.

"You just need to be open-minded, Lee," she said as we settled into our seats.

"Aren't I always?"

"Do you really want me to answer that?"

"Probably not."

"Listen, we've all lost loved ones along the way—your parents, my grandparents, Mr. O'Nelligan's wife. It's natural to wonder what becomes of us after death."

"This crowd isn't just here to wonder—they've come to meet Casper the Friendly Ghost."

"Lower your voice!" Audrey told me. "You'll offend someone."

"Who? Casper?"

"Look, my sister Clare swears that when she was ten our grandmother appeared by her bed and stroked her hair. Then the next day, do you know what we found out?"

"That your grandmother had just died."

"Have I told you this before?"

"No, but isn't that how all these ghostly stories end? With some loved one appearing smack-dab at the moment of death?"

I never got Audrey's reply, because, just then, a wide, curvy woman in her late fifties sashayed onto the stage and commandeered the microphone. Her dyed hair was only a shade or two shy of canary yellow, and she had squeezed herself into a garish red gown draped with a black boa. The woman winked at the audience and declared in a throaty bellow, "Good evening, chums! It's time to shake up the spooks! Are you ready? Why, sure you are!"

"Now, who would this be?" Mr. O'Nelligan asked us. Seated to my left, he looked typically dapper and O'Nelligan-ish. The man never lacked for vest and tie, which tonight he had augmented with a tweed jacket. Slim and compact, he was somewhat into his sixties, about twice my age. Deep soft eyes, a balding forehead, and a trimmed gray beard gave him the look of an antique apostle.

Audrey leaned over me to answer him. "That's the one and only Sassafras Miller."

"Quite the moniker," Mr. O'Nelligan observed.

"It is, isn't it? In her younger days, she had parts in a few movies, second banana roles, but her chief fame comes from the Carefree Cabana."

"Carefree Cabana? What, pray tell, is that?"

I joined in. "That's a speakeasy she hosted back during

Prohibition. They say in her prime she was a real queen bee. Ran a nonstop party."

Sassafras played to the crowd. "I'm here to welcome all you mortals to the Otherworld's Fair. Ain't scared, are ya? Good! 'Cause the spirits can smell fear. Which is better than smelling *like* fear, such as two or three of my ex-husbands. Ha!" She didn't wait for laughter but plowed blithely ahead. "Now I'm going to introduce you to the fella who put this whole shebang together. Nobody else has the smarts to pull off something like this, and, frankly, nobody's got the greenbacks, neither. 'Cause this gent is *stuffed* with cash! Here he is—inventor, investor, and indulger— Mr. Trexler Lloyd!"

To our applause, a tall man in a cowled cloak walked briskly onstage and gave Sassafras a small nod that sent her scurrying off. Once the room had quieted, he drew back the cowl to reveal a strong Roman nose, thin lips, and dark hair worn unusually long in the style of an orchestra conductor. An individual in his fifties, he looked immensely confident and as comfortable at a microphone as Sinatra himself.

"Good evening, friends and truth seekers," he began. "I am Trexler Lloyd, and tonight is the feast of Samhain. This is a time of spirits."

By way of punctuation, a hidden organ squeezed out a few melodramatic notes.

I whispered into Audrey's ear, "This is really too much."

"Hush, Lee!"

"What's next? Bats?"

"Hush!"

Well, as it turned out, it wasn't bats. It was crows. From backstage, some unseen hand released a half dozen of the noisy black scavengers. They swooped and cawed and riled up the crowd before returning from whence they came. I don't know if crows are trainable, but these ones sure seemed well mustered. Or maybe they were just painted pigeons.

Lloyd favored us with a mild smile. "You'll forgive us our little flourishes."

His tone indicated that we were expected to. From what I'd read, Trexler Lloyd was a fellow who generally got what he requested. His sizable wealth saw to that, but so, too, did the intellect and force of character that had furnished that wealth. Over the years, Lloyd had patented a string of complex inventions, the nature of which I don't pretend to understand. There was a chromo-something and a techno-something and several other somethings that had confounded plumper brains than mine. His endeavors also included a number of corporations, charities, entertainment events, ex-wives, and self-penned books. His autobiography bore the revelatory title *Myself and No Other.* Clearly, this was not a guy who hid his light under a bushel.

Lloyd extended his arms to the audience. "Can any among you tell me the meaning of the Celtic holiday of Samhain?"

Several hands popped up directly.

Our host did a quick appraisal of the volunteers and shook his head. "No. Not our guest mediums and clairvoyants. Someone else." The hands dropped.

A high-pitched male voice to my right called out, "Ask *him*! He'll know."

I turned and saw a short, round man approaching us from down the aisle. His head was shaved bald, though a dark, bristly mustache hung from his lip. The crumpled black suit and crooked purple bow tie certainly didn't flatter him. He was, unfortunately, pointing in our direction.

"Ask that one!" He sounded almost angry.

For one panicky moment, I thought that I was the target of his extended finger. Then I realized it was Mr. O'Nelligan he wanted.

"Yes, him," the man said. "That old widower."

My friend stood and cleared his throat. In terms of knowledge and scholarship, Celtic or otherwise, O'Nelligan was not the man to fool with. Additionally, since he had logged time as both an actor and a teacher, his presentation was impressive.

"Samhain is the celebration of harvest's end." He spoke loudly and clearly. "As marked by the Irish and other Gaelic populations. Some believe it to be the time when the boundaries between the spirit world and our own are most obscured."

"Excellent, sir!" Lloyd gave a little bow from the stage. "And I take it that you are a son of Erin yourself, Mr. . . . ?"

"O'Nelligan. And I am," our friend said, then reseated himself.

"You are a gentleman of wisdom, Mr. O'Nelligan. What is your trade?"

"He's a detective!" Audrey cried out. "More or less. He works with *this* man."

She meant me, and I wanted to dive under my chair. My fiancée never missed an awkward opportunity to advance my career. But here's the truth of things: While I was the one with the official private investigator's license, the real McCoy, sleuthwise, was actually Mr. O'Nelligan.

"Well, there are no secrets to ferret out here, detectives. We are authentic!" Lloyd smiled mechanically and again addressed the whole room. "As you observed, good people, Mr. O'Nelligan—who is of Celtic blood and who knew well the answer I sought—did not raise his hand. And yet . . . and yet . . . he was chosen from the crowd by that most celebrated of mediums, Dr. C. R. Kemple."

Audrey nodded toward the bald man and whispered, "That's

him, Lee! Dr. Kemple. I recognize him now from the posters. You have to admit it's impressive how he picked out Mr. O'Nelligan."

"Oh, come on," I said. "Mr. O'Nelligan *exudes* Irishness. And scholarliness, to boot. Anyone could have guessed he might know the answer."

"Yeah? Well then, how did he know Mr. O'Nelligan was a widower?"

I had a very good answer for that. I'm just not sure what it was.

Trexler Lloyd called out to Kemple. "You have more mysteries in store for us, Doctor, correct?"

The round man grumbled something that might have been "yes." Apparently, the mantle of mediumship lay grumpily on his shoulders.

"Tonight is Samhain," Lloyd informed us again. "The otherworld is near. The spirits of those we loved surround us, waiting to be recognized and embraced."

"How do you embrace a spirit?" I asked Audrey under my breath.

She answered with an elbow to my ribs.

Lloyd continued. "Perhaps tonight there is someone waiting for each of you. Someone whom you falsely believed you had lost forever. Mark my words—no one is ever lost! Life and death are two sides of the same coin. I am quite convinced of that, and, certainly, I am not a man easily convinced. I ask you all now to divide yourselves and enter one of the side rooms here. In each, an expert in spiritualism will take you in hand. Scatter now, friends, scatter! Wonders await . . ."

As it turned out, no wonders awaited me that night; for, in heeding our host's call to scatter, the aforementioned eager octogenarian spun about and, with her umbrella, dislodged my glasses and jabbed me in the eye.

After several minutes of gauging my pain, Audrey came to a reluctant decision. "We'd better just go home, Lee. You're half blind and bloodshot."

"I concur," Mr. O'Nelligan said. "Rather than risk your well-being, we should forgo the event. Alas . . ."

To be honest, for me, there was no *alas* about it: I was more than happy to skip out on this cavalcade of ghost chasers. While leaving the hall, I glanced back with my unjabbed eye and noted a trio of persons conversing together in a corner: the theatrically cloaked Trexler Lloyd; the rumpled Dr. Kemple; and Sassafras Miller, garish in scarlet.

"The energies are high tonight," Kemple was saying. "The dead are anxious to make contact."

"At least the males," Sassafras said with a giggle. "Men are always anxious to make contact. Even the defunct ones."

Kemple was not amused. "Must you always be so crude, woman?"

"You think that's crude? You've led a mild life, Doc. Hell, if you'd seen half the things I've seen, your eyeballs would melt!"

"Mild, am I?" the grumbly medium responded. "Just wait. One day very soon, you'll see what Trexler and I have—"

"Enough!" Trexler Lloyd stared the other man down. "Let's go attend to our duties. If the energies are indeed high, then we don't want to squander them. Correct?"

Sassafras flipped her boa around her neck. "You're always correct, hon. You're the correctest guy I know."

What a motley crew, I thought to myself. Ironically, within weeks, one of those three would be dispatched to the otherworld, and Mr. O'Nelligan and I would be seeking the killer.

CHAPTER ONE

WORD HERE ABOUT MR. O'Nelligan.

I first met the man roughly a year prior to the Otherworld's Fair. When Audrey introduced us, he was sunk in a massive armchair in his book-jammed living room, a volume on his lap, a pipe in his hand, and a calm smile on his lips.

"Many welcomes, Lee Plunkett," he said. "I've been longing to meet Audrey's lad."

Having crested thirty, I didn't really consider myself a "lad," but I didn't contradict him.

He took a draw on his pipe and went on. "Bespectacled and reedy as you are, you bring to mind a fledgling Yeats."

Not knowing if I'd just been complimented or maligned, I grinned stupidly and shook his hand. I gathered he was referring to my round eyeglasses and spare body, but had no idea what a "yates" might be.

He must have noted my confusion, for he added, "I refer to William Butler Yeats, the greatest of Celtic bards. The name Plunkett is an Irish one. Are you not familiar with the island's best poet?"

"I'm a few generations removed from my roots," I explained, "and my father wasn't one for poetry. Can't say I know much about it."

Mr. O'Nelligan gazed at me in gentle pity and trotted out some Yeats.

> "Wine comes in at the mouth
> And Love comes in at the eye.
> That's all we shall know for truth
> Before we grow old and die."

Then he offered us not wine but tea and blarneyed on about one thing or another for half an hour.

As Audrey and I were taking our leave, the Irishman gripped my hand and told me, "Remember what they say, Lee Plunkett—only the mountains never meet again. Do you know what that expression means?"

"Afraid I don't," I answered.

"Nor I, but I like the ring of it."

I must admit that, after that first visit, I wrote the old fellow off as an odd duck.

Born in County Kerry, Mr. O'Nelligan had a colorful career history that included not only actor and teacher but train conductor, bricklayer, door-to-door saleman, and who knows what else. Also, he had fought in his homeland's civil war back in the twenties, though this seemed to be an episode he preferred to forget. Once, when Audrey had asked him why he wore a beard in these modern times, the old Irishman had muttered something about a knife scar and changed the subject. He had immigrated to New York with his wife back in '44. Widowed after a decade, he moved up to Thelmont, our modest-sized Connecticut town, for a life of books and conversation. He lived in a small pine-crowded house three doors down from Audrey and her parents. Audrey and he had become fast friends, uniting over the joys of well-brewed tea and leisurely chatter. I, on the other hand, after that first meeting, never expected to have much to do with the gentleman.

But you just never know. As our acquaintance grew, Mr. O'Nelligan became an unofficial partner of sorts in Plunkett and Son Investigators, of which I—the Son—was the only surviving member. My father, Buster, had taken me on in '54 to give direction to my drifting life, but had died of a heart attack two months before I met Mr. O'Nelligan. In that first year following Dad's death, I really hadn't done much to champion the family business, struggling just to handle the infidelity and missing-object jobs. Then, on Audrey's suggestion, the keen-witted Irishman eventually stepped in to offer his assistance on a couple of cases. By the time of the Otherworld Murders, Mr. O'Nelligan had been on board for several months and had already proved himself invaluable. Annoyingly, he wouldn't accept a single dime for his help.

"I've set aside adequate funds to sustain my silver years," he'd argue whenever I suggested compensation. "I'm just grateful for the chance to exercise my aging cerebrum." Infuriating.

* * *

AN ARTICLE ON the front page of the *Thelmont Times*, December 1, 1956, edition, ran as follows:

TREXLER LLOYD DIES IN FREAK ACCIDENT

Braywick, Conn.—Trexler Lloyd, noted inventor and entrepreneur, was electrocuted yesterday evening, November 30, while operating one of his own inventions, in what has been described as a demonstration of spiritualism. Lloyd's interest in the supernatural was highlighted last month by the Otherworld's Fair, an event that he sponsored featuring various mediums, mystics, and practitioners of the occult. His death occurred at about 8:10 P.M. at his home in Braywick while in the company of several associates including Dr. C. R. Kemple, a self-professed medium, and Miss Brenda "Sassafras" Miller, former actress and celebrity. Mrs. Constanza Lloyd, the deceased's wife, was also present, though not at the moment of death.

The device that electrocuted Lloyd was known as a "Spectricator" and, according to witnesses, was invented by Lloyd for the purpose of accessing "the death dimension." No reliable evidence has been presented as to its effectiveness, other than the unfortunate part it played in Lloyd's own passing. Police speculate that a fault in the device's electronics caused the fatal mishap. More information will be forthcoming.

Audrey and I were halfway through a Saturday breakfast at the Bugle Boy Diner. She finished reading aloud the article and sighed. "Doesn't get much weirder than that, does it?"

"Not much," I agreed, not knowing then that more weirdness was due, and that I would have a ringside seat for it.

Audrey was looking fetching that morning, and I sure hope I told her so. Her wavy brown hair, cut fairly short in the modern style, had a nice bounce to it, and her button nose never looked so buttony. The scarf around her slender neck, red with yellow polka dots, was one of my favorites and, in my unrefined opinion, always gave her a bit of dash.

"Trexler Lloyd was a strange man," she said, "but a necessary one, I'd say."

"How so?"

"The world needs inventors . . . creators. It's how we progress."

I talked through a mouthful of muffin. "Progress is overrated. Everyone's always going on about rocket ships and robots and such, but there's no need to rush the clock."

She gave me a scowl. "No one will ever accuse *you* of rushing any timepieces."

I'd led myself right into that one. I knew, of course, what she was referring to: our long-term engagement. We'd pledged ourselves in the spring of '54, and here it was the tail end of 1956 with no official wedding day in sight. We seemed to be in contention with *The Ed Sullivan Show* for the longest-running variety series. There was always one obstacle or another to keep us from storming the aisle, lack of cash being the preferred excuse. Even now, when I'd actually been able to set aside a fair amount due to a couple successful cases, I still was hemming and hawing. At twenty-eight, Audrey was more than ready to commit. I, on the other hand, just couldn't seem to make that great leap. *Soon*, I kept telling both of us. *Very soon*.

I retreated to the safety of Lloyd's demise. "Well, the man's bought his own ticket to spiritland."

"That's a rather callous remark, isn't it?"

"Probably. But it's ironic that someone who'd put so much effort into seeking out the company of ghosts—"

"Should turn himself into one with some stupid mistake?"

"*Now* who's being callous?"

"I'm not callous—I'm sensible. He shouldn't have been fooling around with untested electronic devices, even if he *was* a genius. Who ever heard of a Spectricator, anyway?"

I shrugged. "Certainly not me, but then I'm not exactly one of our nation's great scientific minds."

"I heartily concur," Audrey said oh-so-sweetly.

"Gee, thanks. Believe me, though, it's all bull. All this ghostly, bump-in-the-night malarkey is just meant to separate some poor bozos from their paychecks."

"Now, how can you know that? People like Trexler Lloyd and Dr. Kemple may be in touch with things we can't even imagine. Like that story about my grandmother. Is it really so impossible that the deceased might be able to contact us?"

"In a word, yes."

Audrey tossed a balled-up napkin at my head, missing by an inch. "You're so sure of yourself, aren't you, mister?"

Truth be told, there wasn't a whole lot in the world that I was, in fact, one hundred percent sure of. So when something that I *did* feel reasonably confident of—such as, let's say, the iron-clad finality of death—I liked to stick by it.

"Nonetheless, it's too bad Trexler Lloyd perished." I said. "Even if he *was* reckless with his hardware. Do you agree, Miss Sensible?"

Audrey tried her luck with a second napkin ball. This time she connected.

FOUR DAYS LATER, as I was strolling up Audrey's walkway to pick her up for a matinee, Mr. O'Nelligan intercepted me with a firm hand on my chest.

"Ah, Lee, m'lad! I heard you were coming to fetch dear Audrey, so I lay in wait. You can commence your courting in a moment, but first I've some news."

"The good kind?"

"At present, that isn't for me to judge. We do have a case, though. I received a telephone call not a half hour ago."

"You did?" This was unusual. Normally, I was the one who fielded new clients.

"I did. And it's regarding a man of much import. Unfortunately, a dead one."

Somehow, before he even said the name, I knew, just knew, that it was Trexler Lloyd.

Per Mr. O'Nelligan's arrangements, he and I went to my office that evening to meet with George Agnelli, the man who had contacted him. When I say office, I don't mean to suggest anything stately or slick or, to be honest, even professional. It was the same narrow room where my father had started his business fifteen years before, and somehow I hadn't gotten around to making changes. Once, Audrey had tried to describe it to someone but ended up halting midsentence and sighing, "Actually, there's nothing to describe." That summed things up pretty smartly. There were four murky green walls, one curtainless window, a dinged-up wooden desk, a typewriter, a telephone, a table lamp, a cranky swivel chair, a couple of other chairs begging for some varnish, and a gray metal cabinet with stubborn drawers. The one piece of decoration that Dad had provided was a framed portrait of Teddy Roosevelt, of whom he'd often admiringly declare, "That guy had *buckles*! Real *buckles*!" I've no idea what that even meant. The only reason I could afford an office at all was because old Yowler Yarr, the landlord, had been a crony of Dad's who kept the rent down at a pauper's fee. As it was, I'd had to let the part-time secretary go, so who knows how much business I'd lost while the phone jingled away unanswered in the empty space.

George Agnelli arrived promptly at the agreed-upon time. Strangely enough, according to what he'd told my colleague, Agnelli was a professional sleuth himself, a Braywick police detective nearing the end of his career. His sixty-odd years—and perhaps the burdens of his profession—had settled heavily into the deep crevices of his face. His gray hair was thinning, and his eyes had a weary, basset-hound-like droop to them.

I started the conversation. "It's pretty unusual to have one detective hire another."

"Sure, I know that," Agnelli said. "But there are reasons . . ." Then he stopped and, for a moment, I thought he wasn't going to give any.

"Reasons?" I reached for my notepad.

He blew out a mouthful of air, like he was dispelling some little demon. "Can't believe I'm doing this. It's just that it's the end of my career, see? Thirty-eight years. You want things to end clean. You want to slip off your badge and feel it wasn't all for nothing. Because you've been a good cop and tried to play it square. Maybe you've made mistakes, screwed up a case or two when you were younger. But you want your last run to be a good one, you understand?'

I really didn't. "Why don't we backtrack? What led you to seek out Mr. O'Nelligan?"

"Okay, I started to go into this on the phone, but he wanted to wait till you were in the mix. He said you're the boss here."

I wanted to say, *In name only,* but let it go. "Something about the Otherworld's Fair, right?"

"Yes, I was there last month when O'Nelligan here stood up and talked about the feast day . . . what's it called?"

"Samhain," Mr. O'Nelligan answered.

"That's it. I remember that gal with you said you were detectives, and that stuck with me. O'Nelligan seemed like a sharp fellow, so when I decided I needed help, he came to mind. Since I'm going behind the department's back, I wanted someone from out of the area. Plus, it felt like fate in a way, the fact that he was there the one time I saw Trexler Lloyd alive."

"Why were *you* there?" I asked. "At the Otherworld's Fair."

Agnelli looked down at his hands. "My wife passed away last spring. Well, with all this stuff about spirits that Trexler put out, I just . . . Oh, hell, I don't know. A fellow misses his wife, he gets a little lost, maybe."

"I understand," Mr. O'Nelligan said, and I knew he did. "Now, you just said 'the one time I saw Trexler Lloyd alive,' implying, perhaps, that you've encountered him dead?"

"Right. We were the ones called out Friday night, my partner and me. By the time we got there, Lloyd was sprawled out cold in that cloak of his, and Felix Emmitt, the coroner, was already closing up shop. That crazy apparatus was still sparking, and Emmitt had declared it death by electrocution."

"That's how the papers wrote it up," I said.

"Sure, that's how everyone wrote it up."

"But you have your doubts?"

Agnelli looked pained. "You don't put in thirty-eight years without developing an eye for something wrong. We barely got to glance at the body before that Kemple nut starts yelling at us not to disturb Lloyd, that we'll muddle his death energies or some such nonsense. Plus, with Sassafras Miller sobbing up a storm, and the coroner saying it's a done deal and packing up the corpse, we didn't have much time to take it all in. We interviewed the witnesses afterward—Lloyd's inner circle and a handful of clients who'd come hoping to contact their loved ones—but everyone chalked the death up to faulty wiring."

"But not you and your partner?"

"Forget Tommy Bells. He's a kid, twenty-six, who only made detective a year ago. Thinks he knows it all, but doesn't. No, Tommy took everything at face value."

"So, what made *you* suspicious?"

Agnelli blew out another demon. "Well, first of all, Felix Emmitt being there."

"Why wouldn't the local coroner be on hand?"

"Because he didn't just arrive after the fact in his official capacity. He was already there. Emmitt was in the room when Trexler Lloyd died."

No one spoke for a moment as that sank in.

"Did you get an explanation out of him?" I finally asked.

"He said he was there as a client, that it was just a coincidence."

Mr. O'Nelligan clicked his tongue. "Be wary of coincidences, for every vine has its seed."

"Exactly," I concurred, not really sure what I was concurring with. "So, were you able to follow up on examining the body?"

Agnelli looked deflated. "No. By that next morning, Lloyd had been cremated."

"Overnight?" Mr. O'Nelligan tilted back his head. "That seems quite hasty."

"That's what I thought," Agnelli said, "but apparently Lloyd had made it clear that in the event of his death, he wanted it done immediately. Even had something legal drawn up to that effect."

I paused in my note-taking. "But this was an untimely death. Wouldn't the authorities hold up the cremation until everything had been sorted out?"

"Which authorities?" Agnelli snickered. "You have to understand that Trexler Lloyd flung a lot of cash around our county. I won't say he owned the place, but let's just say his wishes were respected. Even as a corpse. That night, Lloyd's Spanish wife was insisting that his instructions be followed, and crazy Kemple was babbling on about cosmic bonds and flames and spirits. Emmitt had already called the cause of death, so nobody was going to get in the way of Lloyd's final request—not the police chief, not the mayor, not anybody."

"I get it," I said. "The whole thing smelled bad to you, though."

"It reeked." Agnelli's eyes narrowed. "It goddamn reeked. You don't go thirty-eight years without developing a nose. But when I tried to push this thing, the chief told me there was no evidence of anything amiss. On the face of it, he's right. But still . . ."

Mr. O'Nelligan laid it out smoothly. "But still, you wish to see events brought to their just conclusions."

"That's it. The chief told me to relax and just coast toward my retirement. I've only got three more months to go. So, you see, I can't do anything when I'm on the force that could screw up my pension. On the other hand, I don't want the trail to go cold on this. That's why I'm turning to you fellows. The thing is, I don't want to give you too much info up front. I think it's better if you examine everything with fresh eyes. I've got a little extra cash put aside to pay for your time. It's worth it to me to go out right."

"A commendable sentiment," Mr. O'Nelligan said.

Agnelli reached into his coat pocket, pulled out several folded twenties, and set them on my desk. "That's to get you started. Let me know when you need more. You'll have an ally of sorts in Lloyd's secretary, Doris Chauncey. She had a funny feeling about Lloyd's death, too. You can get her to help you with the who's who and all. On the sly, I've suggested to her that someone outside of the department might be looking into things. With the rest of that crowd, don't mention me. You'll have to figure out how to present yourselves when you're poking around."

My Irish comrade offered a warm smile. "We don't merely poke, sir. We prod."

CHAPTER TWO

THE NEXT MORNING, WITH Mr. O'Nelligan beside me, I aimed down Route 7 toward Braywick. It was a gray, overcast late autumn day (or early winter, depending on your level of pessimism), but something about being behind the wheel of my 1952 baby blue Nash Rambler always made me feel sunny. Before I'd acquired it, it had suffered a minor accident, and the previous owner—an unfaithful lout with money to burn—had simply bought himself a new car and sold away Baby Blue (as I'd named her). Audrey's mechanic father got hold of it and, after making the few nicks and scrapes nearly undetectable, sold it to me at a price reserved for potential sons-in-law.

I'd reached Trexler Lloyd's secretary, Doris Chauncey, by phone, and she'd be meeting us at the Lloyd residence. Or, I should say, at *one* of the Lloyd residences, for he had apparently owned half a dozen homes scattered across the East Coast.

"Must be nice to be insanely rich," I said.

"I wouldn't be too envious of wealth," Mr. O'Nelligan cautioned. "As a case in point, Trexler Lloyd's fortune did not shield him from his demise. Perhaps it even hastened it."

"Meaning?"

"Meaning who knows what motivations we'll discover."

"You realize, of course, that this could all amount to what it appears to be—an electronic mishap, pure and simple. Agnelli seems well-meaning, but he could be overthinking this whole thing."

"Perhaps. Nevertheless, since we now represent that gentleman's interests, it's our sacred trust to follow this road to its end."

My friend was a great one for sacred trusts and honorable pursuits. As for myself, I was just trying to earn my keep in the world. At least, that's what I preferred to tell myself.

Mr. O'Nelligan forged on. "Also, you must admit that the presence of the coroner at the moment of death does raise questions."

"Sure, I'll admit that."

"And the whole spiritualism aspect does give pause."

I snorted. "You think some phantoms zapped Lloyd?"

"I do not, but, to paraphrase the bard, there are more things in heaven and earth, Lee, than are dreamt of in your philosophy."

"Please now, don't go flinging your Yeats at me first thing in the morning."

"Yeats? For the love of God, man, that was Shakespeare!" He looked fairly disgusted with me. "*Hamlet,* act one, scene five, to be precise."

I couldn't resist. "I don't know Hamlet from a ham-and-cheese sandwich."

"And you take pride in that?"

"Not necessarily, but I don't slam myself over it, either. I'm just a regular fellow—no frills, no thrills. And I haven't logged time on the stage or in the classroom such as some superior types I could mention."

This got a chuckle out of him. "Superior, am I? You surely wouldn't say that had you seen, for example, the first role I ever landed in New York. In that particular instance, I played the part of a ne'er-do-well—enamored, of course, of whiskey, as all Irish stock characters here seem to be—who went about life garbed as a giant goldfish."

I could barely grasp the concept. "A goldfish? You? Was it some kind of farce?"

"It was a tragedy. At least for me. I was hoping for a role crafted by Beckett, or perhaps Eugene O'Neill, and instead I drew an inebriated goldfish."

"You know I'll never be able to look at you again without imagining scales."

He flashed me a look not without warmth. "Ah, you've a spry mind to you, Lee Plunkett. Don't let anyone tell you differently."

A light rain began to sprinkle down on the road. I turned on my wipers, and their metronome rhythm became backdrop to our conversation.

"So, where do *you* stand on ghosts?" I wanted to know.

Mr. O'Nelligan smoothed his whiskers. "If you're asking do I believe in them, well, many things have I heard that would sway a man as to their existence. And in my own ramblings, I've beheld a thing or two that lean toward the supernatural."

"You've seen a ghost?"

"Bit of a long story, lad. Perhaps one best saved for another time."

I grunted in dissatisfaction. Mr. O'Nelligan seemed to have a lot of tales that fit into that category: "best saved for another time."

He tried to placate. "Some evening 'round the hearth I'll lay it out for you. A blazing log and a mug of bold tea—those are the proper trappings for such storytelling. Now, as to the authenticity of Mr. Lloyd's explorations of the afterlife, I cannot say. The crows and blue smoke of the Otherworld's Fair are by no means proof of anything."

"Exactly!" I was glad to hear this. "That's what I was trying to tell Audrey. She's a little too willing to give these so-called spiritualists a free pass. I've been trying to make her see the light."

"Ah, now, be careful, Lee, in pushing your fine lass toward any lights. She has a good head on her shoulders, and, I'd say, is quite capable of pursuing her own illumination."

Mr. O'Nelligan was unabashedly fond of Audrey and always quick to bound to her defense. Knowing I'd gain no ground in this debate, I shifted the conversation. "When I spoke to Doris Chauncey on the phone, she seemed kind of ill at ease, but willing to help us. I got a sense that she pretty much runs things at the house."

"A commanding personality?" asked Mr. O'Nelligan.

"No, just an organized one. She sounded soft-spoken, actually, but she assured me she'd be as efficient as possible in assisting us. I think she used the word 'efficient' three or four times."

"Well, for a secretary, efficiency is a worthy virtue."

"Good to hear, because this girl is apparently soaking in it."

As if on cue, the rainfall suddenly decided to do a little soaking itself and upgraded to a heavy downpour. For the rest of the ride we stayed pretty much silent as I squinted behind my glasses to keep the road in sight. An hour's drive delivered us to Braywick—and, ultimately, the secrets of Trexler Lloyd's death.

TO ACCESS THE Lloyd property, you first had to pass through a set of locked black gates bordered by a pair of squatting dragons. These stone guardians, with their twisted jowls, jagged ears, and bulging eyes, struck me as less than welcoming. They, and the high wrought-iron fence itself, looked to be fairly recent additions to the grounds. As Doris Chauncey had promised, someone was waiting there at exactly 10:00 A.M. to open the gates for us. As I slowed the car to a halt, this person approached us, and I rolled down my window. The rain, though having let up a touch, still fell steadily, and the man meeting us protected himself with a slicker and an umbrella.

As he leaned down to speak to me, I took note of his narrow face, pointy nose, and horn-rimmed glasses, and the fact that he wore a blue cloth scarf tied around his head in the manner of a storybook pirate. The man's age was hard to pin down—maybe thirty, maybe forty. His features were scrunched up in a look of disdain, whether for the precipitation or for me, I couldn't say. Overall, a pretty quirky-looking individual. This didn't surprise me, seeing as he was part of Trexler Lloyd's crew, who, judging by C. R. Kemple and Sassafras Miller, seemed a colorful oddball lot.

"You pick it?" he asked in some sort of European accent.

"Excuse me? Pick what?"

"Pick it for Miss Chauncey, yes?"

"Pick *what* for Miss Chauncey?" For a fleeting, foolish moment, I wondered if I was expected to gather a bouquet for the secretary, perhaps as a chivalrous gesture.

"Mr. Pick-it! Yes?" His voice rose in frustration.

"Aha!" Mr. O'Nelligan leaned over me and addressed the agitated buccaneer. "It's Mr. *Plunkett,* good sir. This, indeed, is the man Miss Chauncey is expecting."

Our greeter nodded solemnly. "I am Rast. Martin Rast from Switzerland. I take care of the house and the land, you understand?"

"You're the groundskeeper?"

"I am." Without further comment, Rast marched over to the fence, opened the lock, and swung back the gates for us.

As I drove slowly through the dragons, I glanced in the rearview mirror and saw Rast climbing onto a bicycle. He followed us up the driveway, steering with one hand and maintaining his umbrella with the other, as the rain beat down on him. He looked like a circus performer who'd gone astray.

I turned a bend and lost sight of him. The driveway proved to be a long lane weaving through a stretch of tall sycamore trees. Several twists and turns delivered us to the house. Lloyd's domain was not what I was expecting. Large enough, certainly, but not quite a mansion, the building had an elderly, jumbled appearance that didn't exactly broadcast great wealth. It seemed to have bypassed any particular architectural style other than, perhaps, New England Brooding. The paint job looked to be well over a decade old, with a gloomy, gray hue that registered somewhere between twilight and smoke. By contrast, the immediate grounds of trimmed shrubbery and stone-lined, presently dormant flower beds had obviously received recent care—no doubt by the hand of Martin Rast. We parked and climbed up onto the porch. The brass door knocker was the head of a woman with long, wild tresses and lips parted wide in either terror or ecstasy. I felt uneasy gripping the damned thing.

In immediate response to my knocking, the door swung open and Doris Chauncey greeted us. She proved to be a young woman in her early twenties—younger than I'd expected from our phone conversation—short and somewhat stocky, with plain but not unpleasant features and straw-colored hair tied firmly back. Her simple navy blue jacket and skirt suggested propriety and restraint beyond her years. This was not a young person you'd expect to see letting loose at a Friday night sock hop. We were gestured in, and I furnished introductions there in the foyer, a sparse, moderate-sized space with a wide oak staircase curving up to the right. The secretary then led us down a dim-lit hallway, talking rapidly in a half whisper as we went.

"Detective Agnelli said to expect someone, so when your call came, Mr. Plunkett, I was very heartened. Something just doesn't feel right about Mr. Lloyd's accident."

"So we've been led to believe," Mr. O'Nelligan said.

"Now, please understand, I don't have any gifts like Dr. Kemple or the other mediums are supposed to have, just a *feeling*. So I said I'd help you. Detective Agnelli made it very clear that this was all on the sly. It is, right?"

"On the sly," I echoed. "That's definitely what we're on."

Miss Chauncey stopped abruptly and turned to face us. "I can keep secrets," she said earnestly. "I really can."

Mr. O'Nelligan gave her a little bow. "We presume you are the embodiment of discretion, young miss. Your assistance will be invaluable."

The secretary blushed with guarded pleasure. "I try to be of service to my employer. I take that very seriously. And even though Mr. Lloyd is gone, well, I still . . ." She trailed off and cast her eyes down, and I wasn't sure exactly what emotion was gripping the girl.

My comrade continued for her. "You still wish to be of service to him. We admire that."

Doris looked back up directly into Mr. O'Nelligan's eyes. "Yes. Thank you. Most people don't understand what service is really about. They don't see how doing one's best for another can be an honorable thing."

Mr. O'Nelligan smiled gently. "Back in County Kerry where I hail from, there was a fiddler named Timmy Keefe who, whenever someone was having a poor time—loss of a loved one or illness or just deep, nagging melancholy—would set himself before their door and give them a good long playing. It didn't matter if it was a kinsman or a stranger, old Timmy would rosin up his bow and set out to do his mercy. He was what we'd call born simple, but what he teased out of that fiddle was pure cleverness. Not so much in technique, though that was fine enough, but in *intent*. He knew how to serve, you see. When Timmy passed on, the church fairly burst with all his mourners."

Good Lord, but that Irishman could rattle on prettily. Moved by the tale, Doris Chauncey blushed an even brighter shade. We continued down the dusky hall into a more generously lit room where Doris offered us seats. The oak-paneled walls were crowded with high, overstuffed bookshelves, and numerous high-backed chairs edged the black and crimson Arabian carpet. Aside from a couple of bleak pastoral paintings, the room's chief accessory was a taxidermized raccoon perched on a pedestal. Its jaws were frozen in a disturbing grimace that revealed more sharp, nasty little teeth than I really cared to see. While Miss Chauncey and I seated ourselves at once, Mr. O'Nelligan, literature addict that he was, aimed himself at the books. Judging by their spines, many of them were cheap, run-of-the-mill paperbacks, while others seemed to be antique volumes, bound in fine leather with gilt lettering. The lesser and greater offerings were mixed freely together. Mr. O'Nelligan pulled out one book, then another, flicking quickly through each one before returning it gingerly to its place.

When he finally settled, he gestured sweepingly toward the shelves. "An eclectic collection, indeed. Everything from a first edition of Poe's *Tales of the Grotesque and Arabesque* to some lurid potboiler entitled *Ghost of the Burlesque Babe,* and also texts on such subjects as shamanism, faith healing, and ectoplasmic photography. Eclectic, I should say, within a defined range—that of the occult."

"That's right," Doris Chauncey said. "Over the last couple of years Mr. Lloyd had developed quite an interest in the supernatural. Just about the time I came to work for him. He referred to himself and his followers as the Séance Society."

"This was an official organization?" I asked.

"No, just a name he thought had a certain flair. Of course, séances weren't his only focus. He experimented with all sorts of mystical things."

"Such as the Spectricator?"

The secretary nodded. "Yes, that was his special project with Dr. Kemple."

"Ah, yes. Dr. C. R. Kemple." Mr. O'Nelligan folded his hands in his lap. "Lee here and I observed him briefly at the Otherworld's Fair last month. I must confess, I pegged him as a man of rather sour temperament."

Doris avoided the bait. "I really couldn't say," she said softly. "I didn't attend the event. Mr. Lloyd preferred I remain here to tend to business."

An unconvincing detour. I wasn't going to let her off that easy. "Come on, Miss Chauncey, you've probably had loads of

opportunities to observe that character. Kemple's kind of a charlatan, isn't he?"

Mr. O'Nelligan tossed me a look that said *you're going too far*
but didn't intervene.

I pressed on. "Remember, Miss Chauncey, we're working together here."

The secretary drew in a deep breath, then gave me what I
wanted in a great gush. "He's a wretched little man! Wretched!
I never understood why Mr. Lloyd set such store by him. Oh, I
know they say he has special abilities, but I really can't confirm
that one way or the other. Maybe he's a fraud and maybe he's not,
but he certainly is an evil-hearted little beast!" She caught herself up and gave a nervous laugh. "I'm so sorry, it's just that I
tend to keep my opinions of Mr. Lloyd's associates to myself, and
so, well . . ."

"It's quite all right," Mr. O'Nelligan comforted. "Sometimes
it's good to unburden the soul."

"I must have just sounded like something out of a Gothic
romance."

"Ah, the Gothics!" Mr. O'Nelligan exclaimed. "There are
some excellent offerings in that genre. How can one not be
drawn to the mists and moors of the Brontë sisters? And, argu-
ably, the Gothics set the stage for dear Jane Austen herself."

Miss Chauncey became almost gleeful. "I've read *Pride and
Prejudice* six times! And *Sense and Sensibility* at least half that!"

"Admirable!"

For the next couple of minutes, Mr. O'Nelligan was in hog's
heaven, flinging about literary allusions with someone who actually read books. I myself leaned toward pulp magazines featuring cowboys, air aces, and two-fisted private eyes who were far
grittier than I'd ever be.

I had to interrupt this. "About Dr. Kemple?"

Mr. O'Nelligan came back on board. "Of course. You just said, Miss Chauncey, that the doctor was evil-hearted. 'Evil' is rather a weighty word, you must admit."

Doris grew serious again. "Perhaps. But you haven't spent time under the same roof as that man. He's constantly in a dark mood and treats people as if they were nothing but inconveniences. I'm not even sure if Dr. Kemple is really a doctor. I really wouldn't be surprised if he just uses that title to sound important. Then there are the stories . . ."

"Stories?" Mr. O'Nelligan cocked his head.

"There are rumors that he drinks wine out of a cup made from a human skull."

"An unsavory practice, admittedly. Though, if true, it would put him in the company of Lord Byron, who himself possessed such a cup."

"I've never seen him actually do it, so it may not be real." There was a note of regret in her voice. "They also say he does strange rituals in the woods."

"What woods?" I asked. "These woods?"

"Well, no . . . Oh, he's just a creepy little man! He's not fit to be with other human beings. Unless, possibly, the dead ones." Here she released another awkward laugh. "Sorry. It's a joke. Because he supposedly talks to spirits, you see."

"Sure." I tried to sound tickled. "Now, what about Trexler Lloyd. What was he like?"

Doris Chauncey stared off for a moment before continuing in a subdued tone. "Mr. Lloyd was a complicated person. It was an honor to work for him. Really."

"But what was he like?"

Our eyes met, and I saw that hers had become slightly misty.

"Like no one I've ever known, Mr. Plunkett. And probably like no one *you've* ever known. I can't believe he's not with us anymore. It's been only five days, and already it feels like he's part of history. I guess some people are just . . . legendary."

This all sounded pretty vague and highfaluting to me. "But what kind of man was he? Was he pleasant? Tyrannical? Gentle? Angry?"

"All of those things," Doris answered. "Does that sound foolish?"

I wanted to say, *Yeah, a little,* but my better self responded. "No. I guess any man is a mix of all those traits." As soon as I uttered it, I realized that, shockingly, I'd just said a wise thing.

Mr. O'Nelligan, who bled wisdom, gave me an approving little nod.

The young woman continued. "Mr. Lloyd was very exacting. That's how he put it himself. He'd say, 'I am exacting in all things.' It was like a motto for him. If you didn't do things just right, well, you'd hear about it."

"A big shouter?" I suggested.

"Sometimes. But usually, he'd just speak to you in a certain way. Harsh. He could be extremely harsh. There were people who did something wrong in his eyes and he'd just cut them off from him. And sometimes—" She stopped herself suddenly. "No, this is wrong! I shouldn't be talking ill of the dead. Every-one knows that."

Mr. O'Nelligan responded soothingly. "Please hear me, lass. We're here to do right by your deceased employer. As my friend nicely put it, each man is a mix of things. If we understand the truth of Trexler Lloyd's life, the dark and the light of it, we've a better chance at discovering the truth of his death."

Doris seemed to accept this. "He could be kind, too. You

should know that. Once, he gave me the whole day off with pay just because it was the birthday of the man who invented the mechanical reaper. Imagine! He liked to do quirky little things like that. You see, Mr. Lloyd was capable of showing real kindness."

"No doubt. And it's up to we who still breathe to recall the merits of the dead. It's as the verse tells us, the good is oft interred with their bones." Mr. O'Nelligan glanced over at me. "Shakespeare," he added firmly.

Doris now rose and walked over to one of the bookshelves. After a brief search, she selected a book and delivered it into my comrade's hands. It was Lloyd's autobiography, *Myself and No Other.*

"If you want to know something about Trexler Lloyd, you should read that. You, too, Mr. Plunkett."

"We'll do that," Mr. O'Nelligan promised.

Footfalls in the hallway indicated that someone was about to join us. I turned towards the doorway and saw—and, yeah, I know how this sounds—the most beautiful woman on the planet.

CHAPTER THREE

THE WOMAN WHO'D JUST entered the room was not gorgeous. Nor glamorous. Nor any of the flashy words that magazines and novels trot out to describe beauty. Breath-taking? Well, yes, maybe that works, because I believe I actually did lose a breath when she walked in. Now, I'm not the most refined of fellows, but I want to say there was something downright *artistic* about her. Again, I know how that sounds.

To list her attributes—a sweet, oval face; pure black hair; graceful hands—really can't convey what struck me about her. You could produce a similar catalog for any number of beautiful women. If I had to zero in on one specific about her, I'd go for the eyes. They were deep and black and drew their light from somewhere very distant. I don't just refer to the foreign land of origin that her features and dusky complexion suggested, but to someplace—and, I swear, this word did actually pop into my brain at that first encounter—otherworldly. I guessed her to be in her late twenties, maybe thirty. Most of her form was covered in a black dress edged with lace, which, coupled with her general demeanor, implied a quiet somberness.

Doris addressed her. "Constanza . . ." The poetry of the name made a perfect match for the woman. This, then, was Lloyd's Spanish widow.

"I heard voices," she said, her accent quite strong.

We all rose from our chairs, and, not surprisingly, Mr. O'Nelligan was the one who made the first gesture of condolence.

"Mrs. Lloyd, we are sorry for your loss." He took her right hand in both of his own. "Your husband was a man of great standing, and his absence will, no doubt, be felt in the world. How does your heart fare today?"

That question, asked by any other human, would have come off as frilly, disingenuous, and/or brazen, but when posed by my companion, it registered as nothing less than sincere. The thing of it is, that's exactly what it was. Our investigation aside, my friend honestly *did* want to know how this young woman's heart was faring with the loss of her spouse. Mr. O'Nelligan had an extraordinary way of drawing people in, and his show of sympathy obviously moved Constanza. Her lip trembled as she drew her free hand up to join the one already held.

"Some days it is very *dificil*," she half-whispered.

"Understandable," Mr. O'Nelligan said. "The loss is fresh. We can but offer our best prayers for your comfort."

Constanza held his gaze, apparently taking some solace from the presence of this old bearded stranger. After a few moments, she gently withdrew her hands and fetched a handkerchief from a pocket to dab her eyes. "Who are you men?" she now asked.

Doris Chauncey quickly tendered introductions.

Constanza eyed me, and I thought I might melt just a little. "Mr. Plunkett is the one you told me of, yes? The one with the powers?"

"That's right," the secretary said.

Before I could say anything, Doris shot me an anxious look of warning.

Constanza appraised me seriously. "Doris tells me you have felt my husband."

Dumbfounded, I looked at Miss Chauncey to field this one.

She complied somewhat haltingly. "Oh, yes, Mr. Plunkett . . . I told Mrs. Lloyd how you contacted me yesterday . . . about receiving impressions from Mr. Lloyd's spirit. How you have special abilities, you know, and felt that Mr. Lloyd needed some help to move on."

"It would be good to help Trexler move on," Constanza said. "Doris says you wish to talk to the people who were with him when he died, yes?"

"Yes, that would be helpful." I tried to sound as confident as a man with special abilities would be. "Extremely helpful."

"Very well," Constanza said. "But I was not in the room when it happened, so I do not have much to say. I suffer now from *un dolor de cabeza*. What do you call it? A headache. I must lie down again. Doris will help you." Then, like a figure in a dream, she spun around and vanished across the threshold. And that was that.

I turned to Miss Chauncey. "So, just when did I acquire these 'powers'?"

She looked down, like a child who'd done mischief. "I'm sorry. I intended to tell you before you spoke to anyone. Detective Agnelli said it would be better if people didn't know you were detectives."

"So you turned me into a psychic?"

"In Mr. Lloyd's circle, a person with those abilities is very accepted. I thought people would be more forthcoming with you if they thought it wasn't another investigation. After all, everyone's already spoken to the police."

Mr. O'Nelligan shook his head slowly. "I don't like this. Deception is a road that oft curves back upon itself."

"I'm not crazy about it, either, Miss Chauncey," I said. "What about my partner here? Does he have superpowers, too?"

"No, just you," the secretary said meekly. "I didn't want to make things too complex. I just said that Mr. O'Nelligan was your assistant who helped you keep your powers focused. Look, I'm terribly sorry. I was trying to be helpful, but I've gone and complicated everything. Should I tell everyone I misinformed them?"

My colleague sighed. "No, I think that would turn sentiment against us before we'd even begun. For the time being, at least, our course is set. But, Lee, I would caution against playing up the psychic angle too stridently."

"Are you kidding me? Do you really think I'm going to throw myself into a trance and start spitting out predictions?"

"You don't need to," Doris assured me. "I've just told people that you access vibrations from beyond. You don't actually predict things."

"Well, good, then. I'm more than happy to be a medium-grade medium." Since no one acknowledged my wit, I moved on. "They must have made for an unusual couple—Constanza and Trexler Lloyd."

"I suppose you mean the joining of beauty and brains." The secretary's tone took on a note of defensiveness. "But it's not that unheard of, is it? Look at Marilyn Monroe and Arthur Miller. They just got married this past summer, and it's the same sort of thing, right?" She paused reflectively. "Though, to be truthful, I wish she'd stuck with Joe DiMaggio."

Once we'd reseated ourselves, it was time to extract my trusty notebook. Mr. O'Nelligan silently thumbed through Lloyd's autobiography, content to let me handle the next round of questions.

"Okay, Miss Chauncey, please give us your account of Friday night's events." I think I was trying to sound like my father, who was always solid with the private eye patter.

Doris Chauncey smoothed her dress and began. "Mr. Lloyd had arranged for a presentation of his Spectricator. A few clients were scheduled to attend."

"People who'd paid to come?"

"Yes, there was a fee. That probably was on Dr. Kemple's insistence."

"Does Kemple live here?"

"Thankfully, no. I mean, he'll stay at times for a night or two, but he's been living in a rented room a couple of towns over."

"So, leading up to the presentation, what occurred?"

"Mr. Lloyd had dinner two hours before. A little after six, I think."

I started jotting down a timeline. "Who dined with him?"

"There was Mrs. Lloyd and Sassafras Miller—she's been living here for about a year—and myself."

"Do you often eat with the Lloyds?"

"Sometimes. They're very egalitarian that way."

"I noticed you called Mrs. Lloyd by her first name."

"We've become very close." There was a touch of pride in her voice.

"Okay, so there was a quartet for dinner."

"Well, Dr. Kemple did have soup with us, but then excused himself." She paused. "Actually, he wasn't that polite. He just got up, said he had to prepare for the night's events, and walked out."

"What sort of preparations was he making?"

"I've no idea, but they probably involved Mr. Lloyd's expensive brandy."

"Did he often use liquor to strengthen his powers?"

Doris giggled. "He likes his spirits. Get it?"

I did. "And after dinner?"

"Constanza retired upstairs, and Mr. Lloyd joined me in my office to give me some dictation for a business letter. I'm not sure where in the house Sassafras went off to."

"What about Kemple? Where'd he go to do his 'preparing'?"

"To his guest room, I suppose. He was planning to spend the night."

"Anyone else in the house at that time?"

"Just the staff—Trowbridge, Martin, and the Gallagher cousins. They're two local girls who help out with the cooking and serving sometimes. Our regular cook has been tending to her ill husband and was off that night."

"We've met Martin—Rast, isn't it?—the groundskeeper. The man has an interesting look to him."

"He's really rather nice when you get to know him."

I smiled halfheartedly. "I'll trust you on that. Who's Trowbridge?"

"Lewis Trowbridge. We call him the butler, but he's also the chauffeur and whatever else the Lloyds need him to do. He's very English and very formal. Mr. Lloyd liked that about him."

"That's everybody?"

"Everybody who's *here*. Of course, Mr. Lloyd has staff at his other homes, but lately he's been spending most of his time in Braywick."

"So you were working in your office with Lloyd. Then what?"

"Then, after about twenty minutes, Mr. Lloyd went to the Portal Room."

"Pardon?"

"Oh, sorry. The Portal Room is where he held his special gatherings. He believed it was the best room for accessing those who've passed on. Like a portal to another world. It's right through there." Doris pointed to a door between two of the bookshelves.

"You can show us it in a moment. What time would this have been?"

"A little after seven."

"Lloyd died at ten past eight. What did he do for that last hour of his life?"

"He held court, as he liked to say. Different members of the household went in to see him."

"Who exactly?"

"Let's see." Doris began to tick off people on her fingers. "Trowbridge went in first, I think. Then Dr. Kemple, then me. After that it was Martin, then Sassafras. It was quite a parade. Nobody was with him more than five or ten minutes, I'd say."

"Let's back up a little. What was *your* purpose for seeing him?"

"Well, I'd been busy typing when Mr. Lloyd called me on the intercom—there's one in my office and another in the Portal

Room—and told me he wanted to see me. I had to squeeze around a giant eye to get to him."

"Want to explain that?"

Doris smiled at her own coyness. "Mr. Lloyd had just purchased a sculpture of a huge eye. Trowbridge and Martin had tried earlier in the day to bring it inside and ended up breaking a stained-glass window. Mr. Lloyd was pretty angry about that, but I could barely keep from laughing. It was like watching Laurel and Hardy!" Her mood suddenly shifted as darker memories came forward. "Of course, that stained glass didn't matter in the end. Nothing would matter for Mr. Lloyd. Anyway, Trowbridge and Martin were giving it another try then. They'd been dragging the sculpture down the hallway, and it got stuck in front of my office. So, when Mr. Lloyd summoned me, I had to squeeze around."

"And then . . ."

"Dr. Kemple was leaving the Portal Room when I entered. Mr. Lloyd seemed agitated about something and told me to call Paul Foster, his lawyer."

"Why didn't Lloyd just tell you that over the intercom?"

"Mr. Lloyd liked to give instructions in person. He wanted me to tell Mr. Foster to come over at his earliest opportunity. When I asked if I should give any further explanation, he said, 'Tell Foster I want to change my will.'"

Mr. O'Nelligan looked up from his reading and caught my eye. Changing one's will was always a point of interest.

"Did Lloyd say why he wanted to do that?" I asked

Miss Chauncey shook her head. "No, not to me. I went back to my office and called Mr. Foster, and he said he'd be over first thing in the morning. They were still struggling with that big eye in the hallway, and finally Martin went to ask Mr. Lloyd what to do with it. Trowbridge just stood there muttering and grumbling at the silly thing. I even saw him kick it. Then Martin came back and said Mr. Lloyd was in a bad temper and just wanted them to put the sculpture in the big hallway closet for now. About that time, Sassafras went to see Mr. Lloyd for some reason or other. A few minutes later, she came and asked me to join Mr. Lloyd for the leveling."

"Okay, you've stumped me again. *Leveling?*"

"Once more, please forgive me, Mr. Plunkett. I keep forgetting that all these odd little terms we use here wouldn't be known to most people. Leveling is a kind of meditation we'd do before certain events. Whichever of us was at hand would be asked to take part."

"Who participated in the leveling Friday night?"

"Sassafras, Dr. Kemple, and I. And, of course, Mr. Lloyd. Dr. Kemple seemed grumbly about it, but he came all the same."

"Was Lloyd still agitated at that point?"

"No, by the time we joined him he was already very focused and calm. Whenever he leveled, Mr. Lloyd never let himself be distracted. We meditated for ten or fifteen minutes. The Spectricator presentation was scheduled for eight o'clock, so, a little before that, Sassafras opened the door and rang the temple bell. It's from ancient Tibet, and Mr. Lloyd would use it ceremonially to start off certain events. Once in a while, he would have someone besides himself do it. So Sassafras rang the bell, and Trowbridge brought in the clients."

"Where had the clients been before that?"

"They'd only arrived in the last few minutes. Trowbridge had them wait right here. As I say, the Portal Room's just beyond that door."

Mr. O'Nelligan slid his book under his arm and rose. "What say we enter that sad place of misfortune?"

AT FIRST I couldn't make out much, since the only illumination in the Portal Room came from a single high window whose thick burgundy curtains were half drawn. Lloyd had died here, in the area of the house he believed was most accessible to spirits. I felt a bit of a chill, but that probably came from the cold rainstorm just outside the walls. Probably. I also took note of a trembling shadow or two that I didn't much like. These disappeared when Miss Chauncey flicked a light switch to reveal a sizable space furnished with a number of chairs, a couple of small tables, and several wrought-iron candle stands.

And one other notable feature. Centered atop a marble base, an elaborate-looking apparatus—a four-feet-high metallic cube—sat like an abandoned idol to science. A chaos of coils, wires, dials, meters, glass tubes, antennas, and God knows what else protruded from all sides; as the thing's crowning glory, the amplifying horn from an old gramophone jutted from its top.

Doris nodded reverentially at the contraption. "The Spectricator. It was Mr. Lloyd's latest invention. It's supposed to draw down the voices of the deceased. Friday was to have been the first witnessed demonstration."

"Miss Chauncey, level with me," I said. "You seem like a smart modern girl. Do you buy into all this haunted rigmarole?'

She shrugged. "I'm not really sure, but you know what they say—there are more things in heaven and earth . . ."

Whoa now. I shot a glance at Mr. O'Nelligan. Had that old rapscallion fed her that line? Though I realized that he hadn't had the opportunity to, I still didn't trust him. He offered me a gratified smile.

I returned to my questioning. "No one besides your employer had seen the Spectricator activated?"

"Only Dr. Kemple," Doris replied. "The two of them had worked on it together over the last few weeks."

Mr. O'Nelligan now joined in. "This machine was, presumably, the cause of Trexler Lloyd's death. It's deactivated now, I imagine."

"Oh, yes. It's been unplugged."

My colleague walked over to a corner table and lifted from it an ornate brass bell and small mallet. He struck the bell once, producing a resonant peel. "So, Sassafras Miller rang this, and the butler led in the clients. What occurred next, Miss Chauncey?"

"Dr. Kemple hooked Mr. Lloyd up to the Spectricator. He was seated right there." She pointed to a purple upholstered chair close to the machine.

"How was he hooked up?" I asked.

Again the secretary pointed, this time to a long black cable hanging from one side of the metal box, its end connected to a thick metal band. "It clamped onto his wrist," she said quietly.

Skipping that medieval image, I moved on with my next set of questions. "Were there any indications then of electrical problems?"

"I don't know, because we left the room then. The staff, I mean. We left Mr. Lloyd and Dr. Kemple alone with the clients. Oh, and Sassafras was with them as well."

"So you weren't here when Mr. Lloyd was killed?"

"I was still in the house, but not in this room. We were all out in the foyer—Trowbridge, Martin, and I. Also, the Galla-

gher girls were just about to head home. Then we heard Sassa-
fras scream, and she ran out and said, 'He's been electrocuted.'
Then everybody hurried back in here. Except for the Gallaghers.
I think they got frightened and left, but everyone else came."

"What did you see when you reentered?"

"Mr. Lloyd was sprawled out on the floor. Mr. Emmitt was
kneeling over him while Dr. Kemple kept everyone else back.
And Sassafras was crying through it all."

I latched onto one of those individuals. "Tell me about Felix
Emmitt. Why was he here?"

"It's my understanding that he came as a client."

"The county coroner enjoys séances?"

"It wasn't exactly a séance. Besides, I guess that someone
whose career focuses on death might have a keen interest in the
afterlife."

"A fine supposition," Mr. O'Nelligan chimed in. "But didn't
it strike you as a touch coincidental that he happened to be present at the very moment of Mr. Lloyd's passing?"

"I suppose at first I just thought of it as lucky. I mean that he
was there to take care of things. Afterward, I begin to have
doubts."

"Who were the other clients present?" I asked.

"There were the Greers, a couple who'd lost their son in
Korea. And there was Loretta Mapes, who lives in Stamford.
She's a Negro." For that last word, Doris's voice dipped ever so
slightly in volume, as if guarding against some eavesdropper's
disapproval. "Mrs. Mapes seems very nice," she added hastily.

I winced a little at her awkward attempt at tolerance. "Anyway, your boss was on the floor and . . ."

"Mr. Emmitt pronounced him dead. I went directly to my
office to call the police. Then I went upstairs to inform Mrs.

Lloyd. Even though it was a terrible situation, I was trying to be as efficient as possible."

Aha! That golden word again. "How did his wife take the news?"

"How do you expect she took it?" For the first time, Miss Chauncey sounded testy with me. "She was devastated, of course. And this was the second time she'd lost a husband. Her first was a matador gored in the ring back in Spain. Really, it's true." She sighed. "When I told her about Mr. Lloyd, she fell apart in my arms and kept saying, 'I can't look at him. I can't look at him,' and I told her she didn't have to. But then Sassafras came up—she was a wreck herself—and said Mr. Emmitt wanted to have the spouse identify the body."

"Couldn't any number of people have handled that?" I wondered.

"That's what I thought, but I figured he was just going by the book. Sassafras and I helped Constanza downstairs and brought her in here. It was horrible for her, but she glanced at Mr. Lloyd for a few seconds and made the official identification. Then things got even more chaotic, if you can believe it." She looked at me to see if I did. "Detective Agnelli and his partner arrived and tried to check things out. Then Dr. Kemple started yelling at them not to disrupt the death aura, or something like that. He even produced a legal document stating that Mr. Lloyd wanted to be cremated immediately after death. Constanza told the detectives that her husband's wishes had to be met. At that point, Detective Agnelli asked to use a phone to check in with his chief. I led him to my office, but first I got Sassafras to take Mrs. Lloyd back to her room. I joined them there a couple of minutes later."

Mr. O'Nelligan now took on the questioning. "Were you present at that moment when the body was taken away?"

"No, I remained with Constanza. Though I did happen to glance out her window and saw the hearse driving off."

"How long after Mr. Lloyd died would you guess that to be?"

"About a half hour."

"Only a half hour? That hearse was obtained rather briskly."

"No, it was already here on the premises. It's one of Mr. Lloyd's personal vehicles. He bought it last year as a kind of joke."

"A decidedly dark joke, indeed," mused Mr. O'Nelligan.

Doris gave a little shrug. "Well, with his interest in death and the afterlife, it actually didn't seem all that peculiar. But, living here like I have, maybe I've grown a little too used to the morbid and the bizarre."

"Yeah, maybe." My eyes wandered back to the Spectricator, that mechanical monstrosity that was built to summon the dead. "Maybe just a touch."

CHAPTER FOUR

E HAD JUST STEPPED BACK into the waiting room when a force of nature named Sassafras Miller burst in on us.

"Crap almighty! It's raining zebras outside!" The large blonde tore off a dripping raincoat and tossed it onto a chair. She was garbed in something ruffled and radiant—shell-shock orange, I'd call it. "Not just cats and dogs but ever-lovin' zebras! I just got back from town, and Rast tells me we got visitors. Come on, which one of you gents rubbed auras with Trexler? Was it you?" She eyeballed Mr. O'Nelligan. "I'd guess you've cornered a spirit or two in your time, right? Why sure you have."

"Regrettably, no," the Irishman said. "I am the most mundane of men."

Sassafras's eyes widened. "Is that a brogue? God, I do love a brogue! I had a lover once, Mad Dan McFinney, who had the sweetest little brogue you ever heard. Unfortunately, some other hoodlum shot Dan in the throat back in '32. New Year's Eve it was. Didn't kill him, but that brogue was pretty much butchered. You happen to know Mad Dan?"

"Never had the pleasure," Mr. O'Nelligan replied. "Alas, there are several Irishmen here in America with whom I've never crossed paths."

"Ha!" Sassafras slapped his shoulder roughly. "You're the clever boy, aren't you?"

My sixtyish friend didn't say whether he was or was not a clever boy, but did offer his assailant a thin smile. Sassafras now faced me, and I could see that, beneath her well-applied rouge and lipstick, she was clearly closing in on sixty herself.

"So, Mac, *you* must be the one with the voodoo. Doris here says—oh, wait!" Sassafras pushed past me and made a beeline for the dead raccoon. She patted its small vicious head three times, then turned back to me. "Excuse me, champ, but it's my habit, you know? Whenever I enter this room, I gotta pet that little bastard, pardon my French. I guess I'm superstitious, but, hell, if you're gonna be superstitious, this is the place to do it. Hey, kid!" she addressed Doris Chauncey. "Did you tell them this is a genuine haunted house?"

"No. I didn't." Miss Chauncey lifted Sassafras's dripping raincoat from the chair and hung it on a coat rack. "Because I don't know that it's true."

"Oh, c'mon, hon, you've lived here, what, two years? All that time, you've been surrounded by tons of spiritualist types, and you still won't give our resident ghosts the courtesy of believing in 'em? That's out-and-out unfriendly."

"Don't be so haughty," Doris admonished. "*You've* never experienced anything here, either. You've said so yourself."

Sassafras chuckled. "Yeah, but when you tally up all the

crazy doings I've been through in my life, it's no wonder ghosts give me a wide berth. Look, I know I'm not the most sensitive of females, and I guess you gotta be sensitive for the spirits to reach you. At least that's what Trexler always said." She caught herself up and released a low sigh. "Poor Trex. Now, maybe he's one of them." She spun back to me. "Did you see him floating around? Hey, what's your name, anyway?"

"I'm Lee Plunkett."

"Forget the Plunkett. Last names are extra baggage. I'll call you Lee. And what's your friend's handle?"

He answered for himself. "Just Mr. O'Nelligan."

"What, your mama didn't give you a first name? Never mind. I'll just call you Blarney 'cause I think you're full of the stuff. Anyway, you can corner Martin later and get him to rattle off all the spooks in this house. I can't keep track of 'em all, but ol' Switzerland knows the whole roster."

"We'll do that," Mr. O'Nelligan vowed. "But first we were hoping to get your own impressions of what happened Friday."

"Sure, sure," she bobbed her head. "It's a crying shame what happened to that man. Prime of his life, and he had to go get fried like an egg."

"Sassafras!" Doris scowled at her. "Do you always have to be so coarse?"

"Some call it charm. Listen, honey, if I wasn't joking, I'd be bawling, you know that. I was awful fond of ol' Trex. Hey, Lee!" I caught her attention again. "You didn't say exactly how he showed up for you. Was it in full phantom mode? Or maybe ectoplasm? It's supposed to be a kind of supernatural substance, but I saw a photo once and it just looked like something you'd cough up after a bad night on the town. So, give, how'd Trexler contact you?"

I realized that in keeping with my newly minted vocation of psychic, my response had better sound authentic. I could feel Mr. O'Nelligan and Doris staring at me as they, no doubt, wondered what precisely I was going to cook up here.

I thrust out my answer, "Emanations!" and paused to let it wash over the room. What hat I'd pulled it out of, I'd no idea, but judging by the look on Sassafras Miller's face, it was a dandy choice.

"Right, em-a-na-tions . . ." She drew it out, sounding both puzzled and satisfied.

I went in for the kill. "Yes, emanations from the afterlife. I felt Lloyd's presence, and he told me he needed assistance to move on to the next stage."

This jazzed up Sassafras. "He actually spoke to you?"

That was perhaps going too far. "Well, no . . ." I scrambled to keep from losing ground. "His emanations . . . his emanations told me."

I watched her face to see how this last bit played.

When Sassafras said, "Then you need to help him," I knew I'd passed my first test as psychic.

Mr. O'Nelligan, uneasy, I was sure, with this subterfuge, shifted the conversation. "We understand, Mrs. Miller, that Friday night you had dinner with—"

"Whoa now. It's *Miss* Miller," the woman informed him. "I shed four husbands in my time—buried two, divorced two, just to keep it even—and I dropped each of their names afterward like a hot potato. I always end up with Miller, like I started with back in Plum, Pennsylvania. But if you call me anything other than Sassafras, I'll clam up like Garbo."

Mr. O'Nelligan knew when to pick his battles. "Very well . . . Sassafras. As I was saying, we—"

"Here's the deal. You want to talk to me, you gotta come to my bedroom." The aging speakeasy queen gave us a wink. "I've got something I want to show you."

Doris Chauncey rolled her eyes. "You gentlemen do what you need to do. I'm going to finish up a list I was making for you."

"That's swell, kid," the other woman said. "You toddle off and leave 'em to me. Two men and one Sassafras—I like that math!"

Dear God, where was this heading? Well, first off, back down the hallway, where Doris split off from the rest of us to enter a room on the right. As she opened the door, I glanced in and viewed a neat little office, as prim and proper as the secretary herself.

Sassafras led us farther down to a door on the left. "They didn't give me a bedroom upstairs like the other ladies. I guess for a gal like me it's better to sleep closer to hell than heaven." She guffawed and gripped the knob. "Know what I mean? Why, sure you do."

I'D FIRST HEARD about Sassafras Miller back when I was a kid, maybe fifteen years old. As a matter of fact, I remember the exact moment. This would have been, I think, in 1940, when my father was still a Hartford police detective. We were a year away from Pearl Harbor, two years away from moving to Thelmont, where Dad set up shop as a private gumshoe, and three years away from the leukemia that would take Mom at age forty-two. I think it must have been a Sunday, because we were all home—my parents, my sisters, and I—and because Sunday was always pancake day. The girls and I rushed to the breakfast table at Mom's first summons, but my father dallied in the adjoining living room. From my seat, I could see him sunk in his fat, fading easy chair, his nose buried in a newspaper.

"Geez, this Sassafras Miller is one out-of-control dame," he called out. "You read this, Gertie? She got nabbed up in Canada for stealing a dogsled. A dogsled! Her and some Brazilian politician she was gallivanting around with."

"That's terrible," Mom said, distributing the flapjacks. "What's a Brazilian doing up in Canada, anyway? Don't those people like their weather hot?"

Dad lowered his paper. "Well, I bet Sassafras kept him good and steamy, if you know what I mean."

"Buster! The kids!" Mom was often shielding us from her husband's worldly observations. "Now come eat."

My father shuffled in to join us.

"Sassafras is a neat name," my eleven-year-old sister, June, declared. "I wish *I* was a Sassafras."

Marjorie, age seven, corrected her. "No, you don't, either, Junie. 'Cause that lady's a *whore*."

The word hung in the air like mustard gas.

Our group speechlessness was finally broken by my father, who turned to me and demanded, "Did you put her up to this?"

"No!" And I hadn't. "Why do you always blame me?"

He answered with a slanderous grunt.

My mother spoke calmly but firmly. "First of all, Marjorie, that lady isn't exactly . . . what you just said. And, secondly, where in heaven's name did you ever hear that word?"

Seemingly oblivious of her crime, our little princess shrugged and stabbed herself a chunk of pancake. "I dunno. I think maybe from Mrs. Flint." This was a neighborhood elder famed for her religious zeal. "She said how they all come from Babylon. She named a whole bunch of ladies, and Sassafras was one. Mrs. Flint said they're all whores of Babylon."

At this point, Mom's voice rose an octave as she instructed Marjorie never, never, never to use that word again as long as she lived, even if it did have biblical significance.

Burdened with that long-lingering image of dogsled indiscretion, I now entered Sassafras Miller's bedroom. I think I expected something plush and brothel-like, the decor all blazing reds and midnight blacks, with a giant canopied bed meant to beckon lost sailors, but that wasn't at all what Mr. O'Nelligan and I walked into. Instead, the room we found ourselves in was subdued and delicate—here a vase of dried flowers, there a shelf of tiny glass figures—with a narrow bed covered by a faded pink and white bedspread. Atop the plump pillow sat a trio of stuffed toys—a bear, a rabbit, and a mouse—each adorned with a pastel ribbon. The overall feel of the room was childlike and somewhat fragile.

Sassafras pulled open a bureau drawer and lifted out something swaddled in a white silk scarf. She sat down on the edge of her bed, unwrapped the object, and held it up for us to see. It was a gold statuette of a man, a little over a foot tall.

"Is that an *Oscar*?" I asked, failing to keep incredulousness out of my tone. After all, Sassafras Miller's film career had been a lackluster one at best.

"Yesiree, it certainly is." She lowered the statuette and stared down into its shiny little face. "Trexler gave it to me. It's genuine. I've no idea how he dredged one up, but that man had his ways. I had lousy little parts in four stinking movies, but Trex said it didn't matter. He said this was an award for being indefinable. That's how he put it—'Sassafras, I award you for being completely indefinable.'"

"An accurate sentiment, no doubt," Mr. O'Nelligan said.

Sassafras raised her eyes to us. "Look, in my time I've known heaps of men. Heaps of 'em. I was pretty damned gorgeous once upon a time—and I ain't even bragging. I've had movie stars and gangsters and tycoons that were all crazy about me. I know I've gone to paunch and my best years are behind me, but in my day, I was a real firecracker. Yeah, I had 'em all, but I never had an authentic genius. And that's what Trexler was. He existed on a completely different level, y'know? Like he could see the whole world inside out. To have a man like that think of me as something special . . ." Here her voice broke a little, but she caught herself just short of tears. "No. No. I told myself I wasn't going to cry any more for him. He wouldn't have tolerated it."

Mr. O'Nelligan spoke tenderly. "Madam, if you need us to—"

Sassafras waved him off. "I'm okay. Honest." She rewrapped her Oscar, got up, and replaced it in the bureau. "I keep him burrowed away. The little fella's my hidden treasure." She turned back to us. "Listen, I don't want to give the impression that Trexler and I had anything going on, or that I hoped we might. I'm under no delusions, y'know? I mean, have you seen my competition? Who in his right mind would trade that Spanish rose for this wilting petunia?" She laughed softly. "But I sure amused the guy. You gotta give me credit for that. Trex definitely found me amusing. "

I felt it was time to march out some questions. "How long had you known Lloyd?"

"I met him maybe four years ago, but it was really in the last year or so that we became pals and I moved in here. He'd seen me hosting a cabaret down in Jersey and decided I might make a good emcee for when he took his supernatural lectures on the road. He'd really gotten deep into this ghosty stuff over the last couple years. To me it was like we were doing medicine shows, only instead of tonics, we were peddling phantoms. But that was fine with me. I'm always up for a good flimflam."

"How do you spend your time when you're not out on the lecture circuit?"

Sassafras grinned. "I putter, Lee! I'm the best damned putterer of the twentieth century. I lounge around, raid the icebox, read the gossip magazines, and jabber away at whoever I can corner in this creaky old ghost trap."

"We understand that Friday night you had dinner with the Lloyds and Miss Chauncey." I glanced at my notebook. "Around six. How did Lloyd seem to you then?"

"He seemed swell. He was looking forward to unveiling his spooktricator."

"Where did you go after dinner?"

"I came back here and read for about forty-five minutes." Sassafras indicated a thick book on the nightstand. "It's my fifth shot at *Gone with the Wind*. I keep promising myself I'll finish it, but a thousand pages is a helluva chore. I think Scarlett O'Hara will be a wrinkled old biddy by the time I wrap it up."

"Forge on!" Mr. O'Nelligan encouraged. "Literature is like a bucking stallion. Stay in the saddle and you'll see it to its end."

"A bucking stallion! Wow, you sure can fling a phrase, can't you, Blarney? Hey, if you're such a literature fan, I've got a copy of *The Kinsey Report* somewhere I could scrounge up for you." Sassafras snickered. "I kinda think of it as my biography."

I got us back on course, "So, after reading, you went to the Portal Room?"

"Yeah, I wanted to take part in the leveling. That's a sort of meditation."

"So we've heard. Do you level a lot?"

Sassafras wagged a finger at me. "Now, I know what you're thinking—'This dame can't keep her mouth shut to save her life, so how's she gonna sit silent for even a minute.' Well, we'd only do it for about a quarter hour at a time. I can put up with anything for fifteen minutes. Hell, that's longer than some romances I've had!" She was back in form.

"Was Lloyd alone when you went in?" I asked.

"Yep."

"Earlier, Miss Chauncey and Rast each saw him individually, and both found he was in a foul mood. Was that the case when you went in?"

"Hard to say. He was just sitting there pondering. Maybe a little moody, I suppose. I asked him if after the leveling I could ring the bell to call in his clients, and he said, 'Sure, why not, Sassafras.' 'Cause he knew that I'm partial to that little Chinese bell."

"Tibetan," Mr. O'Nelligan corrected. "The bell comes from Tibet."

"I never get that right. Anyhow, then I ask Trexler should I go gather up some of the gang for the leveling, and he says to get on it. So I went out, snatched Doris and ol' Dr. Grumble, and we went to the Portal Room and did our little thing."

"Was Lloyd still calm then?" I asked.

"Oh sure. I mean, I won't lie, Trex could be a real stormy guy when he wanted to be. But when he was meditating, he was always cool, calm, and collected. We leveled for maybe fifteen minutes, then at eight I popped up and rang the bell. Trowbridge had the clients next door in the waiting room, so he led them right in and things got under way."

"The butler didn't remain?" Mr. O'Nelligan asked, clarifying a point.

"No, he buttled and scrammed. Doris left, too. Then it all

happened pretty quick. After everyone was seated, ol' C. R. Kemple hooked Trexler up to the machine and said a few words to the group about how he and Trex had created this thingama-jig that would change the way we communicated with the dead."

"Did Mr. Lloyd say anything?"

"Yeah, I think so. Probably. Then they flicked a few switches, and while C. R. was jabbering on about this and that, it hap-pened. The *electrocution*." The word distorted the woman's whole face. "All of a sudden, there's crackling and sparks flying and poor Trexler's slumped over dead in his chair."

I noted a variation in the tale. "He was seated? Miss Chauncey said he was sprawled on the floor."

"Well, after all the sparks, Felix Emmitt kind of eased him to the floor to examine him."

"Emmitt was the first at his side?"

"Yeah. It was good that he was there. He's a coroner, y'know. He said right off the bat that Trex was dead, and I gotta admit it hit me hard. I was wailing like a nut. I ran out into the hall and called to Doris and the others. Pretty soon the room's filling up with people and detectives, and C. R. is yelling at everybody, and we're dragging Constanza in and out, and it's all just horrible. Doris and I ended up with Constanza back upstairs, and that's all I really know."

"A chaotic scene, indeed," Mr. O'Nelligan observed. "And you have no doubts that electrocution was the cause of death?"

Sassafras looked thrown by the question. "What do you mean? Didn't I just say that? That damned machine scorched Trexler's heart. That's what Felix Emmitt told us. What else could it have been?"

"I'm just underlining the facts," my partner said. "This old noggin isn't what it once was, so I like to accent the pertinent points for myself."

Sassafras narrowed her eyes. "You don't fool me, pally. I know you, sure as sin. . . ."

For a moment I thought our jig was up. Though I somehow hadn't registered it before, it now occurred to me that Sassafras would have recognized Mr. O'Nelligan from last month's event. She would have remembered him standing to describe Samhain, and also how Audrey had identified him as a detective. I waited for the blow to fall.

"Yeah, I've got your number," she continued. "You're one of those vintage gents who pretend to be getting soft in the brain pan, when they're really sharp as daggers. Ain't I been listening to your fanciness for the last half hour?"

So, apparently, Sassafras's powers of observation weren't too well-honed. She hadn't recognized my friend after all.

Mr. O'Nelligan smiled somewhat sheepishly. "I didn't intend to feign dullness, madam."

"What's your racket anyway, Blarney? Lee here gabs with ghosts, but what are *you* tagging along for?"

I answered that. "Mr. O'Nelligan helps keep my powers grounded." This was actually true, except for the fact that I had no real powers other than the ability to fill a notebook legibly.

Sassafras zeroed in on me again. "Okay, I gotta know, Lee, when you were chatting with Trexler's emanations, did he, well, did he . . ." She glanced away. "Did he mention me?"

I fumbled at an answer. "Uh, not really. That is . . . it was emanations, you understand. The emanations didn't mention anyone in particular. At least, I don't—"

She let out a strained laugh. "Oh, I'm just having fun with ya, bud. I mean, why would he care about one crazy old dame when he's probably got a whole harem of spooks to bide his time with now? I'm just joking." But she wasn't.

"Thank you for your assistance, good lady." My friend offered her a chivalrous little nod. "I trust we can speak again if the need arises?"

"Sure. You guys know where to find me." Sassafras plopped herself back down on the edge of the bed.

As Mr. O'Nelligan and I were leaving the woman's room, I glanced back and caught her scooping up one of the stuffed animals. For a second or two, seeing her there in her quiet little space, cradling a toy rabbit, I saw not Sassafras, the raucous speakeasy mistress, but a small-town girl named Brenda Miller, far from a place called Plum.

CHAPTER FIVE

E REJOINED DORIS CHAUN-cey in her office and accepted a list with contact information for everyone who'd been present at the house Friday evening. The address for Foster, the lawyer, was also included.

"I called everyone last night and told them to expect to hear from you," Doris said. "The only one I couldn't reach was Felix Emmitt. I told everyone it was very important that they cooperate with you and answer all your questions. And I used my little fib, Mr. Plunkett."

"Right, the sweet little fib about me being psychic." I sighed. "Alright, thanks for the list, Miss Chauncey. Are any other members of the staff here now?"

"Only Martin, but Trowbridge should be back before long, and Mrs. Perris the cook will be here most evenings."

"Okay. We'll go talk to the groundskeeper right now and

catch the others later. And we'll want to come back soon to see Mrs. Lloyd, of course."

Doris ushered us back outside. The rainfall had now lifted, leaving in its place a strong, moist wind.

"You should find Martin in that shed over there." She pointed to a small outbuilding on the edge of the front lawn. "He's working on one of his projects. And please don't hesitate to ask me for anything. Anything at all. I want to be of as much assistance as possible."

We thanked her and made our way to the shed. Stepping inside, we squinted against the glare of several naked lightbulbs dangling from the ceiling. Crouching on the concrete floor, brush in hand, Martin Rast was methodically applying a coat of yellow paint to one of a half-dozen wooden boxes. Noting our presence, he stood and beckoned us over with a wide sweep of his arm.

"Come! See my work here. These are my inventions. Mr. Lloyd was an inventor, and so also am I."

With his brush, he pointed to the box he was painting. It stood about two feet high, and I saw now that its wooden frame held in place four glass plates. Through the glass, a cone of extremely fine metal mesh could be seen. The tip of the cone had a small opening, while the base seemed fastened to the wood bottom.

"What is it?" I had to ask.

The spectacled pirate smiled thinly but proudly. "I call it my Fly Bastille. But these flies do not break free, no, no. The plan is that the flies are much attracted to enter the cone. They see it through the glass and go in, but they cannot find their way back out."

Mr. O'Nelligan cast a skeptical eye on Rast's creation. "It

seems to me they could simply track their path back through the entrance."

"But they do not!" the Swiss man declared. "Why not, you say? No one knows. It is a secret of nature. But I have done the test myself."

"Not many flies around in early December," I noted.

Rast scowled. "There are the horse stables just through the woods. Even in December, stables can make flies. Do the neighbors care that their insects attack here? No! Miss Doris is plagued by these flies. She is a nice girl, so I make my boxes for her. And they must be yellow. Flies like yellow."

Having no ammunition to counter that claim, I moved on to other matters. "Miss Chauncey says you were helping to move a sculpture on Friday."

"Great idiot eye!" Rast spat out. "I do not like that eye. Maybe Mr. Lloyd finds something to love about it, but me, I cannot see it."

I smiled sympathetically as if I, like all sane men, hated that eye as well. "You had trouble moving it, we heard. A window was broken."

Rast lowered his eyes. "That gives me sadness. I do not like to hurt the house."

"Mr. Lloyd got angry about that?"

"A little. Yes."

"Later, after dinnertime, when you went to see him in the Portal Room, was he still angry about the window?"

"Oh no, Mr. Lloyd did not grab a grudge."

"Grab a grudge?"

Mr. O'Nelligan intervened. "I believe, sir, the phrase is 'hold a grudge.'"

Rast nodded vigorously. "Yes, yes, thank you. No grudge

was held. And I had already fixed the window. But Mr. Lloyd was in a bad mood about something else, I think. About someone else maybe."

"Someone else? Who?"

Rast tossed up his hands. "I cannot know. It is just my feeling."

Feelings. Sensations. Emanations . . . I was getting tired of the whole shebang. "Did you speak for long in the Portal Room?"

"No, because he threw me out. But first, he told me to put the idiot eye in the hallway closet, and that's what we did, Trowbridge and myself. Soon after, the guests come, and Trowbridge takes them into the Portal Room. A little after that, he comes back and talks with Miss Doris and myself. Next we hear screaming. It is Miss Sassafras Miller, and she runs out and says Mr. Lloyd is electrocuted. Then we all run in. There now!" Rast clapped his hands together. "I have told you all I know. Now tell me all *you* know, Mr. Plunkett. Miss Doris says you speak to Mr. Lloyd, yes?"

I ran through my now standard spiel regarding emanations, adding a nice flourish or two about Lloyd having misplaced his path to the afterlife, and waited to see if Rast lapped it up.

He stared at me for a long moment before responding. "It is too bad Mr. Lloyd is lost. But why does he not seek out Reverend Hayes or Little Violet? Even Miss Winifred would probably be kind to him."

Mr. O'Nelligan and I exchanged a glance. Had we missed something? I thought for a second about pulling out Doris's list of who's who, but held back.

Rast added to the cast of characters. "Gillmond, of course, would be no help, because he is always so angry with everything. But certainly Old Ezekiel—"

Mr. O'Nelligan halted this cavalcade of new names. "Wait now, sir. Are these members of the household you refer to?"

"Yes, in a way," Rast said quietly. "They are the dead ones."

"Dead ones?" My eyebrows headed north. "You're talking about ghosts?"

Suspicion clouded Rast's face. "Of course. They are the spirits of the house. But why do you act with surprise, Mr. Pick-it? You are supposed to have abilities. You were just in the house, so you must have felt their energies, no?"

"Oh, yes, certainly yes. It's just that, well . . ." I petered out. This psychic ruse was fast becoming a burden.

Rast bent down to rest his brush on the edge of a paint can, then pulled himself erect and aimed his horn-rimmed glasses at my saucer-shaped ones. "You went to the Portal Room to see where Mr. Lloyd died, yes? Then you must have noticed Miss Winifred. She died there, too. Very sad lady. She had the melancholia and killed herself with the poison."

"Of course. The sad lady," I said without conviction.

Rast didn't let up. "And Little Violet? Did you not find her in the hallway? She likes to run up and down. Wild dogs killed that poor girl. Sometimes you can see her scars. Sometimes you cannot. Then there is Gillmond. He is the one to stay away from, because he once beat a man to death with a cane. When he was alive, I mean. I do not know of him killing anyone as a spirit."

"Well, that's certainly a relief."

"Then there are the poltergeists. The ones who take objects and hide them. They are very annoying."

"They sure are," I felt required to agree. "Those annoying poltergeists."

The Swiss adjusted his glasses, the better to see me. "I do not think you are someone with great abilities. Forgive me, but I must say that."

Mr. O'Nelligan came to my rescue. "Mr. Plunkett's powers are of a subtle nature." I could tell he wasn't happy getting into this, but, after all, he wasn't lying—my powers were so subtle they were downright unnoticeable. "But what of your own sensitivities, Mr. Rast? Do you actually see these spirits?"

"I do. Sometimes I might just hear Miss Winifred crying or Reverend Hayes saying his Bible, but mostly I see them all. Please, say nothing of these things to Miss Doris. I do not share much with her, because she is such a nice girl and should not be made frightened. "

"We shall spare her," my colleague promised. "How is it you know the names of these spirits?"

"Some told me themselves, but I looked in the town records to find the others. Some once lived here, like Miss Winifred and Violet. Others, like the reverend, were guests who never left."

I'd be lying if I said that this whole conversation wasn't unsettling me. Sobbing suicides and angry bludgeoners weren't the type of beings I relished getting to know.

"How old is the house?' Mr. O'Nelligan asked.

"Over one hundred years." Rast retrieved his brush and moved on to another box.

"A hundred years," I repeated. "I can believe it. The place looks ready to crumble. And a paint job sure wouldn't kill it."

Rast turned and fixed me with a hard stare. Oh, right, this was the groundskeeper, the man whose responsibilities probably included the upkeep of the house.

In response to my galloping insensitivity, he waved his brush at me. "Mr. Lloyd preferred to leave the house as it is. No paint.

No big repairs. He said that way the energies would keep strong. I think so, too."

"Well, he was a lucky man indeed to have you to see to the grounds here." O'Nelligan the diplomat now worked his magic. "Even with our brief view of the environs, it's clear that a skilled hand cares for this place. Not even the shadows of a rainy December day can hide that fact. Lee Plunkett here was saying as much to me not ten minutes ago. He was really quite impressed." Apparently, my comrade could conjure up his own little fibs in times of need.

Properly honored, Rast studied me in a new light. "Maybe you do not know spirits so well, Mr. Plunkett, but it is good you know other things. Still, I do not believe Mr. Lloyd comes to you."

I didn't try to argue. "Did you like the man?"

Rast gave another thin smile. "One does not really like a person such as Trexler Lloyd. One admires him and what he does in the world. "

Mr. O'Nelligan gave a little nod of understanding. "How long had you been with him?"

"Two years almost. I am very blessed to be here. Very blessed. I have my own tiny building out back. Before that, I was living not far away, you see, and I worked as a church custodian. When I heard a great man was moving here who was interested in spirits, I knew I should ask to work for him. Now here I am."

Rast turned back to his latest fly box and swept his brush grandly across the wood. Yes, there he was, a man content at his work. An odd little man, to be sure, but then oddness seemed to be par for the course for the dwellers of Lloyd House.

* * *

THE RAIN HAD lifted by the time we made our departure. Rast had left the gates below open, and just as we were about to drive through them, a long, shiny hearse came barreling around the corner straight at us. There was no time to ponder the irony of being killed by a funeral car. I swerved madly and the opposing driver did the same, so that, miraculously, a head-on collision was avoided. Both vehicles came to a screeching halt side by side just inside the gates, and Mr. O'Nelligan and I climbed out, as did the sole occupant of the hearse—a tall man in his late fifties with sleek black hair, silver streaked, and a prominent curved nose. His looks, coupled with his wind-tossed black trench coat, made me think of a raven.

"Everyone's alright, I trust?" The man's English accent was refined and melodic.

I itched to say, *Sure, no thanks to you,* but held myself to an icy "Yes."

"No harm done, then," the man decided. "Do take care on this narrow driveway, though. I almost didn't see you."

"That's because you were hurtling toward us like a bloody locomotive." Mr. O'Nelligan was suffering no fools just now. He looked fairly shaken by the near-collision. "Are you the butler?"

"Yes, I'm Trowbridge. And who would *you* be, my Irish friend?" There wasn't a drop of warmth in the asking.

Mr. O'Nelligan tendered introductions, keeping his own warmth firmly under a bushel. He confined the explanation of my subtle abilities to a few subtle words.

Trowbridge sighed. "Ah, yes, Miss Chauncey mentioned someone would be coming. I had presumed with Mr. Lloyd gone that the visits by mediums might taper off, but, well, here you are."

"I would think that a virtual platoon of mediums might now

be expected." Mr. O'Nelligan's natural civility struggled to re-plant itself. "What with a new, rather eminent phantom now stationed here."

"I don't squander my time on phantoms," Trowbridge said dryly. "None of their lot has deemed it necessary to contact me, and I return the favor by ignoring *them*. It's a satisfactory arrangement."

"I see," my colleague responded. "Then that would number you, along with Miss Chauncey, as one of the household's skeptics."

"I can't speak for the girl. I imagine she believed whatever Mr. Lloyd instructed her to believe. Not much backbone to that one. But then, of course, backbone is certainly not a requirement for the position of secretary."

"And what of the position of butler?" Mr. O'Nelligan was taking on this snooty son of a gun. "What characteristics would you deem essential for your own vocation?"

Trowbridge didn't flinch. "Discretion, precision, and a sturdy deportment, to name but a few. Oh, and I almost forgot detachment. Yes, detachment goes a long way. And lastly . . . it never hurts to be English."

The glove had been thrown. These two men, born of nations with a shared history of armed strife, now stood staring each other down. I instinctively took a step back to distance myself from their standoff. Just when I feared they were about to re-spark old tribal violence, Mr. O'Nelligan drew himself back into detective mode.

"On Friday evening, approximately an hour prior to Trexler Lloyd's death, you spent a few minutes alone with him. What was the nature of this visit?"

"Tea."

"Tea?"

"Tea," the butler repeated. "It's a hot aromatic beverage favored by my people and, I believe, your own, Mr. O'Nelligan. If memory serves me, I was bringing Mr. Lloyd some Earl Grey."

"That's all that transpired between you—the passing of a teacup?"

"If memory serves."

I stepped back into the fray. "O-kay . . . How was your employer's mood then?"

"Exemplary," Trowbridge replied flatly. "Quite even keeled."

Pulling teeth, that's what this was. "When you returned after Lloyd was electrocuted, was there anything that struck you as unusual?"

Trowbridge drew in a breath and, for the first time, seemed to let down his haughty facade. "Only the manner of the death itself. Tethered to that preposterous machine—what a wasteful way to die."

"Will you miss him?" As I said it, I realized how strange that sounded, but it's just how it came out.

The Englishman drew in the wings of his flapping coat and spoke to the wind. "Any man's death diminishes me."

"John Donne," Mr. O'Nelligan said, by way of identification. "Are you inclined toward the metaphysical poets, then, Mr. Trowbridge?"

The butler's tone shifted back to its earlier smugness. "As a rule, I leave metaphysics to the likes of yourselves. You and that crew that whirled around Mr. Lloyd, but occasionally I'll admire the random verse if it strikes a chord. Now, I must be off. Some individuals have honest work to pursue."

Trowbridge got back into the hearse and continued up the

driveway. I noticed that he didn't much bother to lessen his speed.

"Glad that's over," I said when he was out of sight. "I thought fists were going to fly."

"It's not that the man's English, you know." Mr. O'Nelligan shook off the wind and turned back toward our car. "We're in a new land, and I grab no grudges, as our Swiss friend would say. It's just his unbelievable arrogance."

I followed, nursing a grin. "Yep, I thought for sure you were going to use your dukes on him."

"Now, Lee, that would be the style of savages," my comrade said. "In truth, I'd much prefer a good old Irish shillelagh."

"What's a shil-lay-lee? Is that some kind of musical instrument?"

"Oh, dear Lord! No, it's a walking stick which doubles as a cudgel. Oft used in battle."

"To battle butlers?"

Mr. O'Nelligan smiled wickedly. "When the occasion demands."

CHAPTER SIX

THE LAWYER'S OFFICE WAS only five miles up the road, so we made that our next stop. Paul Foster, a narrow, stooped man nearing seventy, met us without fanfare. Yes, he'd been expecting a visit from us, and, yes, he had a few minutes to spare.

"Normally, I wouldn't discuss these matters openly," Foster insisted as he offered us seats, "but, in this case, the widow wishes me to. Not that I have much to tell, I'm afraid. I really don't go in for all that supernatural business. Although my mother claimed to have seen her brother a week after he was killed at Gettysburg."

"We appreciate whatever information you can offer," I said, "and it doesn't need to be of the ghostly variety. Have you been Trexler Lloyd's lawyer for long?"

"Only the last two years," Foster explained. "That's when he moved here to Braywick. Apparently, he was making a clean sweep of things and wanted someone local to handle his legal interests."

"That must have been quite a boon for you," Mr. O'Nelligan suggested. "To take on such a well-placed client."

Foster had a pleasant smile. "That's an understatement. To be honest, having been put on retainer by Mr. Lloyd allows me to ease into my golden years very comfortably, and I'm truly grateful for that."

I pulled out my notebook and flipped to the timeline. "Roughly a half hour before Lloyd died, he asked his secretary to call you. About seven thirty. Is that right, Mr. Foster?"

"Yes, she told me that Mr. Lloyd wished to change his will. Not all that unusual a request. As a matter of fact, he made some changes just last month. But on Friday, Doris said that he was somewhat agitated and wanted to see me as soon as possible. I told her I had an engagement that evening, but I'd be by first thing in the morning. Of course, tragically, that never happened."

"So the will stands as it was?"

"Correct," Foster said. "And no one seems to know what changes Mr. Lloyd intended."

"You say he made some in November. What were they?"

"Well, I should explain that about a month ago Mr. Lloyd transferred the bulk of his assets to a bank in Madrid. That's a sum approaching a million dollars, by the way. The major revision in the will was that, in the event of his death, his wife must return to Spain to access her inheritance, and that she should do so within two weeks of his passing."

Mr. O'Nelligan leaned forward. "A curious provision. So Constanza Lloyd is planning to head back to her homeland in the next week or so?"

"Yes, I believe she has a flight scheduled for this coming Wednesday."

This was fresh news. Why hadn't someone mentioned it earlier?

The lawyer continued. "Everything was lined up to support expediency—the bank transfer, the probate requirements, everything. When a man of Mr. Lloyd's standing set his mind on something, well, it usually happened."

"Did he make any other changes last month?" I asked.

"Yes, he had me draw up a document expressing his desire to be cremated within hours of his death. My understanding was that this was somehow in keeping with his views on the afterlife. But that's more your field than mine, Mr. Plunkett."

Oh, right. My field with all the emanations. "Who else benefits by the will?"

Foster rested a finger against his cheek. "Well, let's see. Mr. Lloyd's two ex-wives were long ago paid off and are quite out of the picture. His only living relatives are an aunt and two cousins in Florida. A bequeathment of a thousand dollars has been made to each of them. Miss Miller—Sassafras—receives a like amount. Several institutions and organizations have also been mentioned in the will—some of a charitable nature, others more on the 'ghostly' side of things, as you put it. Beyond that, a number of portions have been set aside for members of his staff, both from here and from his other homes."

"Anything substantial?"

"Not really. The monetary allotments average a few hundred dollars each. From his Braywick staff, the secretary, butler, and cook are all recognized. The groundskeeper receives no cash, but he inherits the house here."

"Rast? The house doesn't go to Constanza?"

"No, as I've said, she'll be returning to Spain and will have no use for it. The five other homes will be sold and the funds eventually transferred to Madrid. And, truth be told, the Braywick house isn't really that valuable an acquisition. Besides its obvious state of disrepair, it does suffer from a bit of a reputation, you know."

"That it's haunted?" I asked.

This time Foster's smile was more subdued. "Even when I was a boy, I heard rumors. I believe there was a suicide or two there. And they say a child was once killed on the grounds. By a dog pack, I think."

A chill raced through me. I glanced over at Mr. O'Nelligan, but he appeared immune to the echoes of that ancient house. Well, Rast certainly was a fitting choice to get the keys to the place, seeing as he was already well acquainted with its bodiless tenants.

"Bleak rumors, indeed," my colleague noted. "Although I presume that the house's reputation was the very reason Mr. Lloyd acquired it."

"Without a doubt," the lawyer replied. "He found the most unpleasant house in town and snapped it up. Well, gentlemen, I have some work I need to attend to."

We all rose and exchanged handshakes.

"Thank you for your time," I said.

Foster shrugged. "For what little worth it's been. After all, my expertise is in the legal world, not the ethereal. I don't pretend to know what happens after death. But, if Lloyd's soul really is drifting loose somewhere, I do hope it finds peace. That's no more than anyone deserves."

IT BEING LUNCHTIME, we stopped at the cozy little Braywick Tavern, ordered two chicken pot pies, and reviewed our morning.

"I'm pretty weary of this mystic bit Doris drummed up for me," I said. "People are expecting me to haul down a dead man's spirit and tuck it in for eternity. That's not in my usual job description."

Mr. O'Nelligan brought his fingertips together in a pose of contemplation. "Ah, but perhaps it is. After all, isn't it our job here to properly tuck in Trexler Lloyd's memory by discovering the true manner of his death?"

"Only you would take a perfectly fine complaint and turn it into a sonnet."

"A sonnet consists of fourteen lines. I've only offered a couple."

"Oh, dear Lord," I groaned.

Our waitress delivered a cup of tea for my companion and a glass of ice water for myself. Water had been my father's only beverage at meals, and I'd carried on the tradition. I think it was Buster's one nod toward moderation. Afterward, of course, he'd knock back a few beers alongside cronies with names like Lefty and Dukey and Kokomo Joe, but for eating it was straight H_2O.

Mr. O'Nelligan, who was as far from a Lefty or a Dukey as one could get, hovered contentedly over his steaming tea. "Well, we've an intriguing list of personalities involved with this case, from the constrained Miss Chauncey to the untamed Miss Miller."

"Don't forget Constanza," I said, maybe with a little too much zest.

"Aha! Yes, the compelling Constanza." My companion wagged his teaspoon at me. Teaspoons, napkins, paintbrushes—lately, I was getting a whole arsenal of commonplace items aimed at my face. "Beware, Lee Plunkett, beware! Don't think I didn't notice your transfixed stare when that young lady entered the room. Be on guard. Do not let beauty blunt your sharp perceptions."

"First of all, my perceptions aren't all that sharp to begin with, but thanks for pretending. Secondly, I'm an engaged man."

"Yes, for nigh on two and a half years, I understand. You've managed to make quite a profession out of that, haven't you, lad?"

I snatched up my own spoon and wielded it menacingly. "I'm a tiger when riled."

Mr. O'Nelligan displayed his fear by stirring his tea and ignoring me. "Then we have the men of the household, Trowbridge and Rast, each offering his own peculiar persona. Not to mention the storied Dr. Kemple."

"Yeah, he sounds like a pip. Plus, we haven't even explored the clients. But, listen, colorful cast aside, I still don't see that we've got anything here. We've interviewed a half-dozen people and haven't gone an inch beyond Agnelli's hunch and Doris's 'feeling.'"

"You can add my intuition to the mix."

"Oh, come on. Aren't we mired in enough of a supernatural swamp without sprinkling in your Irish intuition?"

"The intuition I'm referring to isn't necessarily of the Irish variety. And it's not supernatural. It's more a matter of experience and evaluation. To me, there's a certain fitfulness to the Lloyd house."

Our pot pies arrived, and we dug in.

I returned to our topic. "Fitfulness? You mean beyond any possible ghost activity?"

"Yes, beyond ghosts. There seem to be living secrets and complications in play here. I gamble that something is rotten in the state of Denmark."

"Hey! That one I know. Hamlet says it, right?"

"It is said in the play *Hamlet,* true, but the line is actually spoken by Marcellus, a minor character."

"Cut me some slack, will you? By the way, you seem to be flinging around a lot of Shakespeare lately. Don't tell me you're trading in your Irish darling Yeats for an English writer?"

Mr. O'Nelligan calmly lifted a forkful of pie. "Seeking to goad me, are you, Lee? Let it be known that I can quote freely from either Yeats or Shakespeare as the occasion demands, 'though I am old with wandering through hollow lands and hilly lands.' There's your Yeats right there. Now, back to the task at hand, what have we learned today about Trexler Lloyd's final hours?"

I laid it out. "That Lloyd was looking forward to the unveiling of the Spectricator. That in the hour prior to his death, he was visited individually by most of the people of the house. That somewhere along the line, he got into a nasty mood. And that, in the midst of that mood, he wanted to change his will for unknown reasons."

"Yes, noteworthy points all," my comrade acknowledged. "And ones we must delve into. But I find myself ever returning to the coroner, Emmitt, and his conspicuous presence at the moment of death. Remember, that's what first drew Detective Agnelli's attention, and that's the path I suggest we next pursue. Miss Chauncey said she hadn't reached Emmitt, so perhaps we should just arrive at his doorstep."

In agreement, we polished off our meals and drove to Felix Emmitt's home address. There, in the ten seconds that the door was open to us, a curt, middle-aged woman informed us that her husband had gone to Vermont and could not be reached. Returning to the car, we discussed our next move.

"Let's go for Dr. Grumble," I said, swiping Sassafras's nickname for the moody medium. "We can just show up at his door and ambush him."

"*You* can ambush him, Lee. Remember, Dr. Kemple picked me out of the audience at the Otherworld's Fair."

"And he heard Audrey refer to you as a detective."

"Exactly. Although that honor is one I must humbly decline, being but your assistant in these endeavors."

I cast my eyes toward heaven. "Deliver me from this man's modesty. But I get your point. Kemple will know what our true business is here."

"Not if you approach him on your own."

"But I was there, too. Won't he recognize me?"

"I think not."

"Why? Because I'm nondescript?"

"No. Because you blend in well with the world around you."

"Here in the U.S.A., we call that nondescript."

"Come now, Lee, don't be so self-effacing. Will you ambush the man or will you not?"

"Okay, I'll take it on. What'll you do while I'm seeing Kemple?"

"I'm not yet ready to give up on our coroner. I think I'll revisit Mrs. Emmitt in a few minutes to beseech her for more information."

"Are you kidding? That woman didn't exactly welcome us in with a plate of cookies. She won't talk."

"It never hurts to make a second effort." There was a little gleam in Mr. O'Nelligan's eye.

I left my colleague on the sidewalk, agreeing to meet him back at the Braywick Tavern in an hour and a half. It would be a walk of two miles to there from the Emmitt house, but Mr. O'Nelligan always welcomed the chance to stroll. I drove on in pursuit of C. R. Kemple.

*　*　*

A TWENTY-MINUTE JAUNT up I-95 brought me to the town of Darien. There, I located the unimpressive boarding-house where my quarry took his lodging. His landlady, a small, ditzy woman, told me that Dr. Kemple was presently out, but seeing as I was his pal (I'd implied no such thing) I might as well wait for him in his room. As she unlocked his door, humming discordantly to herself, I thanked my stars that my own landlady treated each of her tenants' rooms as a little Fort Knox that no stranger should breech.

Left alone, I surveyed Dr. Kemple's domain and was not dazzled. The bed was unmade, and its jumble of blankets suggested a bad night's slumber. From overstuffed bureau drawers spilled socks, shirts, and underwear; a pair of checkered trousers lay in a ball on the uncarpeted floor. By way of decoration, several wrinkled posters had been tacked to the walls, all advertising the appearance of THE FABLED DR. C. R. KEMPLE, MASTER MEDIUM at one event or another. The most striking of these featured a photo of the good doctor with eyes crazily wide and hands raised as if he intended to strangle any onlooker. The legend underneath demanded, COME! HE WAITS FOR YOU!

My father would have relished a situation like this: easy access to a sketchy character's digs with no one there to worry about. Stealthily but merrily, he would have yanked open drawers, read hidden letters, rummaged through the closet, and even pried up a floorboard or two if he felt so inclined—all in the name of professional sleuthing. I, on the other hand, was a milder sort of shamus. A nervous thrill, chiefly unpleasant, shot through my abdomen as I contemplated the opportunity before me. I could almost feel Buster's dark disappointment if I failed to seize the moment. Sparing the floorboards, I settled for an inventory of those objects within eyeshot.

The items on the nightstand were unexceptional: an alarm clock, a glass of water, a bottle of aspirin, and a paperback novel entitled *Queen of the Tenth Planet*. The cover offered a garish depiction of green-faced aliens marching out of a spaceship and, regally in the foreground, a curvy green vixen wearing a crown and little else. Clearly, Kemple respected the loftier elements of science fiction. Atop the low bureau, an equally common display included a pair of cufflinks, a coin jar, a crumpled cigarette pack, a hairbrush, various toiletries, and a couple more sci-fi paperbacks. Disappointingly, I didn't notice any human skull cups in the lot. There were two things, though, that I did take note of: a local newspaper with a notice circled in red, and a spooled tape recorder.

The notice stated that Dr. Kemple would be appearing at a local bookstore in two days to "display his amazing, uncanny connection with the dead." As an added incentive for attending, the bookstore promised a discount on all ghost story collections. Next turning my attention to the tape recorder, I pushed the PLAY button and was greeted by a piercing metallic whine interspersed with loud crackles. After a minute of this torture, I reached out to silence it, but hesitated when an echoing voice rose from the machine. It sounded strained and distant, but I could make out the words.

"The afterlife is a place of memory and mystery. You who still dwell on the earthly plane can only guess at its wonders. I, who no longer live, shall tell you of what lies beyond. I, Trexler Lloyd, now speak to you from the dead . . ."

CHAPTER SEVEN

IT WAS INDEED LLOYD'S VOICE —at least as I remembered it from the Otherworld's Fair.

"I was once composed of flesh and sinew like you. But no longer. Now I am part of the bubbling mists—dammit!"

With that last exclamation, the voice ceased to be unearthly and became, instead, all too humanly annoyed.

"Not bubbling . . . billowing! I meant billowing mists. Okay, then . . . The afterlife is a place of memory and mystery. You who still dwell . . ."

He was reciting the speech all over again, telling me once more how dead he was. I raised the volume to hear better and, in doing so, drowned out any outer sounds. Sounds such as, for example, the approach of footsteps in the hallway. Midway through Lloyd's description of the afterworld, the door flew open and there stood C. R. Kemple, his eyes nearly as wide and crazy as his poster depicted. Without a word, he walked promptly to the bureau, pulled open the top drawer, and extracted something I didn't want to see.

It's one thing to have a spoon or paintbrush pointed at the bridge of your nose; it's another thing entirely when it's a pearl-handled pistol. Facing the barrel of a gun, it's odd what grabs your focus. Of course, the weapon itself commands attention, that goes without saying, but at that particular moment what riveted me was Kemple's bow tie. No lie. It looked to be the same purple number that he had worn at last month's event, and, seconds away from potential oblivion, I now found myself wondering if it was the only one he owned.

But only for a second. Then the enormity of the situation rushed in on me, and, in my mind, I began madly apologizing— to Audrey, to Mr. O'Nelligan, to my dead father—for letting myself die so stupidly. I began to jabber for my life.

"Plunkett . . . I'm Plunkett. Doris Chauncey called you about me. She did, right? You can put the gun down now."

Kemple didn't see it that way. "I could kill you for breaking into my room."

"You don't want to do that," I said, in hopes that he didn't. Realizing that the tape was still playing, I reached over and turned it off, guessing this wasn't the best time to ask about its content.

"I could kill you," he repeated. His bristly mustache twitched, and I worried his trigger finger might do the same. "You're the one the Chauncey girl said communicated with Trexler."

Glad to be recognized as a harmless fellow medium, I let out a groaning sigh. "Yes, Dr. Kemple, I only stopped by to—"

He didn't lower the pistol. "Nobody needs you! I'll communicate with him, no one else. No one! Understand?"

I was not about to argue. "Yes, I understand."

Kemple waved the gun at the door. "Leave right now."

He didn't have to tell me twice. I've always been a huge fan of not getting shot.

MR. O'NELLIGAN AND I were sitting in my car in front of the Braywick Tavern, comparing notes. I let him go first, figuring that my account of gunplay and the talking dead would lose none of its vigor by waiting a few minutes longer.

"I've learned Felix Emmitt's whereabouts," my colleague informed me. "He's in the town of Brattleboro, Vermont, staying in the woods there in a cabin owned by a relative. The place lacks a telephone, so we'll have to make the journey up there to accost him. The directions, though a touch labyrinthine, will, I trust, be adequate."

"Wait—you got this out of his wife? How?"

Mr. O'Nelligan's smile shone like the sun over an Irish meadow. "A bit of conversing. A bit of commiseration. Apparently, Mr. Emmitt is not the easiest man to cohabit with, what with his deep thirst and a penchant for the gambling table. I merely lent the good woman my ear, and she was quite forthcoming."

"Don't tell me she offered you tea and cookies."

"Brownies," he corrected. "Walnut brownies. Quite pleasant."

I had to laugh. "How long's Emmitt been up there?"

"Since Sunday. He took a leave of absence from his work and told his wife he needed a break. Said he wanted to get in some fishing."

"Fishing? In December? In Vermont?"

"Have you not heard of ice fishing, lad? It's all the rage up north. Anyway, he just upped and left, saying he might be gone for an extended period."

"So, two days after he declares Trexler Lloyd dead, Emmitt hears the call of the wild and scampers off to an isolated cabin. Very interesting."

"Isn't it, though? Now, what of your visit to Dr. Kemple?"

I gave him the rundown, leaving out the part about the bow tie but adding an insinuation that being held at gunpoint was something I took in stride.

Mr. O'Nelligan wasn't buying that. "The consequences could have been dire! It was risky to have placed yourself alone in that room."

I tried to sound cocky. "Risky's my middle name. With a first name like Leander, I needed something daring to balance it out."

My friend's tone grew hard. "Your cavalier act doesn't fool me, you know. In the past, I, too, have had guns pointed at me, and I know damned well there's no flippancy there. You look down that barrel, and it's as if the very tunnel to hell is opening for you. So don't play the jester with me."

Coming from this usually genteel man, the harsh reprimand stung. I stared at the steering wheel and said nothing.

Mr. O'Nelligan's voice softened. "But why am I berating *you*? It's myself I blame. Knowing the nature of that man, I should have accompanied you. I should have looked after you. What would I have told dear Audrey if . . ." He didn't finish, and I didn't want him to.

I pulled us back to business. "The tape was perplexing."

"Yes . . . the tape. What's your opinion of it?"

"I don't think it was Lloyd's ghost, if that's what you're asking, but I'm pretty sure it was Lloyd's *voice*. Why he was saying he was dead, I've no idea. He seemed to be practicing his monologue, trying to get it just right."

"How did Dr. Kemple react to you listening to the recording?"

"Well, as I mentioned, he wanted to shoot me. But I don't know if that was specifically because of the tape or because he found me interloping."

Mr. O'Nelligan nodded thoughtfully. "We'll have to exercise more care around Dr. Kemple in the future."

"Agreed. When should we head to Vermont?"

"I suggest tomorrow morning. It's over a three-hour drive. We can return home now and prepare for an early start. You've had enough excitement for a single day."

"Too true. But tomorrow, before we head north, I'd like to make a few stops. First at the Lloyd house again. I want to bring in someone who knows electronics to take a look at that Spectricator. I have in mind an old friend of my father's. Also, we can make a couple of detours to meet Lloyd's clients, the Greers and Loretta Mapes. Sound okay?"

"You're the boss, Lee Plunkett." My friend smiled, warming another Irish meadow.

AFTER DROPPING MR. O'NELLIGAN at his house, I decided to swing over to the Thelmont Five-and-Dime to catch Audrey before she got off work. Like all good five-and-dimes, this one was situated right in the heart of Main Street. And like all good small-town Main Streets, Thelmont's was a corridor of modestly thriving shops, most painted colonial white, bunched together along sidewalks wide enough to stroll with your honey. Many of the businesses had second- or even third-generation ownerships, and each storefront, I'd wager, looked about the same as it had thirty years before and probably thirty years hence. I parked and strolled past the familiar buildings—the Bugle Boy Diner, Owen's Barber Shop, Selgino's Stationery, the Sugar-Apple Bakery, Huntington's Crystal Shop, and Rowland's Drug Store (where I'd first met Audrey). As I was entering the five-and-dime, a trio of laughing, jostling boys came spilling out, each of them sporting the latest in American boyhood fashion: the coonskin cap. Like a lot of other modern fads, the Davy Crockett craze eluded me. Why were kids so gung ho on wearing something that looked like it had been peeled off a highway? Smiling and shaking my head, I watched the boys rush down the street and vanish around a corner, losing themselves in the wild frontiers of Thelmont.

Audrey was busy with some customers, but Mrs. Jerome, the owner, took me in tow, insisting I see some newly arrived item. The tiny but tough seventy-year-old fairly dragged me across the store, past scores of compartmentalized bins bulging with hardware, toys, trinkets, household items, and a thousand other what-have-yous. As always, I found my eyes leaping from one bin to the next, impressed by the sheer multiplicity of objects. The Jeromes had started the store nearly three decades before; and when Mr. Jerome died in '52, his widow hired Audrey to help run the place. It was a good match for both women.

"Look at this, Lee." Mrs. Jerome halted us halfway down one aisle and plucked something out of a bin. "Can you guess what it is?"

The thing had plenty of bolts and springs and movable parts. I took a stab at it. "A tool?"

"Well, of course it's a tool, you goop. But what kind?"

I almost said, *Why, it's a miniature Spectricator,* but figured the reference would be lost on her. I shook my head in defeat. "Sorry. No idea."

Mrs. Jerome clicked her tongue. "I thought you would know, since you Plunkett men are so mechanical."

"That was my father." I must have explained this to her a dozen times. "He could fix anything. Me, I'm dangerous around tools and machinery. Can't even turn on an electric fan without giving myself a haircut."

She ignored all that. "It's a handkerchief folder! See? You slip your handkerchief in here and it folds it smooth for you. So you never have to iron one again."

I don't believe I'd ever ironed a handkerchief in my life, but I said, "Very clever gizmo."

"It is, isn't it?" Mrs. Jerome placed the tool gently back among its fellows. "I ordered eighty of them."

"Wow. Thelmont will boast the snappiest handkerchiefs in the state."

The old woman narrowed her eyes. "I know perfectly well when I'm being poked fun at. But just think about it—on your wedding day, for example, wouldn't you want a nice, crisp hand-kerchief to put in your breast pocket?"

Uh-oh. Here it came. The wedding talk . . .

"Say, when are you going to marry that nice girl of yours, anyway? She's twenty-eight, for Pete's sake! At her age, I had three children already. You'd better get cracking."

I saved myself by asking if there were any Vermont road maps in stock. While Mrs. Jerome went to fetch one, I returned to the front to find Audrey customer-free and finishing up for the day. Stepping out from behind the counter, she walked over to the magazine rack and pulled out several comic books.

"These should do nicely."

"Who are those for?" I asked.

"Mr. O'Nelligan."

"Come again?"

"Mr. O'Nelligan. I told him I'd drop by with the new issues. He has a running account with us."

"Are we talking about the same Mr. O'Nelligan who's read every classic novel at least three times and can quote whole passages?" I glanced down at the topmost comic in her hands. "Are you telling me that Batman's Robot Twin gets equal billing with Beowulf?"

Audrey shrugged. "Mr. O'Nelligan has eclectic tastes."

"Eclectic—that's just around the corner from eccentric, isn't it?"

"Stop it. He's young at heart. You could stand a little of that, you know."

"So you'd prefer me to be immature?"

"That's not what I said. I want you to be mature *and* young at heart."

"Ah, so you want to have your comic book and eat it, too."

Mrs. Jerome reappeared, map in hand. "Whatever is your boyfriend talking about?"

Audrey sighed. "No one knows, Mrs. Jerome. No one ever knows."

Minutes later, we were outside leaning against my Nash and bickering lightly over dinner plans. I wanted to eat out, but Audrey said her mother had supper already going, and I should just come over and join them. I told her I didn't feel like a lot of company.

She didn't get that. "Since when are my parents a lot of company? You like them and you like Mama's cooking. So come over."

"Rather not."

"It's fried chicken," she tempted. "You always love—"

"I had a gun shoved in my face today." I flung that out like a challenge. "Just so you know."

Audrey drew a hand to her mouth and let out a small moan. A look of such deep concern contorted her face that I immediately felt terrible for springing things on her like that. I explained that we were investigating Trexler Lloyd's death and, in a breezy style, recounted the episode with Kemple, assuring her that it really was no big deal. Like Mr. O'Nelligan, Audrey saw right through my nonchalance.

"Oh God, Lee. Don't pretend like it was nothing. I'm scared for you." She burrowed into my shoulder. "I'm always pushing you to take on cases. It's so damned selfish of me."

"You're not pushing anybody, sweetheart. I was born into this job."

As the words hit the air, I instantly knew that I sounded like a rotten imitation of Bogart. Audrey knew it, too, and pressed her fingers to my lips, lest any more tough-guy dialogue dribble out. After a spell of silent hugging, I convinced her that I'd really prefer to just drive home alone, whip up a quick meal, and make an early night of it. We kissed hard, more so than we usually would have in public, then climbed into our separate cars.

I BURROWED INTO my apartment—a comfy enough space, but as blandly indescribable as my office. If you wanted a sofa, a coffee table, or a chair or two, sure, I could provide that much, and, for style, a couple of painted plaques, each depicting a colonial soldier leaning on his rifle, nailed to the living room wall. (These had hung in our family's home when I was growing up and were the only things I'd kept after the sale of the house.) If you required anything more by way of decor, you were flat out of luck.

I fixed myself an underachieving dinner of hot dogs and

beans, then placed several phone calls. First I tried George Agnelli to catch him up on the day's events. No answer. I remembered then that he'd said he was on the late shift tonight. I'd try again in the morning. Next I rang up Dad's old electrician buddy, who agreed to meet us at the Lloyd house at 9:00 A.M. Lastly, I reached Doris Chauncey to say we'd be stopping by in the morning to look over the Spectricator. That done, I turned my attention to a very long, steamy shower. For a good twenty minutes, I let the water beat down on the crown of my head in an attempt to dislodge the image of Kemple and his damned cowboy pistol. What kind of gun was that to be carrying around here, anyway? This wasn't Deadwood or Tombstone or a John Wayne movie set. This was Connecticut, where revolvers were gray and businesslike, not flashy, pearl-handled affairs. Not that I was any connoisseur of firearms. My father, ex-cop that he was, always carried a handgun while on a case, whereas I—unable to envision myself surviving a blazing shootout—armed myself with my wits alone. It was a miracle I wasn't dead already.

Drenched, then dried, I climbed into bed with the copy of *Myself and No Other* that Doris had lent us. Judging by his prose, Trexler Lloyd held himself in the highest regard and, as a matter of course, assumed the rest of the planet shared that view. The book began:

All I have, I can say with complete honesty, is derived of my own hand. If I possess wealth, then lay the blame at my doorstep. If I possess fame, then cry J'accuse! and yoke me with that crime. If I possess brilliance, then hold up a mirror to me and I will brave my own blinding light. The world is a gnarled, complex organism, and it takes a man of endeavor to unravel it. Behold me, for I am such an Unraveler!

I fought against my gag reflex and continued reading. Several pages in, Lloyd defended his own overstuffed ego.

Where o where is the author's humility, my muddled readers might demand. Why does he not curb his self-congratulation? Let me tell you why, my friends. I do not stifle my braggadocio for the simple reason that I have no right to. We are all but receptacles for the eternal pulse of life, and each man must honor his own level of receptivity. My own capacity is quite large—such is my nature and my destiny.

The fellow was a real prince, taking the time like that to explain things to us poor "muddled readers." He went on to describe several formative experiences of his youth, including one in which he purposely put himself in harm's way on an archery court. After dodging arrows and reprimands, Lloyd had found himself strangely content.

For, by my audacity, I had just beheld something of the world's terror and splendor, and I knew I craved for more.

A few chapters in, he began to lament the curse of being so darn famous, admirable, and dazzling, wondering what it would be like to shake that awful burden.

I was struck by the idea of converging myself with a greatly different destiny, of somehow striding forth unencumbered by my own prominence. I found myself yearning for such freedom—as an urchin might pine for some unobtainable toy in a shop window—but, in the end, could not realistically imagine its obtainment. While I would gladly remove myself from the public eye, I would fear forfeiting my legacy. It is one thing to go unmolested by prying admirers; it is another thing entirely to be unremembered by them. So, unless there is some way to fulfill both needs, I must content myself with who I am: Trexler Lloyd, a man unlike other men.

I plodded on for a while, marveling page by page at the guy's vanity, until my eyes went half-mast. I closed the book, removed my glasses, and switched off the light. Then I took my best shot at a dreamless slumber where ghosts, guns, and ego-ridden geniuses held no sway.

CHAPTER EIGHT

THE MAN I HAD IN MIND to examine the Spectricator was Skip Ottoson. What Skip's true moniker was, I don't think I ever knew. As I've mentioned, my father surrounded himself with guys whose nicknames sounded like the lower card of a boxing event: Lefty, Dukey, Lunk, Jammer, Bazooka, etc., etc. A few were decent guys; a lot were not. Dad's taste in friends was never the most discriminating, and a good number of questionable characters always hovered around him. The fact that he was a former police detective turned private dick didn't seem to elevate his choice of compadres. When Mom was alive, she kept the most unsavory of these off our doorstep. After her death, the quality of visitors dipped. Luckily, our Aunt Louise soon talked Dad into letting my sisters move in with her family. I, however, hung in there for five more years to observe the boozy, bellowing, guffawing circus that Dad and his cronies intermittently put on.

One guy I always did like, though, was Skip Ottoson. In his youth, Skip actually *had* been a boxer, probably a featherweight, judging by his small stature. Dad and the other guys used to rib him about his record, which I gathered was unimpressive. My guess is that his disposition was just too gentle to support a career of pummeling other men. Whenever I think of Skip, one particular night always leaps to mind. It was a few months after Mom's death, and Dad was hosting a boisterous poker game with the usual bunch of bozos. I'd been keeping myself cloistered in my room but decided to slip into the kitchen to snag a soda. I was intercepted there by Bazooka Davis, a big, nasty moose I never saw sober.

He eyed me without warmth and breathed a six-pack into my face. "How old are you, kid? Eighteen, right? Ain't you goddamn eighteen?"

"Yes." With Bazooka, it was best to keep your answers short.

"Then why ain't you in the army? You should be over there blowing up Nazis. Why the hell ain't you blowing up Nazis?"

"Don't know," I muttered and tried to slide past him.

He shifted to block my way. "It's 'cause you're a 4-F, ain't it? That's what your daddy said. Goddamn 4-F. Poor eyesight and a scrawny physique—that's what the draft board told you, right? Well, you know what? That's crap! You shoulda found a way to enlist. It's your goddamn duty, damn it."

My guilt about remaining stateside was strong enough without this palooka adding to it. I tried again to escape. "Excuse me, Mr. Davis."

He wouldn't budge. "Other boys are dying in the goddamn muck and you're here doing—what the hell do you do, anyway?"

"I work in the hat factory."

"Hat factory? Christ!"

Out of the corner of my eye, I saw my father paused in the hallway, listening to his buddy berate me. Though he had never said so directly, I knew he couldn't have been too happy about having a 4-F for a son. On the other hand, I always felt that maybe he was a little relieved. After all, he'd just seen his wife die painfully, and the thought of his only boy bleeding on some foreign field couldn't have held much appeal. When our eyes met, he looked quickly away and continued down the hall.

Bazooka kept at it. "Hat factory? A goddamn hat factory?"

Having my dad abandon me to this bullying buffoon triggered something. I snapped back, "Yeah, Mr. Davis, I make hats. Maybe I could make you one. Maybe something tall and pointed."

A slender ray of comprehension pierced his sloshed brain. "A dunce cap? You calling me a dunce?" He clenched his fists and pressed in on me.

That's when Skip appeared, seemingly out of nowhere. He stepped between us and placed a restraining hand on the big drunk's chest.

"Easy now, Bazooka. Easy now." Skip had a low, soothing voice only a couple of notches above a whisper. "Lee here's a good kid."

"He's a punk."

"Nah, he's a good kid. He's Buster's boy. Poor kid lost his mom."

"Goddamn 4-F."

"It happens, Bazooka. It happens. Go get yourself another beer, why don't ya? That'd be good, huh?"

In my opinion, another ingestion of hops and barley was the

last thing Bazooka needed. Apparently, he thought different. Forgetting my existence, he grabbed another beer from the fridge and lumbered away.

Skip turned to me and ran a hand through his close-cropped hair. "We dodged a bullet there, didn't we, buddy?"

I mumbled my thanks.

"Forget what he said, kiddo. Working in a hat factory's just fine. You make anything for the army?"

"Sure. Service hats and garrison caps."

"See? There you go! You're helping the war effort right there. More than ol' Bazooka's doing, I tell ya." He gave me a wink and a grin, and right away I didn't feel half so lousy.

WHEN MR. O'NELLIGAN AND I pulled up to the Lloyds' gates at 9:00 A.M., Skip Ottoson was already there waiting for us. The gates were still locked, and Skip was leaning against his beat-up old Pontiac, scrutinizing the stone dragons. As we shook hands, I realized that the last time we'd done so had been at Dad's funeral well over a year ago.

"Real beauties, huh?" He indicated the dragons. "I guess when you've got a few bucks like Trexler Lloyd did, you can toss 'em around on whatever strikes your fancy. It's swell to see ya again, Lee."

"Same here, Skip. Thanks for helping out."

"Hey, listen, Buster was a great buddy to me. Anything I can do for one of his kids, heck, I'm more than happy. Besides, how could I pass on the chance to tinker with some genius's ghost machine?"

As Skip and Mr. O'Nelligan exchanged names and hand-shakes, I glanced up the drive and saw Rast swooping down on his bicycle. Today the headscarf had been replaced by a wide-brimmed straw hat, which, teamed with his angular face, weirdly made me think of Katharine Hepburn. He dismounted and opened the gates for us.

"How go your Bastilles, sir?" Mr. O'Nelligan asked him.

Rast looked pleased to have his efforts remembered. "They are good! I will put them out today, and we will show the flies what a boss they have."

"Splendid," Mr. O'Nelligan said, choosing not to adjust Rast's phrasing. "By the way, we just learned that the house here will now be yours."

"Yes, I am blessed. Mr. Lloyd knew that I would be the best to watch over the dead ones here. No doubt he did."

"No doubt," the Irishman echoed. "And perhaps Mr. Lloyd now dwells here, as well."

"I do not think so. I think Mr. Lloyd's spirit has gone away." Then, looking at me—the flawed phantom-seeker—Rast added, "But if some people want to hunt for him, let them do that."

We drove our cars up to the house. As on the day before, it was Doris Chauncey who received us.

"Your butler never seems to man the door." Mr. O'Nelligan commented. "That's a traditional duty of his profession, I believe."

The secretary ushered us in. "Sassafras wanted to take Constanza out for breakfast, so Trowbridge drove them."

"In the hearse?" I grimaced. "Not a very nice way for a recent widow to go for pancakes."

"Oh, no, not the hearse. We have several cars available here."

"And neither of those two ladies drive?" I asked.

"Constanza doesn't. Sassafras does, but she likes to get chauffeured whenever possible. She's that kind of person."

Skip patted the toolbox he'd carried in. "I'm set to go. Just aim me at that boo machine."

Doris led him on toward the Portal Room, but I lingered behind with Mr. O'Nelligan, who had paused before one of the hallway doors.

"By process of elimination, this must be the closet." He pulled open the door. "Aha! There it is."

I peered in. "Whoa, Nelly!"

A huge, ugly eyeball stared back at us. Its pupil appeared to be a manhole cover from which tin lightning bolts jutted out in all directions, and the eyelashes looked like corkscrews with little propellers welded to the ends.

"Man oh man, it's hideous."

"Indeed it is," my friend agreed. "Perhaps banishing this horror to a closet was Trexler Lloyd's final gift to humanity." He closed the door firmly.

"Yeah, it's quite an *eyesore*." God forgive me, but it just came out.

Mr. O'Nelligan gave me a glare of reprimand. "Cheap, Lee Plunkett. Disappointingly cheap."

Doris Chauncey reappeared. "I left your friend with the Spectricator. He won't harm it, will he?"

"Don't worry about Skip. He has the hands of a surgeon." I wasn't quite sure that was true, but I liked the sound of it. "By the way, we saw Mr. Foster yesterday."

"He's very nice for a lawyer, isn't he?"

"Yes. He said that Mrs. Lloyd is scheduled to fly back to Spain next week. No one told us that."

"I'll hate to see her go," Doris said softly, as if that explained why she hadn't mentioned the departure before. "But it's what Mr. Lloyd wanted."

"But why?" I asked. "Why does she need to return to her home-land to receive her husband's fortune?"

"I just don't know. Constanza says she doesn't, either." She paused and shook her head. "It's unbelievable to think that at this time last week, Mr. Lloyd was enjoying muffins and tea and looking forward to the night's activities."

Mr. O'Nelligan joined in. "Speaking of tea, Miss Chauncey, when your employer summoned you to the Portal Room last Friday evening, did you happen to notice the presence of a tea-cup?"

"No, I don't think so. He had a small stack of letters on a table next to him, but that was all. Besides, Mr. Lloyd never drank warm beverages after dark. He said it muddled one's dreams. He had a lot of beliefs like that. But why—"

Mr. O'Nelligan pressed on. "Might there have been anything in his correspondence that would have agitated him?"

"I doubt it. I gathered up those letters later and looked through them. They were all just minor business exchanges. I can show you."

We followed the secretary into her office, where she handed me a packet of a half-dozen letters. She was right—they were all commonplace bills and receipts.

"While our colleague conducts his examination, could you show us the rest of the house?" Mr. O'Nelligan asked. "It occurs to me that we never received a proper tour."

Doris complied and led us around the first floor. Since we were already familiar with the rooms off the hallway, she fo-cused on the living room, dining room, and kitchen. The fur-nishings throughout were handsome but not lavish, and you wouldn't necessarily assume this was the home of a wealthy man. Here and there, some oddity would pop up—like a Japanese samurai helmet used as a fruit bowl or a gaudy painting of angels dancing with frogs—but, by and large, the trappings were fairly unremarkable. Doris skipped the basement, where Trowbridge had his quarters, and led us upstairs. She offered us the briefest peek into her small, tidy bedroom and, on the other end of the hall, the Lloyds's larger, plusher one. At the latter, our guide gestured to an ornate urn set atop the mantelpiece.

"That's Mr. Lloyd," she said. "I mean, of course, his ashes."

"His wife chooses to keep him near at hand," Mr. O'Nelligan observed.

"Oh, yes. Constanza's been very possessive of his remains. She didn't want anyone else to handle them."

Moving on, we were shown a trio of intervening rooms, which had been commandeered as work areas for Lloyd's projects. Each space overflowed with various tools, electronics parts, manuals, and several unidentifiable objects that looked like close cousins to Mrs. Jerome's handkerchief folder. Our tour completed, we returned to the first floor, where Doris excused herself to see to some task. Mr. O'Nelligan and I joined Skip in the Portal Room. He had just finished his inspection of the Spectricator and was packing up his toolbox.

"Here's the scoop, fellas. I gave this here appliance a pretty thorough looking over, and there's nothing to it."

"What do you mean?" I asked.

"I mean the thing's all smoke and mirrors. Well, no mirrors, maybe, but smoke. This baby was rigged to set off smoke and sparks. There's a timer built in."

"Are you saying it was meant to kill someone?"

"Nah, just spit out sparks and smoke at a certain time. It would look kinda nasty, but there'd be no real current shooting out."

"Still, it could electrocute a man."

Skip wrinkled his nose. "Don't see how. Unless he was standing in a tub of water and screaming insults at the Lord. And maybe not even then. Things are pretty well grounded."

Mr. O'Nelligan ran a hand over the machine. "What about its audio components? This device was intended to convey the voices of the dead."

Skip chuckled. "Well, that's outta my field, friend, but it sure seems like a lot of goofiness to me. I didn't find anything resembling a transmitter. And see this gramophone horn here? Looks pretty slick and all, but the neck of it is blocked by a steel plate."

"So it can't amplify?" the Irishman asked.

"Not at the moment it can't. Matter of fact, outside of the timer, not much is rigged up to work in this thing. Some colored lights will flick on and off for laughs, and some wheels will spin, but that's about it."

Skip flicked a switch and, sure enough, the Spectricator came alive with blinking red and blue lights and whirling gears.

I wasn't greatly impressed. "So that's it?"

"Yeah, that's it," Skip confirmed. "This whole setup reminds me of something you'd come across at a carnival—'Step right up, ladies and gentlemen, and see the marvelous contraption that don't do a damned thing. It'll only cost a nickel.'"

"I'm guessing Lloyd charged a lot more than a nickel," I said.

Skip switched off the machine and picked up his toolbox. "I'll level with ya, Lee, it's kind of a letdown. Here I get a shot at fiddling with something a mastermind built and it turns out to be a sham. Well, so it goes. Anyway, I'm real sorry I couldn't deliver better news to you fellas."

Mr. O'Nelligan waved off the apology. "On the contrary, Mr.

Ottoson. You gave us that most worthwhile of all news—the truth."

AFTER SAYING GOOD-BYE to Doris and slipping a twenty to Skip—with a promise to him that I wouldn't stay such a stranger—I aimed the Nash toward the parkway.

"So the Spectricator's a fraud," I said. "Just a jumble of useless parts with no purpose."

"So it seems," Mr. O'Nelligan agreed. "Unless the components function on a subtle level that your friend Skip couldn't detect."

"By subtle level, you mean up where phantoms hang out, right? So you're saying the Spectricator works?"

"Not at all. I merely play the devil's advocate to keep our brain cells nimble."

"My brain cells are happy just as is, but it's nice to know you fret over them."

"You're very welcome," my friend replied. "You're wrong, however, when you say the Spectricator had no purpose. At the very least, as we just learned, it was meant to discharge sparks and smoke at a prearranged time."

"Right. But what does that mean exactly?"

"That's to be determined. We know that nonlethal sparks were meant to fly, and we know that Trexler Lloyd was declared dead by electrocution."

"I get all that, but what's it add up to? That Trexler wanted a big sparkly, smoky show but somehow got zapped by mistake?"

"I think not. Remember, Skip said electrocution was unlikely."

"Then what does that—wait." Spying a phone booth along the road, I remembered something. "I wanted to check in with George Agnelli."

I pulled over, climbed into the booth, and placed the call. After a few rings, the phone picked up and I heard, "Yeah, hello?"

"Hi, Detective Agnelli, it's Lee Plunkett. Just wanted to touch base. We talked to a lot of Trexler Lloyd's people yesterday, and I'm thinking that your hunch was right. Something definitely smells bad about his death."

"Who is this again?" he asked.

"Lee Plunkett."

"Lee Plunkett?"

"Yes."

"Mind telling me who the hell Lee Plunkett is?" I suddenly realized this was not George Agnelli's voice but belonged to a younger, surlier man. "And what are you doing messing around with the Lloyd case, anyway?"

I didn't reply. In the background, a woman's voice called out, asking who was on the phone.

The man seemed to hesitate. "Don't bother. It's nobody."

"Is it a friend of my dad's? Give it to me, Tommy." Then the woman was speaking directly to me. "Hello? This is George's daughter."

Caught unawares, I wasn't sure what to say. "Um, I was just calling for your father."

"My father, he . . ." Her voice started to tremble. "He had a heart attack yesterday. He's dead."

I said nothing for several long moments, then offered a weak "I'm sorry" and hung up.

CHAPTER NINE

E WERE PARKED BY THE side of the road, neither coming nor going.

Slightly dazed, I'd just repeated the phone conversation to Mr. O'Nelligan, who'd listened intently before asking, "It was his heart, then?"

"That's what she said."

"So, no mention of foul play . . ."

"What?" I hadn't thought of that. "You're suggesting that someone—"

"I suggest nothing. In truth, Detective Agnelli didn't quite strike me as the picture of health when we met. Rather haggard looking, I thought. "

"Then you accept that he died of natural causes."

"I've no reason not to. What was the man at the other end's name again?"

"The daughter called him Tommy." I pulled out my notebook and flicked to some earlier notations. "Here it is—Tommy Bells. Agnelli's partner. That's who it must have been."

"Most likely. And now he knows your name and your involvement with this investigation."

"What are you saying?"

"Perhaps nothing. Hopefully his focus will remain on mourning his partner."

"But you know what this all means, don't you? It means we're done with the case."

"What makes you say that, Lee?"

I stared hard at him. "Didn't you just hear my little report? Our client's dead. We're not working for anyone anymore."

"I don't know that that's true."

"Wait, don't try to tell me we're working for his *ghost.*"

"Not his ghost, but perhaps his spirit."

"Spirits, ghosts, zombies—call them what you like, it's all ridiculous."

"Hear me out, lad. We were summoned to this quest by an honorable man on his last full day of life. I see something quite mythic in that. That man now exists only in memory and history. In a sense, he's nothing but spirit now, but that doesn't lessen the summons, does it?"

"Doesn't it?"

"Not to my way of thinking. I see a sacred trust that we—"

"Hold on. I know you're very keen on the whole sacred trust idea, but we have to face facts. Agnelli's dead. No one's paying our fee anymore."

"Is that all it's about, then? The fee?"

I began to talk very rapidly and very hotly. "Look, we've only been at it for twenty-four hours, and already I've found myself squinting into a gun barrel! I don't think it's outrageous to be compensated for that. Sure, he gave us some cash as a retainer. Well, he retained us for a full day, and now we're done."

Calmly, Mr. O'Nelligan took that all in and withered me with a smile. "It was good to get that off your chest, wasn't it now?"

I groaned. "You're going to talk me into continuing this case, aren't you?"

"I've a little cash of my own saved up. I would gladly put some toward your expenses if—"

"You're killing me. You know that, right? There's absolutely no way I'm taking your money. My soul would go straight to hell if I did that."

He laughed. "Ah, so you *are* capable of metaphysical speculation."

"Too many syllables. Way too many syllables."

"Here's a little tale." He spoke very softly now. "In the Book of Jonah, the titular hero receives a heavenly summons to journey forth and preach atonement. At first he refuses, and who can blame him? The call to a great quest is always intimidating."

"What is this—Sunday school?"

"Hush up, will you? God forbid you should learn something. Anyway, Jonah ignores the summons and flees, catching a ride on a ship bound for the open sea. Then do you know what befalls him?"

"A big whale."

"Well, you're skipping a few parts, but, yes, a whale swallows him. See? You *do* know your tales of antiquity."

"And this is supposed to be an enticement? I should pursue this case—convoluted and uncompensated as it is—so that, in the end, a monster fish can digest me? Gee, where do I sign up?"

"There's no digestion in this story. Jonah lingers unscathed in the whale's belly, gaining humility, before he returns to the quest and makes good. The point is, one can try to avoid the call to action, but in the end it must be heeded."

"Or you have to do jail time in a whale stomach."

"Essentially, yes. Until one is belched out."

I sighed deeply, both lungs, double barrel. "Alright, alright. We'll go on."

"So my analogy convinced you?"

"No, it *confounded* me. You're a golden-tongued villain, did you know that?"

Mr. O'Nelligan straightened his tie and smiled. "You're doing what's right, boyo. Now, onward! Onward to our duty!"

BACK ON SCHEDULE, our plan was to stop and see Lloyd's clients before heading to Vermont. First up were Herb and Adelle Greer, the couple who'd lost their son in Korea. According to Doris Chauncey's notes, they spent most of their time at the small grocery they owned in Cos Cob, the harbor section of Greenwich. Entering the store, we encountered a tall, lean woman in an apron, probably in her late forties, stacking jars on a shelf. Her thin, ordinary face was upstaged by a flurry of brown hair that rebelled against bobby pins.

"Good morning." Her tone was subdued, a bit distant. "Anything I can help you find?" She listened as I gave our names. "Oh, yes. I'm Adelle Greer. We were told about you. You're the man who's communicated with Mr. Lloyd."

Wanting to take the focus off my astounding powers, I asked, "Is your husband here, too?"

"He's out in back. Come on."

She told a girl behind the counter to keep an eye on things

and led us into a back room crowded with stacks of cartons and soda cases. There, Herb Greer—a burly, balding man in a white shirt and suspenders—stood taking notes on a clipboard.

Without looking up, he called out, "We're low on cornflakes, Adelle. Both kinds." Once he'd noticed she was not alone, he looked inquiringly at his wife, who introduced us.

I spoke to both of them. "We'd like to learn a little about your connection with Mr. Lloyd."

"Yeah? Why?" Herb set the clipboard on a carton and hooked his thumbs through his suspenders. "I thought it was his ghost you were interested in."

"Well, yes, but it's helpful to know about the people who were around him when he died."

"Terrible!" Adelle flung out the word. "Just terrible for him to go like that, shocked to death by his own invention. Don't you think?"

"Yes, it was very sad," I agreed.

She shook her head in regret. "And we expected so much from the Spectricator."

"*You* expected so much," her husband said. "I told you all along nothing would come of it."

Adelle frowned at him. "Why can't you ever show a little faith? Besides, we never had a chance to see it work. How can we know that it wouldn't have brought Andy back to us?"

Herb Greer moaned softly and looked away. "Y'know, Adelle, I wish you would just—"

"Just what? Forget my son?" Adelle turned from her husband to face us. "It's been almost three and a half years, but I could swear it was yesterday. I still feel it in my body. The words. The words in that telegram . . ."

"Aw, please, Adelle," Herb half-whispered.

She pressed on, growing more agitated. "Do you know where he died? On the Korean Peninsula at a place the army called Pork Chop Hill. Isn't that a silly name? Pork Chop? Hundreds of boys were killed and maimed there, and they have the gall to call it that. And do you know what's funny? Pork chops were Andy's favorite. It's true! On his birthday, I would always make them. Pork chops and lima beans and . . . and . . ." Just as it seemed that tears would overtake her, she drew herself up and continued, this time more slowly. "He first came back to me this past summer. I don't know why he waited so long, but he did. I was at home, watering our garden, when I felt him behind me."

"Felt him?" Mr. O'Nelligan asked.

Adelle bobbed her head emphatically. "Oh, yes, yes. I actually felt his hand on my shoulder."

"I told her it was probably just the wind," Herb said. "Something like that."

His wife forced a laugh. "The wind? The wind can't pat your shoulder, can it? Well, can it? Besides, it wasn't just the touch. A mother knows when her son is next to her." She tilted her chin up as if challenging someone to contradict her. "Then on Labor Day weekend I actually saw him. I glanced outside the kitchen window, and there he was, running across the driveway. It was twilight and he was moving fast, but I saw him."

I could tell this was all very wearying for Herb. "Lots of young guys live in our neighborhood," he said. "Could have been anybody."

Adelle ignored his suggestion. "The third visit was in October, right here in this room. I was sweeping up one night and saw him standing in that corner, just over there in the shadows. He tried to say something, but he couldn't seem to speak. This time he was in his uniform. Mind you, I only caught him for a few seconds—he was there and then he wasn't—but I saw him very clearly. He wanted so hard to tell me something. My Andy."

The counter girl popped her head in, asking which potatoes were on sale, and Adelle left to assist her.

Alone with us now, Herb stepped closer, and his voice grew low and tense. "Now listen. As you guys can probably tell, I don't go along with my wife on all this. It's hard as hell to lose your son, your only child, but you've got to pick yourself up and keep going. It's been more than three years, and I thought Adelle was doing okay, considering. But then she started in with all this business about feeling Andy and seeing him, and it seems to me like she's losing ground. Like I say, you've got to just pick up and move on, and I don't think she's doing too good with that."

"I'm sure, Mr. Greer, that it must be very—"

He held up a hand to cut me off. "Look, I know you people are into the same stuff that Lloyd was. And I know you think you can talk to him and all his dead pals, but I don't buy it."

I desperately wanted to identify myself to him as a brother skeptic, but I held my tongue.

Greer was building up steam. "For Adelle's sake, I went along with meeting Lloyd and that little weirdo Kemple. Three times, fifty bucks a shot. They'd say this thing or that about Andy, and it sounded pretty scattergun to me, wild guesses at best. But it seemed to comfort Adelle, so we kept at it. Then Lloyd told us about this new equipment he was working on. Said it would draw down Andy's voice from another world. He made it sound very scientific and modern, and, of course, Adelle ate all that up. So we went, just in time to see him shoot a bolt of electricity into himself."

When the grocer paused to catch a breath, Mr. O'Nelligan

squeezed in a question. "Was your wife very distressed at witnessing Mr. Lloyd's death?"

Herb let his engines cool for a moment, then answered. "Not as much as I was worried she'd be. I mean, naturally she was upset. Everyone was—seeing a guy die like that. But she didn't break down or anything. Now, that Sassafras lady, *she* went all out with the wailing and thrashing. More even than Lloyd's wife when she showed up. But, no, for Adelle it was mostly disappointment that she wouldn't be able to talk to . . ." He finished almost inaudibly. "Talk to our son."

Mr. O'Nelligan nodded solemnly. "We understand, sir. And we're sorry for all your burdens."

The hardness returned to Greer's tone. "Yeah? Then how about you don't add to them. Just go, okay? My wife's been through enough disappointment and craziness lately. She doesn't need to be stirred up again. Just go."

We had no time to argue the point. Placing firm hands on our shoulders, the barrel-chested man turned us around and aimed us back into the shopping area. Adelle looked up quizzically from a mound of potatoes as her husband opened the front door and gestured us out.

"Take care, now," he said, almost sounding friendly.

Without an opportunity for good-byes, Mr. O'Nelligan and I walked across the parking lot to the Nash. A sharp little wind was in the air, just biting enough to remind us that winter would soon be closing in. As we opened the car doors, we heard "Please, wait!" and turned to see Adelle Greer hurrying toward us from the grocery.

She came up and took my hand. "I just wanted to say that when you're talking to Lloyd, or anybody else on the other side, if you happen to hear from someone named Andy, well . . ." Her breathing quickened. "He's nineteen. He has a pretty deep voice, so you might think he's older, but he's only nineteen. Just tell him that Mom . . . and Papa . . ."

Then she couldn't say any more. Releasing my hand, she turned and walked slowly back to the store.

"I'M SICK OF this game," I grumbled as we drove on. "I'm sick of deceiving people and making them think I can do something I can't."

"That's understandable," Mr. O'Nelligan said. "I suggest we dispense with this subterfuge after the present round of interviews. At that point, revealing our true purpose may actually play to our advantage."

"I'm all for that. You know what else really ticks me off? Knowing that Lloyd preyed on vulnerable people like Adelle Greer—and charged them fifty bucks each time. Fifty bucks! Why the hell would Trexler Lloyd need to take people's money like that? The guy literally coughed up cash."

"Figuratively. You mean figuratively. If a man *literally* coughed up currency, it would be quite disturbing to witness."

"In Lloyd's case, I'd laugh."

"Remember, Miss Chauncey suggested that charging a fee was done on Dr. Kemple's insistence. It's quite likely that he, not Lloyd, was the recipient of the money."

"Well, then it's Kemple I'd like to see cough up a roll of cash. Or, better yet, both of them, side by side, spitting out greenbacks like twin fountains. That'd be a thing to behold."

Mr. O'Nelligan patted my knee. "It certainly would. I hope that image brings you solace."

CHAPTER TEN

LORETTA MAPES OFFERED US coffee, toast with jam, and a penetrating stare. I accepted the beverage; my comrade, the toast; and, as for the stare, Mrs. Mapes deemed it best to direct that at me specifically. She was a slender woman of about seventy years with ebony skin and pearl white hair. Her attire was a simple beige dress; her only flourish, a silver necklace from which hung a small, delicate cross. She had accepted us into her modest home impassively, saying only that she'd been expecting us. Now, here in her living room, amid dried flowers, framed pictures of family, and a cocker spaniel that dozed at her feet, Mrs. Mapes fixed her gaze on me so intently that I felt she was trying to turn me inside out.

"So." She made the word sound like a command. "You're the one they say Mr. Lloyd spoke to."

I started in with my standard spiel. "Actually, it was his emanations that—"

She nipped that in the bud. "I don't believe you."

"Sorry? I was just—"

"Don't even bother." The gaze sharpened. "I know when someone's got the gift, and you don't."

The day before, I'd had to contend with Martin Rast's doubts and Dr. Kemple's jealousy concerning my abilities, but this was different. Loretta Mapes *knew.* I could see it in her face. She had my number. Seeking help, I turned to Mr. O'Nelligan, who raised his eyebrows to indicate a lack of suggestions.

Mrs. Mapes took a long sip of coffee, never removing her eyes from me. "I know when somebody's got the gift, because I have it myself. Had it since I was ten. I hate when someone pretends about possessing it. There's lots of them out there who fake it so they can get money or seem important. I despise that, and, Lord knows, the spirits do, too. So, tell now, Mr. Plunkett, what's *your* reason? No use lying to me."

At this point, Mr. O'Nelligan set aside his jam-smeared toast and, to my surprise, commenced to tell the truth. "Mr. Plunkett's a private detective, and I am his associate. We were hired to look into the matter of Trexler Lloyd's death because certain individuals believe it wasn't accidental. Lee here was forced to assume the guise of someone who could beckon the dead. It was neither his choice nor his desire, but we felt he needed to maintain the ruse to further our investigation. Clearly, you are someone who cannot be so fooled."

Loretta Mapes set her cup down and wagged a finger condemningly at us. "Worst way to get at the heart of things is to lie! It always comes back on itself. Always!" She turned to Mr. O'Nelligan. "You should know that, with all your gray whiskers. Maybe this other one's not got enough years to know better, but *you* sure do."

"Yes, ma'am," Mr. O'Nelligan said quietly. He seemed to have suddenly become an errant schoolboy stung by a teacher's reprimand.

Mrs. Mapes kept the lecture going, thankfully now aiming it at my companion. "Yessir, you and me, we've got a few decades tucked away. Folks old as us should know a thing or two. We're not out for our first gallop, after all."

"No we are not," Mr. O'Nelligan conceded. "Although, in my case, my gallop has slowed significantly, well below canter and trot, to a mere dawdle."

At this, our hostess let loose a boisterous laugh, completely at odds with the severity she'd just shown. "You sure can twirl your words, can't you, mister? Do they all talk like that over in Scotland?"

"Ireland!" My friend seemed stricken. "I'm from Ireland. County Kerry."

"Sorry 'bout that," Loretta Mapes said. "I just can't keep straight all those different *lands*. The Ire-lands and Scot-lands and Fin-lands. I knew you sprang from one of them."

"Well, madam, it's Ireland I'm from and nowhere else," Mr. O'Nelligan said stiffly.

"Didn't mean to make you huffy. Now, I hear Ireland's a big place for the spirits, isn't it? And fairies, too."

The patriot unruffled himself. "Yes, there are many people there who subscribe to the fairy faith."

Mrs. Mapes nodded. "Somebody once told me that Irish mamas do all sorts of things to guard their babies so they won't be snatched away by fairies."

"That's quite true," Mr. O'Nelligan confirmed. "Of course, such practices were more rampant in olden times. But, to this day, certain customs are still found, particularly in the west, where I hail from. For example, before stepping into another room, a mother might place a pair of iron tongs over a cradle to ward off the 'gentry,' as the fairies are called. Or she might light up a piece of straw and make a smoking cross over the babe to ensure its protection. These things are done in fear that the fairies might steal a human child and replace it with a weaker offspring of their own race."

"I believe in a lot of things," Mrs. Mapes said, "but I don't know if that's one I'd testify to."

"Nor I. But centuries-old beliefs are hard to shake and can sometimes cast a dark shadow. When I was a lad, there was a man of my town named Liam Ruddy who was physically impaired, one leg being stunted and one eye misted over. Also, in manner, he had a strange way about him, an aloofness that made people wonder. From early on, some folk insisted he was a changeling—a fairy child left as a replacement for the true Ruddy infant. I'm sure such talk must have been painful to endure, and I remember children tormenting the poor man with their jibes and jokes. Then, one day, a besotted stableman went too far with his taunts, causing Liam Ruddy to cave in his tormenter's nose with a shovel. Afterward, Liam felt quite terrible for his act and quit the county, never to return. Superstition, when allowed to run rampant, can be a cruel thing indeed."

Loretta Mapes let the story settle in. "No doubt it can. But it can be troubling, too, when people label something as superstition when it's really true."

"Such as?"

"Such as having the gift. Lots of folks have chided me about it, claiming I was making everything up. My own husband, for one. Over the years, I've taken more than my fair share of scoffing from that man. But now, I'm happy to say, he's changed his way of thinking."

"What brought him around?" Mr. O'Nelligan asked.

"Oh, I'd say it was the dying that did it." She laughed heartily at her own mischief. "He passed about three years ago, and he's been very apologetic ever since. Any time we have a chat now, he says he's sorry for not believing me back when he was alive. That's him right there." She pointed to a photo on a shelf of a grinning man whose bulging cheeks filled the entire frame. "Orville weighed in at nearly three hundred pounds, and his knees always vexed him. Now, he's very pleased to be just drifting about light as a big old feather."

I rejoined the conversation. "There's something I don't understand, Mrs. Mapes. If you claim you can speak to the dead, then why become one of Lloyd's clients? Having your own powers, I'd figure you wouldn't need his help."

"First of all, young man, I didn't consider myself Trexler Lloyd's client. He might have called me that, but I was there for my own reasons. I'd heard so much about him and what he was doing with that special gizmo of his that I wanted to see for myself. I met him and that Dr. Kemple once on my own, and then I attended the gathering last Friday. Those were the only two times I ever laid eyes on Mr. Lloyd. Now, as to me 'claiming' I have the gift, well, I'm not making any claims to anybody. Don't need to. I know what I possess."

Attempting to soothe her, I said, "I wasn't doubting you, Mrs. Mapes."

Her eyes narrowed. "Oh, please. Doubt's just leaking out of you, Mr. Plunkett. I can see it plain as day. You need some proof, is that it?" She moved her gaze upward, focusing on nothing at all. "Someone else has passed. Someone besides Trexler Lloyd. It's a man."

Okay, I thought. *People are always dying. Half of them men.*

She had more to say. "Italian. He's somehow involved with what you're doing, and he's got an Italian name. Not a young man. I feel like maybe I've met him before. He just passed."

Agnelli. She would have met him last week after Lloyd's death. He probably would have interviewed her. But how could she know that he had died yesterday?

"What does he say?" I surprised myself by asking.

The woman flipped her hand dismissively. "Oh, I don't know. He's gone already. He was only a wisp. That's what I call the ones who don't stop and chat. Wisps. They just fly by without really checking in. But, I've got to admit, I did fool you a little just now. I made it seem like I summoned him, but I didn't. Actually, I noticed him flitting around you a few minutes ago. I just focused in on him now to get a little bit of who he was. I see you know that man, don't you, gentlemen?"

"Perhaps we do," Mr. O'Nelligan said.

This contented her. "Mhm. I'm the genuine article. Now, as for these charlatans, they've got a whole bagful of tricks they'll use to swindle people. When some bereaved person comes to them to contact a loved one, the fakers will go on and on about 'impressions' and rattle off a hundred questions till they get an answer they like. They'll say, 'I get a strong impression of a man who was a farmer. What, not a farmer? Then how about a carpenter? No? Oh, I meant to say he was a dentist. Well, he worked with his hands, didn't he?' See, they know how to fish for facts. Butcher, baker, candlestick maker—they'll go through the whole dang list, speaking very fast, till they hit the correct thing, then run with it. And, remember, the bereaved's probably desperate to hear from beyond, so they'll buy into whatever the charlatan tosses at them."

"How does your own gift work?" Mr. O'Nelligan asked.

"It just comes natural," Mrs. Mapes said. "I got it from my mother, who was born a slave down in Virginia. Now, here's a story for you. Mama always had something special going on, but it really rose to the top the night she ran off from the plantation. She escaped with three other slaves, and she wasn't but eighteen, the only female in the group. The second night out they came to some swampland, and the men were all for crossing it. There were patrollers in the vicinity, and the swamp would be a shortcut. While the men were debating exactly which route to take, Mama sat herself against a tree and, next thing she knows, there's Auntie Lime, an old slave woman she'd known most of her life, sitting right beside her in the moonlight. The peculiar thing was that Auntie Lime had died two years before. But there she was smiling at my mama in kind of a gentle, sad way. She had only one thing to say—'Don't go in that swamp, child.' Then she was gone, quick as she'd come. Mama tried to tell the others about the warning, but they wouldn't listen and went for that swamp. Mama kept to the roads and the next day fell in with another band of runaways. Some Yankee soldiers delivered them north, where she eventually met my father and married him. Years after the war, she happened to run into one of those three men she'd escaped with and asked him about the others. He told her, 'Oh, those two drowned that night in that evil old swamp. I barely made it out myself. We should have listened to you.' Yes, Mama had the gift. Now I've got it, too."

Mr. O'Nelligan slowly stroked his beard. "Do many others of your kinsmen display this ability?"

"The gift sort of hops around in my family," Mrs. Mapes told him. "I'm the lastborn of Mama's ten children and the only one she passed it down to. None of my own kids have it, but I've got a granddaughter I'm thinking may perceive the dead like I do."

"So you actually see the deceased?" Mr. O'Nelligan asked.

"It's not exactly like that with me. I say I perceive them, but it's not really with my eyes, though I can often make out someone's face crystal clear. Hard to explain. Other times I can hear them speak. Like back this past July when that ocean liner crashed off of Nantucket—"

"What?" I blurted out. "You mean the *Andrea Doria*?"

Mrs. Mapes nodded. "That's the one. I woke up that night from a dead sleep to a whole clatter of voices calling out all confused and distressed. I figured that a bunch of folks must have just perished in some calamity, and I tried to calm them down best I could. Next day I heard on the news about that ship crashing into another one and there being fifty lives lost. Then, of course, I realized that's who I'd heard—the dead of the *Andrea Doria*."

Not for the first time in this investigation, I felt a chill pass through me. Good thing I didn't believe in this stuff.

"Anyway," our hostess continued, "depending on the spirit, sometimes I perceive them, sometimes I hear them, and other times I can smell them."

I suppressed a smile. "Smell them?"

"Oh, yes. The nose can zero right in on the spirit world. I smell my Daddy's pipe lots of times and know he's watching over me. And, just the other day, I darn near suffocated on my Cousin Soolie's perfume, even though an ice truck flattened her back in 1907."

"And what of Mr. Lloyd and Dr. Kemple?" my comrade

asked. "Having met them, what's your opinion of their own abilities?"

"Mr. Lloyd never claimed to have any. He was just interested in the way the living and the dead commingle, and, being an inventor and all, he aimed his talents at trying to better connect both parties. Now, if you're asking about Dr. Kemple, that's a whole different bucket of worms. That man's a funny mix. On the one hand, he's a snake-oil salesman if ever I saw one. Tries to badger you into thinking he's closer to the spirit world than the angels themselves. Trust me, that's mostly bamboozle. On the other hand, I believe he does have a bit of the gift. I can usually tell if a person's genuine."

"Just as you could tell I wasn't," I noted.

"That's right," Mrs. Mapes said. "With Dr. Kemple, I'd venture his abilities would be stronger if he didn't bury them beneath all his bitter nastiness. I tell you, nastiness will kill the gift quicker than an early frost will kill a garden. Another thing that kills it is liquor. I know because that's how I tried to murder my own gift. When I was younger, I didn't take it well when some dead neighbor would peer in my window, or when some lady a hundred years in the grave would sob in my ear the names of her children. So I took to drinking to drown it all out. It was my Orville, during our courtship, who got me to put the bottle aside. These days, I accept what I've got as a blessing from God, and I don't guzzle anything stiffer than this coffee."

"Let me ask you this, madam," Mr. O'Nelligan said. "At the time of Mr. Lloyd's death, did any particular insights come to you?"

Loretta Mapes gazed into her cup. "Well, I must say, when I first walked in that room and saw him sitting there in his cloak next to that big clumsy machine—this was even before the thing started sparking and he tumbled over—I got the feeling that the spirits already had a grip on Mr. Lloyd. Don't know what I mean by that exactly, but it's just how I felt."

"Well, *something* had a grip on him," I said, though I was thinking it was more the man's own king-sized ego than any ghost.

We talked with Mrs. Mapes for several more minutes, reviewing Friday night's events. Her observations lined up neatly with everything we'd already heard. She didn't seem to remember the names of the detectives who'd been on hand, and I chose not to offer the word "Agnelli."

As we stood on her front steps saying good-bye, she locked her eyes on a point several inches above my right shoulder. After a moment or two, she looked into my face. "Was your daddy a big strong-looking man?"

"Yes. Why?"

"He was just ambling by, that's all."

I actually turned to look over my shoulder.

"Oh, he's gone now," Mrs. Mapes said. "I get a notion that he slides by from time to time, just to look in on you."

Not sure how to reply, I gave a little wave and headed toward the car. Halfway there, I turned and saw Loretta Mapes resting a hand on Mr. O'Nelligan's shoulder and speaking very earnestly to him. I made out a few scattered phrases.

"Floating around you . . . Come to peace with . . . Dennis, right? . . . Yes, he's the one that you killed . . ."

CHAPTER ELEVEN

OR THE FIRST LEG OF THE journey north, we chose silence. Mr. O'Nelligan didn't ask about my dead father, and I didn't inquire as to who Dennis might be—though I pretty much assumed he was some fantasy of Mrs. Mapes's. Sunk pensively in our seats, we drove through a messy, sputtering snow as traffic sped around us. Eventually, our mood was sweetened by Elvis Presley.

"Aha!" My companion slapped the dashboard as Elvis warned us off of his blue suede shoes. "It's my lad from Tennessee."

Elvis had become Mr. O'Nelligan's "lad" only a few months ago when he first viewed the singer on *The Ed Sullivan Show*. Now, whenever the radio offered up the hip-wagging rock and roller, my Irishman was all ears.

"That's how music should be," he now said. "The happy songs should kick your heart up into the bright clouds, and the sad ones should bury it in the twilight mist. Young Elvis can do both with equal aplomb. You should really give him more of a chance."

We'd been through this before. Mr. O'Nelligan believed that, because of my relative youth, I should be won over by the whole Elvis craze. But I was not. After seeing a newsreel of teenaged girls shrieking and sobbing at one of his concerts, I thought it best to keep my distance from the phenomenon. The idea of my gray-bearded colleague somehow aligned with legions of tear-smeared bobby-soxers was just a little too much to digest.

"I guess Presley's okay," I said.

"Okay? Only okay? Where is your passion, Lee Plunkett? You should purchase one of his record albums and treat Audrey to an eve of dancing and romancing."

"Dancing and romancing? You didn't really just say that, did you?"

"I stand by my turn of phrase."

"Stick to Yeats and Shakespeare. That's my advice, no charge."

Elvis kept on crooning, a sneer evident in his voice. He was *very* adamant about us laying off of those shoes. When the song ended, Mr. O'Nelligan flicked off the radio and turned to me.

"So, what do you make of Loretta Mapes?"

"Seems sincere," I offered tentatively, "but I don't buy into her spookiness any more than I do with Kemple or Rast or any of them."

"Her remark about a dead man with an Italian name was noteworthy, was it not?"

"Lots of dead men with Italian names out there. For all we know, it was Benito Mussolini wafting around."

"Now you're just being facetious. Surely Mrs. Mapes's statement brings Detective Agnelli to mind."

"You think that's conclusive evidence of her 'gift'?"

"No, but we mustn't close ourselves off to all the possibilities of this case."

"And forget that stuff about my father." I just tossed it out. "She can see all the big and strong ghosts she wants to. That doesn't mean one's Buster Plunkett. Wild guesses, that's all."

"Yes, perhaps. Wild guesses . . ." My friend stared straight ahead and lapsed again into silence. I could guess what he was thinking about. Did he know that I'd overheard Mrs. Mapes's message to him? I wasn't sure and wasn't going to mention it.

Mr. O'Nelligan had asked me to bring along our borrowed copy of *Myself and No Other.* He now opened it and spent the remainder of the trip in Trexler Lloyd's head.

Just as we crossed the border into Brattleboro, Vermont, my colleague slammed the book closed. "Done."

"So, what did you think?"

He pondered a moment before answering. "A fragment of Walt Whitman comes to mind—'I celebrate myself, and sing myself.' That line, which some critics find a bit strident, seems actually meek when compared to Trexler Lloyd's jottings. Whereas Whitman merely celebrates and sings, Lloyd instigates a mile-long parade on his own behalf, replete with booming drums and blaring horns."

I laughed. "Like Mrs. Mapes says, you sure can twirl your words, you flashy old Scotsman."

He didn't laugh back.

WE TOOK A very late lunch or a very early dinner, depending on your viewpoint, at a restaurant called the Gaslight Inn. According to the menus, it offered patrons "The Best Fare of the Gay Nineties." To our waitress, Mr. O'Nelligan questioned the desirability of that claim. He himself had emerged from the nineties, he explained, and there was little of that period that could be labeled mirthful or merry, never mind gay. This got the waitress hooting. Oh, but that O'Nelligan sure had a way with the ladies.

Using the directions that Emmitt's wife had provided, we then drove on in search of his out-of-the-way cabin. By now, the snowfall was coming down in earnest, making for slow going. The landscape around us had become a rolling white sea from which the multitude of snow-painted trees rose like high masts. We eventually turned off the main route onto a winding dirt road and thumped and bumped along for another mile or so. Finally, we found the narrow driveway that led to our destination. The cabin, small and weathered, was set snugly in a grove of tall pines. We knocked on the door but received no response, and a glimpse through the window confirmed that no one was home. I was just about to try my luck with the door handle when the sound of fierce barking rose from behind us. I spun around in time to see a massive black dog, all fangs and fury, bounding across the white terrain. Clearly, we were his target. A few yards short of reaching us, the mutt pulled up to the summons of someone shouting behind him. A man in a plaid jacket now emerged from the tree line and yelled out a name that sounded like "Mauler." In response, the dog gave up on us and loped back to its master.

I called out to the man. "Are you Felix Emmitt?"

"Can't say I am," he called back in a broad rural accent. "That cabin does belong to some Emmitts, though. One of 'em's been up here last few days. Just seen him down at the meadows dropping his line. You friends of his?"

Oh, the very best. "We are" is all I said. "Where are the meadows?"

The man gestured back to the woods he'd just come from. "'Bout ten minutes thataway. C'mon, boy." Then he moved on in the opposite direction, his hellhound trotting beside him.

"I presume that we'll be proceeding on foot," Mr. O'Nelligan said.

"Swell," I huffed.

Pushing forward, we lowered our hats and buttoned our coats against the tumbling snow. The promised ten-minute hike turned out to be more than twice that long, and our Connecticut boots proved to be barely high enough for the Vermont winter woods. Luckily, the fresh footprints of man and dog made a visible trail for us. We came at last to a huge pond—or, rather, some flooded meadowlands—that seemed to feed into a river we could see in the distance. Atop the pond's frozen surface stood several tiny shacks, most with jutting stovepipes.

"Ice shanties," Mr. O'Nelligan observed.

"I know," I said, though I really didn't.

Only one of the stovepipes was issuing smoke. In front of that shanty, a man sat on an overturned bucket, his fishing rod poised above a round hole in the ice. He seemed to be the only person presently on the pond. We made our way out to him, sidestepping the occasional ice hole.

He looked up from his task. "Hello?" A bulky, middle-aged man, bundled up from head to toe, he had a face as round and pale as a full moon, and his wide cheeks hadn't seen a razor in days.

I tried my luck again. "Felix Emmitt?"

He achieved an even more bloodless shade of pale, and I knew we had our coroner.

"Who . . . ?" That's all Emmitt could get out before his line began jerking fiercely up and down, causing him to tighten his grip on the fishing rod.

"It appears you have a bite, sir," Mr. O'Nelligan said.

We watched intently as Emmitt struggled to reel in whatever was fighting him below the ice. Just when it seemed that man might prevail over swimming beast, the line snapped and Emmitt fell backward off his bucket.

"What lurks below?" Mr. O'Nelligan wondered aloud.

Emmitt didn't venture a guess. He got himself to his feet, tossed the fishing rod aside, and studied us with apprehension. "Who are you?"

Feeling the snow settling heavily on my head and shoulders, I pointed toward the ice shanty. "Can we talk out of the cold?"

Felix Emmitt pulled open the door and gestured us in. I was surprised how cozy and warm the little space felt. A small, compact woodstove deserved the credit for that. Emmitt allowed us to take the two available camp chairs while seating himself on an overturned crate.

He repeated his question. "So who are you?"

My colleague turned to me. "Directness seems the best approach here. I think it's time to cast off our guises permanently."

I nodded and laid it all out for Emmitt—our true profession, our assignment, the suspicions about Lloyd's death. I still held back from mentioning George Agnelli since there seemed no reason to betray his trust, even if he was beyond caring.

I honed in on Emmitt's piece of the pie. "Now, would you like to tell us why you just *happened* to be at Lloyd's last week? And don't say it was your fascination with life after death. We don't buy into coincidences. Every root has its vine."

Mr. O'Nelligan cleared his throat. "You mean 'every vine has its seed.'"

"Exactly." I fixed Emmitt with my best Bogart stare (though my large specs may have watered down the full impact). "Give it to us straight. We'll know a lie if we hear one."

Felix Emmitt groaned and buried his face in his hands. "I shouldn't have agreed to it. I see that now."

"Hold up," I said. "You shouldn't have agreed to what?"

He raised his head, and I saw the face of a man defeated and scared. "I've got my sins, there's no denying it. I like my liquor way too much, and then there's the horses. I've lost a ton at the tracks lately. My wife's been on me about everything, and I needed money badly, so when Dr. Kemple came to me with the plan—"

"Kemple came to you?"

"Yeah. About a month ago."

"He came with a plan to kill Trexler Lloyd?"

"Well, yes . . . and no."

That annoyed me. "Which? It can't be both."

"But in a way it was." Emmitt fished a cigarette out of his coat pocket and lit up, trying to settle his nerves. "It was Lloyd's plan. He sent Kemple to me to make the offer. A thousand dollars before and a thousand after."

"Before and after *what*?"

"After I pronounced him dead." He paused, waiting to see if we'd catch on. "Don't you guys get it? Trexler Lloyd was going to fake his own death."

I felt like I'd just been shoved off a cliff. "Keep going."

Emmitt continued. "Lloyd had rigged that contraption of his to sputter and spark, making it look like he'd been electrocuted. Then I was supposed to rush forward and declare him dead.

Kemple told me that Lloyd had mastered some form of meditation where he could slow down his breathing to almost nothing. To the untrained eye, he'd appear lifeless."

"How about the trained eyes of two police detectives?" I asked.

"Even them. That is, if they weren't allowed to hover too much around Lloyd. But I didn't let them, though I think that Agnelli, especially, had some strong doubts about everything."

Mr. O'Nelligan tried to sort this all out. "So you're telling us that Lloyd was, in fact, alive when you declared him dead?"

Emmitt pressed a hand to his forehead, as if trying to hold back a headache. "No, he was dead."

I'd had it. "Okay, pal, you'd better ditch these games of yours. You're involved in something dirty, and it's going to come crashing back down on you." That was me at my most rugged.

"I'm being straight here," Emmitt insisted. "Look, here's how the plan was supposed to go. First I'd declare death by electrocution, then Kemple would produce some legal paper stating Lloyd's intent to be cremated immediately. Lloyd's wife would back that up. Then, once we'd dealt with the detectives, we'd carry him out to the hearse."

"Wait, now." I didn't like this. "Are you saying that Constanza Lloyd was in on the scheme?"

"That was my impression. Anyway, Lloyd would be driven straight over to Frank Johnson's crematorium. Johnson had been paid off like me. The idea was for Lloyd to be carried into Johnson's to keep up the act and just left there. Then, when the coast was clear, Lloyd would get up, fit as a fiddle, and slip outside, where Kemple would be waiting in a separate car to whisk him away."

"Away to where?" I asked.

"That I don't know. Kemple only told me so much. Obviously, Lloyd wanted to disappear without a trace, though I've no idea why. Afterward, Johnson would produce a fake certificate of cremation and a jar of ashes. Then Trexler Lloyd would be just a memory. That's how the plan was supposed to go."

"But something went astray," Mr. O'Nelligan suggested.

Emmitt ground out his cigarette against the stove. "Yeah, something big. When I went over to examine him, I found that Lloyd actually *was* dead."

I tried to process that. "Not just faking it? You mean he really was electrocuted?"

Emmitt shook his head. "Not electrocuted. Stabbed."

"Stabbed?"

"That's my best guess. Probably by a fairly slender blade—a dagger as opposed to a butcher's knife. As soon as the sparks shot out, I hurried over to Lloyd to do my examination. He half fell out of his chair, and I lowered him to the ground. He was wearing a heavy robe, and when I pulled it back I saw blood. There wasn't supposed to be blood."

"Could it have been fake?" I suggested.

Despite being cornered as he was, I caught a glimpse of the man's professional conceit. "I'm a coroner, for God's sake. I know blood when I see it. There were at least three punctures, all in the chest area. I saw them, and so did Kemple."

"How did Kemple react?"

"We just caught each other's eyes, and he looked as shocked as I was."

"No one else noticed?"

"I don't think so. As soon as I saw the wounds, I quickly covered them back up, and that robe was so heavy and dark that nothing had seeped through."

"Why did you hide his wounds?"

"Because I didn't know what the hell was going on! As soon as I touched Lloyd I knew he was really dead and that something had gone wrong."

"For how long had he been deceased?" Mr. O'Nelligan asked.

"I don't know exactly."

"Yet you are a coroner."

"I panicked, okay?" Emmitt pulled out another cigarette, but it snapped apart in his tense grip. "As soon as I saw the blood and the wounds, I panicked. This was more than I'd bargained for. My career was on the line—my whole life—and my brain just froze. Plus, to be honest, I'd had a couple of drinks before I got there. To brace up, you understand? I didn't really do an examination, but what I can say is that pallor mortis hadn't fully set in. He still pretty much had his color. So he probably hadn't died more than an hour before that."

"Well, that we knew," I said. "Lloyd was conversing with people all along, and he gave a little speech right before the exhibition began."

Emmitt thought about that. "I think you're wrong. About the speech, I mean. Dr. Kemple gave an introduction, but I don't remember Lloyd saying anything."

I pushed on. "Anyway, what happened to the plan once you realized you had a real death—presumably a murder—on your hands?"

"Just before the detectives arrived, I found a moment to pull Kemple aside and ask what we should do. All he said was 'Continue with the plan.' So we did."

"And how did you do that?"

"Well, after the detectives backed off, Kemple found a stretcher to carry Lloyd out."

"There just happened to be a stretcher lying around the house?"

Emmitt shrugged. "I guess it was part of the original plan. We carried Lloyd outside and slid him into the hearse."

"You and who else?"

"Kemple and the butler, Trowbridge."

"Who drove?"

"Trowbridge. I rode with him. Kemple drove himself in his own car."

"So the butler was also in on the plan?"

"I'm not sure if he was or wasn't. We drove to the crematorium without talking. Kemple met us there, and we carried Lloyd inside. Then Kemple took Johnson in another room, and I heard them arguing. I didn't want any part of the whole disaster, so I asked Trowbridge to drive me back to the Lloyds's house. Then I got my car and went home."

"But not for long," I observed. "You snuck yourself up to this winter wonderland pretty damned quick, didn't you?"

This drew another low groan from Emmitt. "The day after, I asked for a leave of absence from work and called my uncle about staying in his cabin up here, since no one was using it. I was desperate to get away, you see. I mean, a man had been killed . . ."

Mr. O'Nelligan tilted his chin back in contemplation. "A tangled web indeed. Are we to presume that Mr. Lloyd's body did, in fact, undergo cremation?"

"I think so, yes," Emmitt said. "I figure Kemple just wanted to be done with it all. Same as I did. So tell me, am I going to be arrested?"

"I'm not sure what the charge would be," I said.

Mr. O'Nelligan had a guess. "Filling out false documents

concerning a man's cause of death. That, I venture, is quite an illegal thing for a county official to do."

Emmitt closed his eyes. "I'm a dead man."

"You most certainly are not," my colleague countered. "You're a man driven by his vices to an unethical act. It is Mr. Lloyd who is untimely slain, and it is with him that our sympathies lie. We might wish to speak with you again, Mr. Emmitt. I suggest you don't attempt to flee. Again."

"Good advice," I added. "If we need your company, we'll ask the local police here to contact you. At this point, we don't necessarily need to mention to them your recent improprieties."

I stood and led the way back outside. The snow hadn't let up.

Emmitt stared across the frozen water and spoke softly. "You know, I first started coming up here as a boy. I always loved it— the woods, the fishing, the snow in winter. An old woman who lived just across the river there used to make corn bread for us. She'd serve it piping hot with butter. Last week when I needed somewhere to run to, somewhere to hide, this is the first place I thought of. I always felt good here. I always felt clean."

He stooped and picked up the discarded fishing pole. We left him there, standing alone in the falling snow. He had shifted his gaze down into the ice hole, looking for the powerful thing that moved beneath the surface.

CHAPTER TWELVE

THE SNOW AND THE WOODS and the failing light had conspired against us. The footprints we'd followed in, as well as the ones we'd made ourselves, had been all but erased by the heavy white downfall. Smartly, I'd brought a flashlight along. Stupidly, I hadn't bothered to check if the batteries were working. They weren't.

"It's that way, right?" I pointed into the twilight.

"I defer fully to you in this situation," Mr. O'Nelligan answered. "Snow isn't my strong suit. Back in Kerry, a few inches' accumulation was considered a miracle."

"I think this is the way we came from."

"Good. Good. Trust your feet, Lee Plunkett."

Within minutes, my feet betrayed us. Whatever meager trail we'd been following was no longer evident, and every tree now resembled every other tree.

"Weren't we just here at this spot?" my companion asked.

"Can't be. How could we go in a circle so quickly?"

"The forest can be a mysterious thing."

We moved on. Traveling in such heavy snowfall was like pushing through an endless series of curtains, so that we couldn't see much of what lay before us. The deepening sunset had transformed the woods from a Currier and Ives winter scene into something dark and ancient where humans had no rightful place. Tall, bare specters of maple and hemlock held reign, as the tangle of lower branches clawed at us with every step. We stopped speaking after a while, which amplified the lonesome thud of our footfalls against the snow-smothered earth. Before long, the landscape began to trick us. Whereas our journey in had all been on level ground, the terrain we now found ourselves on was pitched and uneven. We seemed to be ascending, which couldn't be right, so I started to backtrack. Mr. O'Nelligan followed, though the distance between us widened as we pushed on.

Then I plunged. I hadn't realized that we'd been moving along some precipice, but a false step now sent me hurtling head over heels down an unseen slope. It was steep and rough, and I reached the bottom by slamming full body into a wide-based tree. I lay there for a full minute, trying to decide if I'd broken anything. Thankfully, I hadn't. I sat up, realizing then that I'd lost several items in my descent—my hat, my useless flashlight, and, most alarmingly, my eyeglasses. I called out for Mr. O'Nelligan, several times, but received no answer. It occurred to me that in the snowy grayness he might not even have witnessed my fall. He could well have kept going, wrongly assuming that I was still somewhere out ahead of him.

I needed to find my glasses—the world was a foggy mess without them. After first pulling off my gloves for a more sensitive touch, I pushed my hands deeply through the downy snow. The chill enforced my feeling of desperation. Slowly, on my knees, I moved up the slope, digging as I went and intermittently calling out for my companion to no effect. By the time I reached the top, I'd found my hat and the dead flashlight, but not my glasses. Near-blind and lost in an ever darkening, snow-filled wood, my heart sank. I tried to calm myself with sunny logic. *You can't be far from the cabin and the car. No, not far at all. O'Nelligan's probably there already. He'll probably start beeping the horn right away. That brainy old Irishman would certainly think to do that.* Then I remembered that I had locked the car. There'd be no horn beeping any time soon.

An old, undesired memory came rushing in. A decade back, the owner of the Thelmont Camera Store—a healthy, vigorous man in his early thirties—had entered a stretch of woods one winter afternoon to take some nature shots. My father was part of the search party that discovered him three days later.

As Dad described it, "We found him lying there like a baby. 'Cept instead of a pillow, his head was resting on a big fat rock, black with his blood. We figure he got lost in the darkness, tripped, and bashed his fool skull in."

When I complained that he was being cavalier about a man's life, my father replied, "Hey, I was the one out there looking for the guy. Where the hell were you? You're twenty, not a kid anymore. You could've joined the search, same as me."

He was right. I could have. Probably should have. Maybe I didn't because I was too distracted with my own life, or too busy at the factory, or too scared that I might be the one to stumble over a dead body. Whatever it was, it was just another example of my falling short of my father's standards.

"Anyway, that guy shouldn't have gone out so late in the

day," Dad concluded. "Those night woods can really turn on you."

I now drove that episode from my mind and pushed forward. I say forward, but in reality I had no clue as to which direction I was heading. All I knew was that Vermont was renowned for its vast, wild acres of forestlands, and I was a half-blind man groping through a sunset snowstorm. And what about Mr. O'Nelligan? I wanted to believe that he'd reached the cabin safely, but I had no way of knowing if that was true. As he'd said, he was out of his element—literally. At least my friend had his eyes, whereas my own, presently unenhanced, weren't worth beans. I reached my numbed hands into my coat pocket to retrieve the gloves and, in doing so, dropped one of them to the ground. What should have been a simple task of retrieval became a frantic search. Somehow, I just couldn't find that glove, and the idea of the snow claiming yet another part of me spiked my anger. I let loose a tirade of violent curses toward the woods, the snow, the fading sun, and Trexler Lloyd, who, by dying so bizarrely, was responsible for me being here. After a minute or two, depleted by my outburst, I gave up the search and accepted the warmth of my remaining glove.

Then I just stood there, listening to the soft patter of snow touching earth and feeling the cold peck of each flake that reached my face. For a passing moment, I imagined that the whole of nature was gazing down at me, amused at this stupid little marionette who'd worn himself out from his frenzy in the storm. *Shall we guide him or kill him? Either choice will do.* The notion that I was the object of some cosmic debate quickly withdrew itself, only to be replaced by another strange thought: *This is what it's like to be a ghost.* Suddenly, the haunted universe of Lloyd and his cohorts seemed to enwrap me, to seep into my flesh and brain. Who needed a Spectricator when the otherworld was so near at hand here among these eerie, timeless shadows? Perhaps the wandering dead weren't so different from me in my present condition—lost, unfocused, seeing life through a confounding haze. Right now, in this cold, lightless domain, it wasn't hard to imagine myself no longer one of the living. *The woods are lonely, deep as death . . .* Was that the line from that Frost poem? If it wasn't, it should be. This place seemed quite capable of reaching deep into my chest to clutch and draw out that thing called a soul. Wasn't I, in truth, just a ghost waiting to be born? Weren't we all?

But, damn it, not yet. Shaking off my philosophizing stupor, I moved forward. I'm not sure how long I continued on. It could have been twenty minutes, though it felt like hours. After a time, I heard something and stopped in my tracks. There was definite movement up ahead—the distinct sound of a body pushing through underbrush. Mr. O'Nelligan? Or perhaps Emmitt heading back from the ice? I called out an impassioned hello. Instead of a human voice, the response was loud, angry barking. I recognized it at once as the agitated greeting of Mauler the hellhound.

I held my ground as the large animal advanced on me. He came within a couple of yards, then halted and continued his harangue. I shouted out for Mauler's master, but the man apparently was nowhere in the vicinity. In the dying light, the dog appeared to my flawed eyes as an unformed black specter, half hidden behind the veil of falling snow. It occurred to me that this might not be Mauler at all, but some equally ferocious— and less controllable—doppelganger. Slipping my right hand into my coat pocket, I drew out the flashlight—my only weapon—and tensed myself against a possible attack. Just when

I thought the lunge was about to come, the barking ceased and the dog sat back on his haunches. We stayed like that for a good five minutes, appraising each other without sound or movement. Then, taking a chance, I squatted down and extended my ungloved left hand. The hellhound shot forward and licked it.

Within fifteen minutes, my canine escort had led me back to the cabin area. There I found Mr. O'Nelligan, who had managed to reach the spot on his own. He was much relieved to see that the winter woods hadn't claimed me. I retrieved a spare pair of glasses from my glove compartment and, with sight restored, looked around for my four-legged savior. He was nowhere to be seen.

FORTUNATELY, SEVERAL MINUTES into our drive back south, the snow tapered off and the plow trucks came out in force, carving wide paths down the roadways. With the driving less arduous, it was time to review what Felix Emmitt had told us.

"It's a big, sloppy ball of confusion," I started off.

"It most certainly is," Mr. O'Nelligan agreed. "So, if we're to believe our Mr. Emmitt, what do we have?"

"Well, first off, we have Trexler Lloyd creating a crazy, unbelievably elaborate scheme to fake his own death. Elaborate and far-fetched."

"You're right, of course, in that depiction. But do remember that Trexler Lloyd appears to have been a supreme egotist and a genius in the bargain. So what might be deemed staggeringly far-fetched in another man, in Lloyd might be considered . . ."

"All in a day's work?"

"Just so."

"To continue, we have the scheme . . ."

"Aided by a number of confederates. Including his wife."

"Now, we don't know that."

"You mean you prefer not to believe it because she's beautiful."

"I didn't say any such thing."

"You didn't have to, Lee Plunkett."

"I'm ignoring you. Can I get on with my list now? So first we have Lloyd's cockamamie scheme. Next we have an unknown party who thwarts that scheme by thrusting something sharp into Lloyd's chest three times."

"At least three times."

"At least. And, quite probably, the killer is someone we've already met. But how could anybody have secretly stabbed Lloyd in plain view of a roomful of people? That's the $64,000 question. Then we have the coroner discovering that Lloyd's really most sincerely dead. But, being tipsy and terrified, Emmitt still decides to go through with the plan."

"With Dr. Kemple's encouragement," my friend added.

"Right. Kemple. That's the rat we need to ferret out."

"Rats and ferrets—is that all that our human machinations come down to? A joust between small scurrying mammals?"

"Again, I'm ignoring you. Okay, then Lloyd's body gets reduced to ashes, destroying the evidence, so to speak. As to the murder weapon, well, we have none. For all we know, it's lying at the bottom of a lake somewhere. Add the fact that we're employed by a dead cop, sprinkle in a suspect list of crazies and spookmongers, and we've got ourselves a heck of a party."

Mr. O'Nelligan sighed theatrically. "Ah, yes. It's a big, sloppy ball of confusion, is it not?"

"So they tell me. Anyway, do you think Emmitt was telling the truth?'

"He seemed genuinely anxious when confronted. After all, we caught him unawares. For him to produce such an elaborate fabrication on the spur of the moment seems far-fetched."

"Everything about this case is far-fetched."

"True. But if Mr. Emmitt's narrative is accurate, then some earlier pieces of our puzzle may fit into it."

"Which pieces?"

"Well, firstly, the curious detail of Mr. Lloyd transferring his assets to Madrid, coupled with the requirement that Constanza return there to access her inheritance. If Lloyd was indeed planning to fake his death and disappear, then perhaps Spain was his destination."

"Where he'd reunite with his wife and his fortune?"

"That was my thinking."

"It's plausible," I had to admit.

"Another puzzle piece is the recording you heard in Dr. Kemple's room. Lloyd pretending to speak from the dead would seem to somehow fit into the aforementioned scheme."

"That's plausible, too. According to Emmitt, Kemple was knee-deep in this business. I say we ambush him again and shake him down."

"Alright, but let's not do it in his quarters, where weapons are at hand."

"Fine with me. He's making an appearance at a bookstore in Darien tomorrow afternoon. One o'clock—I saw it in a newspaper. We can corner him then. It'll be out in public, where he's not as likely to start waving pistols around so freely."

"Then there's Constanza, and perhaps Trowbridge. The cremator may also warrant a visit. He can wait until tomorrow, but

I suggest we confront the other two tonight. We can drive to the Lloyd home directly. And I say we reveal to everyone that we believe Trexler Lloyd's death was no accident, to see what we stir up."

"When you say everyone, does that include the police?"

"For the time being, I think not. Remember, we still want for hard facts. Detective Agnelli's concerns went unheeded, as our own would probably be. The gendarmes, more than simply distrusting us, may actually obstruct our work."

"Okay," I said. "We can bring them in later."

"So you'll aim us back toward the Lloyds'?"

"Sure, I suppose so." Having just eluded the wrath of the wilderness, I really wanted to go home to a late snack and a soft bed. But, being a private eye, sometimes you have to give up certain luxuries—like food, warmth, and not getting killed.

CHAPTER THIRTEEN

FOR THE SECOND TIME IN one day we were facing the dragons at Lloyd's gate. In the jaundiced beams of my headlights, they looked even less affable than in the daytime. In fact, they looked downright ominous. We had tried to phone ahead a few miles back, but no one had answered. We'd then made the decision to come directly to the gates and figure from there how to gain entrance. We climbed out of the car and appraised the high wrought-iron fence that surrounded the property.

"I could vault it," I quipped.

Mr. O'Nelligan nodded. "I was thinking that very thing."

"Oh, come on. I was kidding."

"If I provide a boost, I'm sure you could—"

"Absolutely not!"

Once again, someone seemed to be mistaking me for my father. Even in his later years, Buster would have welcomed the chance to lay siege to a fortified objective. It would have brought him right back to 1917 and the trenches of France. Me, I liked to limit my leaping, hurdling, and vaulting to a bare minimum. Before the debate could build momentum, a second pair of headlights eased down from the driveway and paused on the other side of the gates. I saw someone lean out of the driver's window.

"Hello? Who's there?" It was a woman's voice I didn't recognize.

Through the gates, I stated our names, which seemed to have meaning to her. She told us to wait a minute, then got out, undid the lock, and met us in the spotlit area between our two vehicles. She was a heavyset woman in her forties with a calm, unruffled air about her.

"I'm Mrs. Perris, the cook here. Doris said something about you people visiting earlier, but she didn't mention you'd be coming back tonight. Are they expecting you at the house?"

"More or less," I said, deemphasizing the "less."

She accepted that. "They're up there now doing one of their levelings, as they call it. You know, it was just about this time a week ago that Mr. Lloyd passed away. Right now they're in the room where he died. They'd probably welcome having you join in."

"You don't participate in these meditations?" Mr. O'Nelligan asked.

Mrs. Perris shook her head. "No. I'm Presbyterian. I have my own spiritual beliefs."

"I see. And you don't mind spending time in yonder den of specters?"

She smiled at his flourish. "I'm a live-and-let-live sort of person. It doesn't bother me if those folks up there try to jump the fence and talk to the deceased. I don't buy it, but it doesn't bother me. All I concern myself with is salmon steaks and peach pies."

Mr. O'Nelligan sighed. "If we could all make that noble claim, I'd venture it would be a far better world."

Mrs. Perris gave me an amused look. "Quite an orator you've got here. Does he always talk so grand?"

"You know it," I said. "Back in Ireland, this man's tongue was a national landmark."

That got a laugh out of her. "You fellows are like Abbott and Costello! Only neither of you is the round one. Wish I could say the same for myself."

Mr. O'Nelligan got back on track. "One last thing, madam. We understand that you were away the night of Mr. Lloyd's death."

"Yes, I've a sick husband at home. I feel bad in a way that I wasn't here when Mr. Lloyd died. Not that there's anything I could have done. Well, I should be off now. I just finished cleaning up after dinner and organizing the cutlery. I need to get home. Jack's taken a turn for the better, but I don't like to leave him alone for long."

Wishing her and her husband well, we parted company and drove up to the house. I had to rap the wanton-woman doorknocker many times before the door finally swung open. This time it was actually the butler who answered.

Mr. O'Nelligan fired the first volley. "How comforting it is to see you finally at your post."

Trowbridge smiled thinly. "My post extends far beyond the doorstep, sir."

"Apparently. May we come in?"

"I have no orders to the contrary."

The man stepped aside, and we entered. As before, I allowed the exchange between these two to go uninterrupted.

"We've been told that the members of the household are gathered in the Portal Room," said Mr. O'Nelligan.

"Your informants have not lied," Trowbridge answered. "Shall I lead you there?"

"No, we know the way ourselves. But first, there are some matters pertinent to yourself that we wish to discuss."

"My, that does sound weighty. Shall we conduct inquiries here in the foyer, or shall I invite you to my room for brandy and cigars?"

Was this the cockiest butler that ever strode the earth? I found myself transfixed by the two men, wondering again if we were in for fisticuffs.

"We'll remain here," Mr. O'Nelligan said.

"As is your pleasure," the Englishman replied.

"To begin with, can we agree to the fact that your employer Mr. Lloyd abstained from drinking warm liquids after dinner?"

"Yes, that was his inclination."

"Good. I'm glad we see eye to eye on that point. We can race ahead to my next question. Why did you lie about the tea?"

"Excuse me?"

"The tea. You know—a hot aromatic beverage favored by both our peoples, but, unfortunately for you, not by Trexler Lloyd in the evening. You weren't delivering tea to Mr. Lloyd when you visited him alone in the Portal Room. What was the real reason you went to see him?"

The butler hesitated, clearly realizing that he'd tripped himself up. "It was a private matter."

"There are no private matters in this affair. I should now reveal to you that Mr. Plunkett and I aren't here because of any occult concerns. He is a licensed detective, and I am his second. We're investigating Trexler Lloyd's murder."

Trowbridge grimaced. "What do you mean? Mr. Lloyd died accidentally."

"He was murdered. And were you not party to the original conspiracy to fake his death?" Wisely or unwisely, my colleague seemed to be flinging all our cards on the table at once.

"Fake his death?" Trowbridge looked genuinely confounded. "I surmise, sir, that you've been drinking something much stronger than tea."

"You deny any involvement in Lloyd's plan?"

"I deny knowing what the hell you're even talking about."

"Very well. We'll step back from that issue for the present. Let's return to your encounter with Mr. Lloyd in the Portal Room. What passed between you two?"

"What passes between a gentleman and his butler is confidential. No doubt such notions of civility are foreign to your experience."

"Enough!" My friend's face reddened. "Let me tell you something, Mr. Trowbridge. Things will soon be heating up. Yes, very hotly indeed. Your employer has been murdered, and yet you choose to prattle on about confidences and privacy. Here's what I know. Last Friday evening, Mr. Lloyd was in noted good spirits until his butler joined him in the Portal Room. After that encounter, Lloyd's mood darkened, and he stated his intention to make changes to his will."

"I know nothing about the will."

"You're not aware that you receive a monetary recognition in it?"

"Well, yes, I'd heard something to that effect, but the sum, I believe, is a modest one."

"As you say. But again I ask, what passed between you and Mr. Lloyd?"

"Nothing of consequence." Trowbridge drew himself up to his full height, a solid four inches above my colleague. "Are we quite done now?"

Mr. O'Nelligan appraised his adversary for several long moments, then smiled coolly. "Since you seem so fixed in your response, I'll beg off for now. But be aware—Mr. Plunkett and I will not forsake our pursuit of the truth. We are a dogged pair, and before long we'll be sharing our findings with the constabulary."

"The cops," I clarified.

Trowbridge now seemed to remember I was there. "I know the meaning of 'constabulary,' young sir." His contempt was obvious. "I myself was once a constable of the crown."

"You wore the badge?" Mr. O'Nelligan asked.

"I did," Trowbridge answered.

I was feeling brash. "What happened? Did they drum you out?"

"Yes," the butler said simply. "Now, if you'll excuse me, I have my duties." He turned abruptly and left us.

I faced my colleague. "So, Trowbridge is a disgraced ex-copper? Interesting."

"Who knows where the truth lies with that man. But, most certainly, his final conversation with Trexler Lloyd is something we must pursue."

"Didn't hold back much from him, did you? You were pretty free with the word 'murder.' "

"In this case I felt that being brutally direct was the best course of action. Trowbridge feels some pressure on him, which hopefully will yield results before long. Now, may I suggest we seek out the widow Lloyd and see what she has to tell us?" My comrade flashed an annoying little grin. "That is, if you can disentangle yourself from the web of her beauty."

WE FOUND THE door to the Portal Room open and the space lit by candles in the tall iron stands I'd noticed earlier. Not far from the Spectricator, four people were seated in a circle around Lloyd's purple-upholstered death chair: Miss Chauncey, Sassafras, Rast, and Constanza Lloyd. Three had their eyes closed; Sassafras, by contrast, was looking distractedly all around.

She noticed us. "Hey, it's Blarney and the kid!"

"Shhhh, Sassafras!" Doris Chauncey reprimanded. "You'll break the leveling."

"Oh right, sorry." Sassafras slammed her eyes shut and struggled to look earnest.

We stood to the side for several minutes observing the ritual, though Constanza, whom my eyes were most drawn to, had her back to us. When Doris finally rang the Tibetan bell she'd been holding, everyone opened their eyes and slowly stood.

Sassafras pouted. "I thought I was going to ring it at the end."

"Sorry, I forgot." Doris now turned to us. "We weren't expecting you."

"Pardon our unannounced arrival," Mr. O'Nelligan said. "We attempted to contact you, but failed. Your cook let us in"

"This is the hour that Mr. Lloyd died," the secretary explained. "Exactly this time last week. We're observing it."

"And seeing if Trex wanted to make an appearance," Sassafras chimed in. "He hasn't dropped by, though"

"I told you he would not." Martin Rast, now in a black beret, removed his eyeglasses and polished them with his sleeve. "He does not linger here. There are other spirits, of course, but not Mr. Lloyd."

A touch of sorrow came into Sassafras's voice. "I was really hoping he'd surprise me one last time." Then, as if afraid of her sentiments being misread, she hurriedly added, "You'd think he'd at least want to visit his wife."

In keeping with our new policy of self-disclosure, I immediately flung out the truth. "We can tell you all now, Mr. O'Nelligan and I are actually private detectives conducting an investigation into Trexler Lloyd's death. And, by the way, I'm no psychic."

Rast was the first to respond. "Aha! Yes, yes! I *knew* you did not know the spirits."

Doris Chauncey, who, of course, was already in our confidence, kept silent, as did the sad, lovely Constanza, who was staring at me intently.

Sassafras scrunched up her rouged face in a look of confusion. "Hold on now. Why do we need another investigation if Trexler died by accident? I mean, having a couple private eyes knocking around is sexy as hell, but I don't see the point."

Not wanting to go as far as my partner had with Trowbridge, I bypassed the term "murder" for a less sensational explanation. "We're treating this as a questionable death." I left it at that. At this point, I wasn't going to mention Agnelli's concerns or Emmitt's testimony.

"May we now have some time alone with Mrs. Lloyd?" Mr. O'Nelligan asked.

The young woman turned to Miss Chauncey and parted her lips in what seemed like an unspoken plea for intervention.

Doris came to her aid. "She's really terribly fatigued. As I've said, tonight is—"

Mr. O'Nelligan let her go no further. "I'm afraid we must insist. There are crucial aspects to this case that only Mrs. Lloyd can assist us with."

"Well, if there's no other way," the secretary said. "But I'd like to be with her to offer support."

"That wouldn't be in anyone's best interests," the Irishman said firmly.

Constanza drew in a deep breath. "Very well. But I don't wish to be in this room anymore."

Mr. O'Nelligan nodded. "We understand. Perhaps we can adjourn to one of the other rooms."

"You can use my office," said Miss Chauncey. "But are you sure I can't—"

My colleague spoke over her. "It's better done with Mrs. Lloyd alone."

Constanza headed toward the door, glancing back once at Doris with a look of deep resignation. She seemed like someone on her way to her own execution.

"WE KNOW ALL," Mr. O'Nelligan said.

He and Mrs. Lloyd were seated; I was half-perched on the secretary's desk.

"You do?" The young widow tried to keep her voice strong but couldn't quite pull it off. Her dark complexion grew pale, and her breathing quickened. I didn't like seeing this. Whether because she was eerily beautiful or because she was a stranger to our land or because she'd lost two husbands before age thirty, the sight of her trapped and desperate didn't sit well with me.

I couldn't hold back. "Don't worry. Everything will be alright."

Mr. O'Nelligan flashed me a look as if to say, *Oh, will it re-*

ally? then continued. "Would you like to tell us about your husband's plan?"

"Plan?" She widened her eyes as if she didn't comprehend.

"Just tell us." My colleague made his voice low and grandfatherly. "It will go much better for you in the end."

Constanza lowered her head, and her long black hair covered her like a veil. Her body began to tremble, and I assumed that she was fighting bravely against tears. I resisted the urge to reach out to stroke her shoulder. Then her head jerked back up to reveal a face wildly distorted with rage, and I nearly slipped off the desk.

She started with "Damn him! Damn him!" then shifted to *"Soy inocente!"* and a string of agitated Spanish that I couldn't follow. Abruptly freed from her beauty, I looked to Mr. O'Nelligan to stem the tide he'd just released.

"Mrs. Lloyd, please," he tried to soothe her. "Just tell us what you can. It will surely lift your burdens."

"I did nothing wrong!" she wanted us to know. "It was all Trexler's plan. I went along because I am his wife."

"Tell us what you know," Mr. O'Nelligan coaxed. "We're not here to judge you."

Constanza eased back a little. "Trexler wanted to go away. To no longer be who he was. He and Dr. Kemple made this plan to pretend Trexler had been killed by his machine. *Un plan muy complicado.* That man Emmitt was to say my husband was dead, and I was to come down to cry over Trexler and demand his body be burned to ashes. Then Trexler would disappear, and we would meet next week in Madrid, where all the money was. He would change his name, and we would go travel the world to places where people did not recognize him. But something went wrong."

"And what was that?" I asked.

"Sometime after they drove Trexler away, Dr. Kemple came back to the house to tell me that my husband was really dead. Someone had truly killed him. Then I cried for real. Dr. Kemple said we should say nothing, because if we did, the plan could become known and we would all be in trouble. So I stayed silent. You understand?"

"Certainly we do," I answered. "Have you any guesses as to who might have wanted your husband dead?"

"No, I have been asking myself this. But Trexler was a powerful man, and powerful men are many times killed by people who hate their power. You know Julius Caesar, yes? He was such a man, and he was stabbed many times like Trexler."

Mr. O'Nelligan took on the questioning. "How do you know Mr. Lloyd was stabbed?"

"Dr. Kemple told me this."

"I see. Did you discuss your husband's plan with anyone? Or the fact that he was stabbed to death?"

"No. Only with Dr. Kemple."

"Not Miss Chauncey?"

"No. Not even her."

"You're close to her, aren't you?"

"I am. I do not have a maid here or anything like that. I take care of myself, which is fine, but Doris helps me with some things. She is my best companion here. Of course, there is also Sassafras, but she talks so much."

"What of your husband?" Mr. O'Nelligan continued. "Were you and he good companions?"

"I am sorry I cursed him just now," Constanza said. "I am just so scared. But he was a good husband to me."

"How so?"

She shrugged. "He gave me things when I wanted. And he would tell me I was special."

"So, he was affectionate towards you?"

"*Afectuoso?* As much as he could be. There was perhaps too much in his mind, because he was always thinking about all the things of the world."

"How long were you married?'

"Almost two years. He was visiting in my country and saw me at a festival dancing. He thought I was beautiful and asked to spend time with me. I had another husband once, but he died fighting the bulls. I have known other men, but Trexler was the only one besides Edmundo who I thought I should marry."

"Have you enjoyed your life in America?"

Constanza took a moment to answer. "When I first came here, Trexler took me many places, showed me many sights. But the more he studied the dead, the less we did such things. We moved here to Braywick, and life became *muy solitaria.* Very alone . . ." She stared off and spoke just above a whisper. "But never think I did not love him."

"We have no such illusions," Mr. O'Nelligan assured her. "One more thing. I think it best that you keep our conversation private. Even with Miss Chauncey."

"I understand. But will you speak to the police?"

"Very soon. Although we'd like to pursue matters on our own for a little longer."

By way of offering comfort, I said, "There's one part of Mr. Lloyd's plan that stayed in place. The money that's waiting for you in Spain."

"Yes, that's true," Constanza replied. "But I have not much thought of it."

Really? I found myself thinking. *Not think about a million dollars?*

"You fly out soon, I believe?" Mr. O'Nelligan asked.

"In less than a week." The young Spaniard smoothed back her long midnight hair, and again her beauty became evident. "I do not think I will ever return here. For me, America will always be *una país de fantasmas.* A land of ghosts."

CHAPTER FOURTEEN

FTER CONSTANZA HAD LEFT, Mr. O'Nelligan and I stepped out into the hall and were greeted by a loud *pssssss*. We turned and saw Sassafras Miller peeking out from her doorway, waving at us to join her.

She shanghaied us into her room. "You guys gonna arrest Constanza?"

"Hold it, now," I said. "First of all, we're not the police. Secondly, what makes you think Mrs. Lloyd would be arrested?"

"You gave her the shakedown, didn't you? You spring it on us that you're really private dicks and that Trexler's death is suspicious, and then you haul Constanza away. Looks to me like you're putting the screws on the culprit. Wouldn't be the first time some pretty little wife did in her rich husband. Not that I'd *want* Constanza to be a murderess. I like her fine enough, even if she is kinda aloof."

"You're jumping to about a hundred conclusions here," I warned. "You read too many mysteries."

"Actually, I don't," Sassafras answered. "But I've been cuddly with my share of felons, so you might say I've got a natural feel for life's seamy underbelly."

I winced. "'Seamy underbelly?' You *must* have swiped that from some cheap potboiler."

She let go a horselaugh. "What a kidder! Hey, listen, now that I know you guys are gumshoes, I've got a couple things to toss your way. First off, I got to thinking about that fly."

"What fly?" I asked.

"The one that was buzzing around when we were leveling."

"I didn't notice any fly."

"I don't mean tonight, silly," Sassafras said. "I mean last week just before Trexler died. There was this fly in the Portal Room, a big, ugly character who took over the place. He was flying loopty-loops and buzzing like a dentist's drill. Of course, it didn't bother Trex, 'cause when he was leveling he wouldn't let a damn thing distract him. That fly even landed on his nose for a spell and Trex didn't flinch. But as for Doris—oh brother! It drove her crazy. I mean, Doc Kemple and I were annoyed by it, but Doris went absolutely crackers. Started swinging her arms like a windmill, trying to shoo it away. I almost burst out laughing. Anyway, that fly was there for a while, and then it just wasn't. And, later, Trex got electrocuted. That's how I got my theory."

I was totally at a loss. "What theory are we talking about?"

"You don't get it? What if when that huge ol' fly disappeared, it flew straight into the Spooktricator and gummed up the works somehow? I'm telling you, this was one king-sized pest. He could have messed up the machine's innards and caused it to backfire on Trexler. So maybe it wasn't foul play after all, just a lethal bug. Whatta ya think?"

For the life of me, I couldn't muster a reply.

Luckily, Mr. O'Nelligan chose to field this one. "A piquant conjecture indeed. Unfortunately, madam, we've discovered that the cause of Mr. Lloyd's death was not electrocution after all. So your theory, while riveting, doesn't quite apply here."

Sassafras humfed. "You just don't like it 'cause you want it to be homicide. That's a detective's bread and butter, ain't it, Blarney?"

"The truth. The truth is our bread and butter."

Sassafras ran on. "Listen, if you're looking for a murderer— and if Constanza doesn't fit the bill—then how about Doc Kemple? Nobody really likes the guy, and he likes nobody right back. Or what about Martin Rast? He's so gaga over his ghosts that maybe he did in Trex just to fill out his collection. Or try the butler on for size. That Trowbridge is one cool customer, as you've probably noticed. Or what about—"

"Madam!" Mr. O'Nelligan held up a hand. "Trust me. We shall leave no stone unturned in our investigation."

"Oh, and here's another thing. I think Betty and Katie stole something."

"Betty and Katie?" The names caught me up short. "Those aren't more of the resident ghosts, are they?'

"Hell, no. You don't need to be afraid of that pair. Unless, of course, pretty girls give you the shivers." Sassafras laughed. "Betty and Katie Gallagher are the cousins who help out sometimes with the cooking and cleaning. They were here last Friday."

"Right, the Gallaghers." I remembered now. "What do you think they stole?"

"Well, that's the thing. I'm not really sure what it was, but

Betty had it wrapped up in a hand towel under her arm. When Trexler keeled over, I ran out and found everybody in the foyer. Doris, Martin, and Trowbridge were there talking, and the girls were just sort of passing through, done with their work and heading out. When I rushed in, I saw Betty clutch close whatever she was carrying and hurry for the door. She and Katie got out of there pretty quick."

Mr. O'Nelligan offered his view. "At that moment, you were screaming sonorously about Mr. Lloyd's death, were you not? Surely, the panic of the situation might have hastened the girls's departure."

Sassafras shook her head firmly. "I saw what I saw. Betty had a guilty look to her, and she squeezed that thing to her breast like it was her own suckling babe."

"But you were in a high state of emotion," I pointed out. "Your friend had just died. Why would you have noticed a small detail like that?"

"I just did, okay?" Her voice tightened. "Maybe because I think it wasn't the first time they took something. A few weeks back, a silver gravy boat went missing after they'd been here."

"Martin Rast would say it was the work of poltergeists," Mr. O'Nelligan observed.

"Yeah, well, Mr. Swiss Cheese says a lot of colorful things. Anyway, I'd seen Betty fiddling around with that gravy boat just before it disappeared. Admiring it, you know?"

"So what do you think she took last Friday?" I asked.

"No idea. I forgot all about it until yesterday when I was driving downtown and saw the girls on the sidewalk. Then I remembered."

"Yes, sometimes a memory will take its time to surface," my

colleague said soothingly. "Have you mentioned your suspicions to anyone else?"

"Sure—to everyone. I even called Paul Foster, the lawyer, but he said I needed actual proof that something was stolen."

"Lawyers *are* sticklers for evidence," I said. "Have the Gallaghers returned to the house since that night?"

"No. Mrs. Perris has come back to handle the cooking. Look, I know you've got enough to deal with without chasing down kleptomaniacs, but I just thought I should tell you."

"We appreciate that," Mr. O'Nelligan said. "We'll seek out the girls tomorrow and have a word with them."

"Don't mention I was the one who told you. Okay, Blarney?"

"Rest assured, we'll leave your name out of the discussion."

"One more thing. You haven't told me how Trexler was really killed."

I made a quick decision. "I think we need to keep that information under wraps for a bit longer."

"Jesus, just tell me! I mean, was he poisoned? Was he strangled? Poor Trex . . ." Sassafras suddenly looked very weary. "Aw, never mind. What's it matter, anyway? He's dead as dirt, and one way'll send you to hell quick as the next." She became uncharacteristically quiet for a few moments, then added, "I'll tell you this, though—if somebody killed Trexler, then they should swing for it. Swing by their damned neck."

WE SEEMED DESTINED to never leave that hallway. Seconds after exiting Sassafras's room, Mr. O'Nelligan and I were confronted by an anxious Doris Chauncey.

"I hope you haven't upset Mrs. Lloyd," she said. "I'm worried for her. Not only has she lost her husband, but now she knows that someone may have killed him. And soon she'll be returning to Spain. Constanza has no close family still alive there, so she'll be widowed and alone."

Mr. O'Nelligan spoke gently. "An unfortunate situation, but one, I believe, in which she does have some experience. After all, Mrs. Lloyd survived the loss of her first husband."

"And she has a considerable fortune waiting for her," I added.

Miss Chauncey let out a deep breath. "I know, I know. Still, I can't help worrying."

"We can see that," my colleague said. "For so young a woman, you have much of the mother hen about you. It brings me to mind of dear Moina McGee, who lived just down the lane from us. Early one morning she stopped on by . . ."

Since Mr. O'Nelligan was launching into one of his "tales o' old Ireland," I knew I had a couple of minutes to spare. I'd just remembered that I'd left my hat on a table back in the Portal Room, so I went to retrieve it.

When I entered the candlelit space, I saw that Martin Rast was still there, seated now in the chair Lloyd had died in. He seemed to be in deep concentration.

Once he noticed me, Rast spoke as if we'd been midway through a conversation. "Yes, I cannot feel Mr. Lloyd at all. I knew he would be gone. His spirit has no reason to remain among the living."

"No? Not even if he was killed by someone who's gone unpunished?"

"Mr. Lloyd was a great thinker. His spirit would not trouble itself with what happened in the past. It would move on to what lies beyond."

"And what *does* lie beyond?"

"Who am I to say? It is the silver mystery. First we live in our bodies, and then we live outside our bodies. We will all be ghosts someday. Ah! Over there." Rast pointed to a shadowy corner of the room. "You cannot see her, of course, but Miss Winifred, the melancholy one, is standing there weeping. She always finds a new reason to be sad. Now she says it's something she has just read in the newspaper. Out west the Indians have killed some general and all his men. I do not know your American history. Who is Custer?"

Despite myself, I shuddered. Half my psyche cried out that Rast probably knew full well who Custer was, and that this was a ploy to impress people with his supernatural talents. My other half retreated to a cold, primitive place where all dark things abide.

Instead of answering his question, I posed my own. "When did you start seeing spirits?"

His response was not one I'd have bet on. "It was the first time I ever kissed a girl. I was young and she was young, and we were lying by the banks of the Rhône. It was late spring—"

Quite certain that I didn't wish to share this intimate slice of life, I rushed the tale forward. "Then a ghost appeared?"

"Yes. It was my godfather, who died on the Matterhorn. He winked at me and said, 'Well done, Martin.'"

Oh, for crying out loud, this was getting preposterous. I plucked up my hat and gave Rast a little salute. "Catch you later."

Seemingly ignoring me, he leaned back in the chair and closed his eyes. "There have not been too many kisses since. But there have been many spirits, and here in this house is where I have found the most. I am blessed to be here. Here with Old Ezekiel and Little Violet and Gerda the milkmaid . . ."

I left him to his reverie.

* * *

ABRUPTLY TURNING A corner of the hallway, I found my-self slamming chest-to-chest into the ever lovely Constanza. It was alarming and tantalizing, and I quickly stepped back and began to sputter out apologies. Like twin doves, Constanza's hands swooped downward to smooth out the front of her dress. It was a motion that both quickened my blood and slowed down my brain. I stopped midword and just stared at her. Astonishingly, she then reached out one hand and touched my face. The sharp intake of my breath must have been audible. Her eyes, large and eternal, locked onto mine, and her plush lips parted to address me in Spanish. She must have guessed that I couldn't understand what she was saying—but maybe that was the point. After the longest five seconds in the world, she dropped her hand and continued on her way. I watched the gentle sway of her hips in retreat and tried not to die.

WE WERE FINALLY bound for home. It had been a long, drawn-out day, no question. In the last thirteen hours, we had debunked a ghost machine, discovered our client was dead, faced down believers and nonbelievers, driven all the way to Vermont, dragged a convoluted scheme out of a crooked coroner, lost our-selves in snowbound woods, driven back from Vermont, and confronted a disturbingly beautiful Spanish widow to prod her into a brief but ugly rage. All this excitement made me almost long for the bygone monotony of the hat factory.

"And what of tomorrow?" Mr. O'Nelligan asked.

I moaned a little. Tomorrow . . . Right, who knew what twists, turns, lies, and legwork still awaited us? It already felt like

I hadn't been home for a month, even though we'd only been away since morning, I thought now of Audrey. How much, if anything, should I share with her of this day's events? Well, certainly not Constanza's hips. Of course, it wasn't like I had anything to be ashamed of there. Not really. I was conducting myself professionally, if not uncomfortably. But maybe Sassafras was right and we detectives couldn't help but exude a certain amount of sex appeal. Did Dad, on any of his cases, ever find himself ensnared in the lure of some gorgeous female? No sooner had that unsettling thought popped up than I kicked it vigorously out of my brain.

I finally answered my partner's question. "Well, tomorrow there's Kemple and the cremator and maybe the Gallagher cousins—though I'm not sure that hunting down gravy boats is the best use of our time."

"One never knows where a trail might lead. After all, those girls were in the house when Lloyd succumbed. Besides, just listen to the names—Betty and Katie Gallagher. Why, when you utter them, you can almost hear the wind in the barley. Those lasses come from old Irish stock and may be predisposed to confide in a fellow Hibernian."

"We'll see. Okay, we can track down the Gallaghers tomorrow before we go for Kemple. If I remember Doris's notes, they work together as waitresses on the weekends. Someplace in Braywick called Burger Babylon."

"Burger Babylon? You jest."

"I jest not. Doesn't the sound of it just make your mouth water?"

Mr. O'Nelligan declined to answer that.

"So, by the way," I said. "Whodunit?"

"You're being flippant."

"Unfortunately, that's all I can be at this point, because I haven't a clue. Which is a helluva pathetic thing for a private eye to admit."

"You're doing fine, Lee Plunkett," my friend said. "Much has come to us this day. Much that needs to be sifted through and pondered over. That's the business of tomorrow. But fear not, lad, we'll reach the end of our road. As it says in the I Ching—"

"The ee-what?"

"The I Ching, the ancient Chinese book of divination. It tells us that through perseverance, the ways of heaven and earth will become visible. Or something to that effect. It depends on the translation, of course."

"Oh, of course."

"But, for now, it's getting late." Mr. O'Nelligan's voice grew low and sleepy. "It's getting late and we yearn for home."

I flicked on the radio, and over the next hour, the Moonglows, the Heartbeats, and the Five Satins delivered us through the night.

CHAPTER FIFTEEN

UDREY CALLED EARLY TO check if we were still on for breakfast. It was, after all, Saturday, our customary Bugle Boy Diner day. Through my yawns, I confirmed that we were good but petitioned successfully for a slightly later meeting time—last night didn't seem nearly as far away as it should. *Myself and No Other* was still perched on my nightstand. To wake myself up, I tried tackling it again, but didn't get past my first paragraph:

I oft times feel as if I were some pulsing source of light that other beings are powerfully drawn to. Many of these human moths are so intoxicated with the glow that they come to believe that we share some unique one-to-one bond. They imagine that I am their staunchest ally, their dearest friend; and, in my kindness, I will often allow such a notion to stand.

Gee, that's swell of you, pal. I slammed the book shut. It was too early in the morning for Trexler Lloyd. At least until I'd dunked my brain in a cup or two of coffee. I showered, dressed, and headed out. Driving to the diner, I experienced a little blip of appreciation as it occurred to me how downright nifty it was to share Saturday omelets with your girlfriend—nay, your perpetual fiancée.

Interestingly, the first time I ever went out with Audrey was the first time I really stood up to my father. It was about eight years back. I was twenty-three and hadn't strayed far from Thelmont more than once or twice. Audrey was three years my junior, firmly outside my circle of friends, but I knew of her existence. I'd graduated high school with her older sister Clare and vaguely remembered Audrey as an awkward kid with a pug nose and puffy hair. She'd slipped off my radar for a few years, only to reemerge at age twenty as someone very noteworthy.

I'd run into her and her sister one late afternoon at Rowland's Drug Store. I was sitting at the soda counter polishing off a malted milk shake, and Clare was desperately hunting the aisles for something to soothe her colicky baby. It was a little unnerving to know that someone I'd gone to school with had already married and spawned. Unnerving, but not unusual, for a small platoon of former classmates had already started in on family life. Though, at that moment, as the piercing wails of the displeased baby bounced across the store, I had no regrets concerning my bachelorhood.

Then Audrey took a seat two stools down and ordered a soda. The puffy hair of old had been nicely tamed, and the pug nose now seemed cute as all get-out. I tried to hold back a glance from becoming a stare.

"Sorry about my niece's crying," she said to me and the counterman. "I know it's awful loud."

The counterman grumbled and walked away. I, on the other

hand, began insisting, almost to an idiotic degree, that I was totally unaffected by the infant's howling. I all but swore that I'd mistaken it for a choir of angels.

"What a liar," Audrey said pleasantly. With that, she both calmed me down and reeled me in.

We talked animatedly for several minutes—about what I can't recall—before Clare summoned Audrey with a loudly whispered "C'mon, Aud. I'm done." The baby had dropped into a peaceful sleep on her mother's shoulder. Absorbed in our conversation, I hadn't even noticed the lack of baby screams.

As Audrey headed for the door, I called out, "We should get together sometime." I surprised myself with my boldness.

"Sure, sometime," she said hurriedly.

I felt my heart sink a little. That sure sounded like a classic brush-off. But then she added, "Sometime soon. We're in the phone book. Give me a jingle, okay?"

And then I knew I was onto something. I called her that very night, and we made plans to meet back at the soda counter early the next evening, sans the bellowing niece. The next day went by painfully slowly at the factory, but finally I extracted myself from the fedoras and top hats and drove like the wind to meet Audrey. We had a bite to eat, caught a Cary Grant movie, walked around the town green for a spell, and ended up on a park bench kissing. It was a great night, and we agreed to go out again. When I got home, Dad was sitting in the living room listening to a *Gang Busters* episode. I grabbed a seat and caught the final minutes. The show, as always, ended with a loud barrage of police whistles, which always pleased Buster to no end.

Knowing that justice had been served, my father flicked off the radio and said, "So, you had a date tonight. How'd it go?"

I was impressed that he'd actually remembered. I had mentioned it at breakfast, but, as usual, his head was wedged in the morning edition, and I'd just assumed that the fight results had trumped my personal report.

"It went swell, Dad. Real nice."

"What's the girl's name again?"

"Audrey. Audrey Valish."

"Valish?" Something shifted for him. "Her father isn't Joe Valish, is he?"

"I don't know."

"Well, is her old man a mechanic?"

"Yeah, I think she said that."

"That's him. Joe Valish is a bum."

"Oh, come on, Dad."

"No, I mean it. He's a goddamn bum."

"Do you even know the man?"

"Damn right I know him. And Jammer Dixon does, too."

"Jammer?" One of Dad's drinking buddies. "What's he got to do with anything?"

"I'll tell you. Jammer bought a used Plymouth off the guy a few months back. Turned out the car was a piece of crap, so Jam tried to sell it back to him. But Valish wouldn't do it."

"Wait, wasn't that the car Jammer crashed against a fence?"

"Aw, that didn't do any real damage. Just a little dink."

"It was an iron fence, wasn't it?"

"So?"

"So, did Jammer hit that iron fence before or after he decided the car was crappy?"

"Before. What's your point?"

I laughed. "My point is this. Jammer buys a car, bangs it all to hell, and then gets ticked off when Audrey's dad won't buy it back. Sounds like one of Jammer's typical bonehead moves."

"You listen." Buster's voice grew harsh. "Don't you ever bad-mouth my friends. Jammer would take a cannonball for me. A goddamn cannonball."

Though he used it frequently, I never figured where he got that cannonball thing from. It seemed a simple bullet would have served the analogy just as well. "I don't want to get into this."

"Well, you're already in it, pal. Of all the girls in this town, you have to go pick one whose father screwed over my good friend."

This was getting to me. "First of all, I've dated a couple of girls in Thelmont, but this is one I think I could really like. And I'm sure her father's an upright fellow. As for Jammer, well . . . You want to talk about cannonballs? I think that guy's got one where his brains should be."

That did it. Suddenly, my father was on his feet, cursing bru-tally, and I was on my feet, and the room was filled with our anger.

"You're a punk, you know that?" His face was burning red. "Nothing but a spoiled punk!"

"Spoiled? Are you crazy? You think we're living in some golden castle?"

"It's good enough for me. And it was good enough for your mother."

"Yeah? Well, now it's a dump."

"You're talking about my home!"

"I pay rent, too! I pay rent and clean up your beer cans and listen to your ancient war stories. That's my life, sad as it is. "

"Well, if it's so goddamn terrible, maybe you should leave."

"Maybe I should."

"Go run to your girlfriend, then, and see if her dad will let you sleep in his garage. Yeah, your little tramp girlfriend."

"Don't call her that!"

"Goddamn little tramp!"

Then, suddenly, we were inches apart, our faces distorted and our fists balled. I drew my arm back as if to strike—an unthinkable act—but went no further. My father's lip began to tremble and he pushed out one word, "Bum." Then, drawing a hand to his eyes, he turned abruptly and left the room.

I moved out two weeks later. Audrey and I went out again once or twice that month, but things just didn't click like they had on that first date. Probably it was me. Then some old beau of hers showed up—an annoyingly likable ex-sailor—and I just sort of stepped to the side. Come summer, I'd quit the factory and headed out west to ramble and reflect. I ended up moving around for a couple of years, drifting from one job to the next. In '50, I returned to Thelmont because . . . well, because it was home. I guess it's as simple as that. I was perhaps a little more settled in myself, a little less twitchy. Audrey and I ran into each other at a party one night, and we ended up dancing together and laughing a good deal. Seems her charming sailor had come and gone, and she was unattached. We decided to give it another go, and this time it stuck. As for my father, he seemed mildly happy to have me back in town. He never said anything about that night of anger, and I didn't either. Silence was what we did best.

AUDREY WAS AT the Bugle Boy when I got there. She'd already ordered me a cup of coffee, and it was still steaming as I sat down.

"That's why I like you," I said. "You always anticipate my needs."

"You like me?" Audrey widened her eyes in mock surprise. "Really and truly?"

"Just a little." I slid a spoonful of sugar into my cup. "Just about a teaspoon's worth."

"Are you referring to the sugar or the liking?"

"Both, I suppose. You working today?"

"Why do you always ask? Don't I work every Saturday? How about you?"

"Don't *I* work every Saturday?"

"Actually, Lee, you don't."

"Well, I am today."

"You're not going anywhere near that Dr. Kemple, are you?"

I stirred my coffee excessively so as to avoid Audrey's eyes.

"You are!" She was about to get into it when the waitress arrived to take our order. Audrey went for eggs over hard instead of her customary omelet. This meant she was distressed.

"Nice warm day for December," I said. "No more snow, no more—"

"Don't change the subject. Why would you go to see that man again? He tried to shoot you!"

"Not technically."

"What do you mean 'not technically'? You mean he didn't actually pull the trigger?"

"That's right."

"Oh, so *technically* I don't need to worry about my fiancé being gunned down, because no actual triggers were pulled last time. Gosh! What a relief. I feel light as a feather now, I surely do." Audrey dropped the sarcasm and leaned across the table. "Lee, I'm really worried. Can't you see that? This is different than other cases you've had. Nobody's tried to shoot you before."

"Maybe not, but I *have* been punched in the line of duty."

"Yes, punching's bad. But shooting's very, very bad. Horrifi-cally bad."

"Don't worry. We're going to see Kemple out in public. In a bookstore, and you know Mr. O'Nelligan would never allow bullets to fly in a bookstore. He'd be too afraid that some old volume of Dickens might get winged."

Audrey stared down into her cup, unamused and unconsoled, and I felt like a class-A rat for putting her through this.

"You just get this job done quickly." Her voice had become very soft. "Quickly and safely. Then stash your fee away so we can save for a house. A nice little house . . ."

I closed my eyes and suppressed a groan. How could I justify to her the fact that I wasn't getting paid for this one? Heck, I hadn't really even justified it to myself. How had Mr. O'Nelligan talked me into it, anyway? Maybe he was a changeling himself—half fairy, half beguiling old trickster—who could tempt other-wise sensible mortals into doing high-minded, romantic, stupid things that were completely at odds with their better judgment.

Speak of the devil. I glanced up, and there looking down at us was the Irish changeling himself.

"Ah, young lovers breaking bread at morn! Is there a more pleasing image for one in his silver years to behold?"

Without missing a beat, Audrey said, "I don't know, Mr. O'Nelligan. Is there?"

"The answer is *mais non*! For French is the language of love."

"Why'd you walk all the way here?" I asked him. "I would have picked you up."

He slid in next to me. "Forgive the interruption. I knew breakfast at the Bugle Boy was your Saturday ritual, so I thought I'd intercept you. And a long morning walk is just the way to stimulate the brain for the day's work ahead."

"Speaking of today's work," Audrey said, "you're not leading my Lee into danger, right?'

"Dear Audrey, it is Lee Plunkett who does the leading on our team. I am but the Sancho Panza to his Don Quixote."

I raised an eyebrow. "Don Quixote—wasn't he nuts?"

"He was heroic," our friend countered.

"Heroic. Yeah, that's me all over."

The waitress delivered our meals, and Mr. O'Nelligan ordered tea. While we ate, he entertained us with a letter from his daughter that he'd brought along. It featured a comical anecdote about Irish country life, replete with goats, geese, a matchmaker, a milkman, and a busload of lost nuns.

After breakfast, Audrey took me aside and gave me one last talking-to for the day. "Look, Lee, I'm not going to tell you to be careful anymore. Because I don't want to sound clingy. But if you're *not* careful—"

"You'll break my neck?"

"Something like that. I love you. And you love me, too, right?"

"Something like that."

Audrey sighed. "This is what I live for—the sweet talk."

She headed off for the five-and-dime, but not without first hugging me so tightly that I almost got a back spasm. Mr. O'Nelligan and I drove to my office so I could check my mail before leaving for Braywick. As I sat at my desk flicking through bills, the phone rang. Surprisingly, the caller was Lewis Trowbridge.

He sounded perturbed. "Finally! Miss Chauncey gave me your numbers, and I've been trying both your office and your house all morning. One would think a private detective would make himself more available to field urgent matters."

"You've got an urgent matter?" I asked.

"Meet me at three this afternoon. I'll be waiting at a tavern called Dapper Dan's out on Route 15."

"I've passed by it. What's this all about?"

"Just be there. Three o'clock. And bring your Celtic cohort with you. I'm sure he wouldn't want to miss out on the intrigue."

Before I could ask what flavor of intrigue he was offering, Trowbridge rang off.

"We have a date this afternoon," I said to Mr. O'Nelligan, who was seated across from me. "The butler requests our presence at a roadside bar."

"Trowbridge? How extremely interesting. Are tails required?"

"The meeting place *is* called Dapper Dan's, but your tie and tweeds should do fine. We may need to push off one of our other interviews, though. Today we were planning to go for the Gallagher girls, Kemple, and the crematorium guy, Johnson."

"I'm feeling rather drawn to approaching the Gallaghers, and Dr. Kemple is essential—he was, after all, the main coconspirator in the scheme to fake Trexler Lloyd's death. If we need to jettison someone, I vote for Mr. Johnson. As it is, I doubt he has much new to offer us. We can swap a cremator for a butler with little loss."

"Agreed."

In five minutes, we were back in my Nash, hitting the road like gangbusters.

CHAPTER SIXTEEN

N HOUR LATER, WE STEPPED
through a door and beheld the
grandeur that was Babylon. Dangling plastic greenery and fake flowers covered every square inch
of the interior, and clusters of artificial trees filled each corner.
Round tables, covered with cheap contact paper meant to resemble marble, crowded the main room and several small alcoves. A sputtering makeshift waterfall had been rigged up in
the center of the dining area, and if you passed too close to it,
you were likely to end up with soaked trousers. High on one wall,
a massive neon sign proclaimed BURGER BABYLON, EIGHTH
WONDER OF THE WORLD.

"Oh dear," said Mr. O'Nelligan for both of us.

A young redhead appeared, cradling a stack of menus. Garbed
in a bright white toga, she exuded perkiness.

"Hiya," she said. "Would you like to try our Mesopotamian
Meal?"

My comrade declined. "No, thank you, young damsel. But please tell us, what inspired the decor of this establishment?'

She shrugged. "The boss tells us we're like the Hanging Gardens of Babylon, whatever that is. He wanted to make the place really classy."

"Did he now?" Mr. O'Nelligan managed something between a smile and a grimace. "Were it only that all man's attempts became achievements."

The girl stared quizzically at him, unsure if a reply was called for.

"We're looking for the Gallaghers," I said.

Her eyes grew big. "I'm Katie Gallagher. What's up?"

I explained our presence minimally, saying only that we were investigators reexamining Trexler Lloyd's death. A few minutes later, Mr. O'Nelligan and I were seated in a tucked-away alcove facing Katie and a second toga-clad redhead, her cousin Betty. Whereas Katie was all rosy cheeks and easy smiles, Betty had a harder, more guarded look to her.

"We can't sit for long," Betty warned us. "The lunch crowd will be showing up soon."

By way of easing into things, my partner asked, "So, what county in Ireland do your people hail from? I'm a Kerryman, myself."

"I wouldn't know," Betty answered. "I don't bother with all that old-world stuff. It was our grandparents who came from there."

Katie turned to her cousin. "It was Cork, wasn't it, Betty? County Cork?"

"Yeah. Probably."

"How old are you lasses?" Mr. O'Nelligan asked.

"I'm twenty and Betty's twenty-one," Katie answered, "but that doesn't mean she's wiser than me." She laughed lightly.

"Are you from Braywick originally?"

"Nope," Katie said. "We came here from Delaware last year and got an apartment together. Connecticut just seemed more . . ." She searched for a word. "Exotic."

Betty cut to the chase. "What do you want to know about Mr. Lloyd?"

I told her, "We'd like your impressions of the night he died."

"Impressions?" Betty snickered. "What kind of impressions could we have gotten? We spent our whole time in the kitchen cooking and cleaning. Not much to be impressed about there."

"How often do you work at the Lloyds'?" I asked.

Katie answered. "Not too often, really. Usually just if Mrs. Perris needs the night off. For me, it's been maybe once or twice a month. I've been doing it since the spring, and the last couple of times Betty's helped out, too. It's convenient for us since we only live about a mile from the Lloyd house."

"And you weren't intimidated by the house's reputation?"

"What? You mean that it's haunted? I actually didn't hear about that till after I started going there. But I always carry a lucky coin that our grandfather gave me. I like to think it keeps away any ghosts or bad things that might be hanging around. The only reason I'm not carrying it now is because there's no pockets in my toga."

"What did you girls think of Trexler Lloyd?" I asked.

"He was kind of nice," Katie said.

"He was kind of stuck up," Betty contradicted. "He seemed to float above everybody else."

"What do you expect, Betty? The man was a genius."

"You think everyone's a genius." The older girl turned to us. "Katie thinks our boss here's a genius just because he once read a book on ancient history." She cast her eyes around the roomful of plastic vegetation. "Though I kind of wish he hadn't."

Katie pressed her case. "No, but really, Mr. Lloyd was a genius. And, for a genius, he was pretty nice. To me, at least. One time there was a whole box of baked pastries left after a dinner, and he insisted we take them home. Remember that, Betty?"

"I do. Still, he was sort of funny."

Her cousin appraised her. "Funny? What, like Milton Berle?"

"No, you ninny, I mean weirdo funny."

Katie pondered that. "Well, yeah, I guess he was. Even so, it was still sad that he died."

"Of course it was sad." Betty sounded peeved. "Who said it wasn't?"

I cut in. "What happened when Sassafras Miller ran in to announce his death?"

"I wigged out," Katie said. "I mean, who wouldn't? She was screaming bloody murder."

"We just left," Betty added. "After all, there was no reason for us to stay."

"No reason," her cousin echoed.

Betty began to stir in her seat. "Is that all? Because we really should get back to work."

Mr. O'Nelligan pinned her down with a smile. "Please now, just one last inquiry. As you were exiting the Lloyd house that night, you, Betty, were observed holding some object bundled in a towel. Can you tell us what that object was?"

The question had an immediate effect on both girls. Katie's sunny face instantly clouded, and her eyes dropped nervously to the table. Betty, by contrast, continued to stare straight ahead at Mr. O'Nelligan, her manner now more hardened, perhaps even defiant.

"Who told you that?" she asked.

The Irishman held her gaze. "Suffice it to say that you were observed. Tell now, what was in the towel?"

Not backing down, Betty took several moments to answer, and when she did it was with a slight smile that hinted of triumph. "Breadsticks. That's all. Just breadsticks."

"Oh, really?" Mr. O'Nelligan grinned right back as if he believed her without reservation.

"Yes, really." Betty expanded her own smile unflatteringly. "There were some breadsticks left over from dinner, and since they were already getting a bit stale, I brought them home. I didn't think anyone would mind. My cousin makes a really nice stuffing out of old breadsticks. Don't you, Katie?"

Katie's "yes" was wafer thin.

Mr. O'Nelligan drew his hands together on the table and lowered his voice. "Cork is a fine county indeed. It leans right up against my own Kerry, you know. I've met many a Corkman— good, solid folk who know how to keep to the honest road. And if, God forbid, they do go astray, they find a way to wander back."

He let that settle in. The older girl, who had abandoned her smile, was hard to read. The younger one never raised her eyes.

The room had become louder with the chatter of arriving customers. A very rotund man in a bright yellow toga ran hectically up to our table. "Let's go, girls! Let's go! I'm trying to run a restaurant here." Then he turned and raced away.

Betty said, "We really do have to go now." She stood, and her cousin followed suit.

"Perhaps we'll talk again soon," said Mr. O'Nelligan

By way of punctuation, I pulled out one of my business cards and held it out. "In case you want to reach us."

Pretending not to hear me, Katie hurried away. Betty accepted the card blandly without bothering to examine it, and then she, too, was gone.

"Did we let them off too easy?" I asked my companion.

"No, we pushed them as far as was prudent. That Betty Gallagher is not a lass easily cornered. Katie, on the other hand, could be persuaded to tell the truth, but not when she's in the shadow of her cousin. We can always approach them again tomorrow."

"Why bother? We're trying to solve a murder, not a spree of silverware swipings."

"Can't we do both while we're at it?"

"What a swell idea," I said. "Since we're not being paid for one case, might as well not get paid for *two*. That way we double our fee."

"Oh, but aren't you the very pillar of logic, Lee Plunkett."

WE STOOD IN the far back of the Billion Words Bookshop, hidden from C. R. Kemple's view by a table stacked with fat dictionaries. Even though it was a small store, the bloated reference works allowed us to view our quarry without his knowledge. Kemple sat on a low stool reading aloud to his audience, which numbered three—if you didn't count the uninterested tyke sprawled at his mom's feet. The tyke was reading a vividly colored picture book; Kemple was reading a clumsily worded pamphlet, which he seemed to have written himself.

"And unto the seventh valley of delusion, all the atoms of the dead will congregate deathily, disjointed for the seasons. What ho! What ho! Rattle these tingled bone slabs!" It went like that. On and on.

"Holy Mother," Mr. O'Nelligan groaned under his breath. "How did the man ever write this drivel? Did he simply stab a pen into a stack of paper over and over again, and then publish the results?"

Mercifully, the reading at last came to a close. The child and two of the three listeners exited (the third turned out to be the proprietor), and Kemple took a moment to browse among the bookshelves. A perverse urge now seized me. I snuck around the shelf he was looking at and positioned myself directly across from him, with the rows of books between us. I waited for him to pull out a volume, and then, on my own side, yanked out a couple of books opposite him. I thrust my face into the gap, so that we were suddenly eye to eye.

"Remember me, Doc?" I asked with an exaggerated grin.

Not expecting a head to be sitting on the shelf, Kemple let out a yelp and took a step back.

Mr. O'Nelligan immediately appeared next to him. "May we have a word with you, Dr. Kemple? A word about your plans with Mr. Lloyd?"

The proprietor called out to Kemple to see if everything was alright.

"We can do it here or outside," said I, the detached head. "Name your pleasure."

"Outside," Kemple said quickly, then called out to the proprietor, "I'm fine. I'm leaving now."

We left the shop and stood together in the small parking lot. Yesterday's snows had given way to an unseasonably warm day. For me, the pleasantness was heightened by the fact that we had this gun-toting rat-dog in our mitts and were about to shove him over a barrel.

"Not so tough when you're not packing hardware, are you?" I asked, again with my best Bogart. "Nobody likes having a pistol waved in their face."

The bald-headed little man gulped, causing his bow tie—yes, purple—to tremble slightly. He wasn't enjoying our company.

"I was well within my rights," he said. "You violated my room."

"Violated your room? What is it, a temple?"

"It's *my* temple!" he growled. "It's where I rest from my duties. But you wouldn't understand that, you stupid man."

"Your *duties*? What duties would those be? Tricking people with your hocus-pocus? Numbing minds with your god-awful writing?" I couldn't hold myself back. "Those are pretty defective duties, if you ask me."

"Imbecile!" Kemple's high-pitched voice climbed even higher. "I wouldn't expect someone like you to comprehend my writings. They come to me directly from the death dimension, from Zexalla, my guide."

"Oh, so Zexalla's your little space pal, is he?"

Mustache quivering, Kemple answered with a withering scowl.

Mr. O'Nelligan entered the ring. "Shall we keep to the matters at hand?"

Kemple turned on him. "You! I know you! You're that mick from the fair. The one I picked out of the crowd."

" 'Mick' is a highly distasteful label," my Irishman said dryly. "Perhaps the term 'denizen of the emerald domain' would better serve."

Kemple sneered. "You talk oh so fancy."

"He does," I said. "He truly does."

Something now dawned on Kemple, and he pointed at my colleague. "You're a detective! That girl said so at the fair. You, too. I remember you now. Both of you."

"That's correct," said Mr. O'Nelligan. "And we're here, Dr. Kemple, to discuss your participation in Mr. Lloyd's plan."

"What plan?" It was a knee-jerk response.

"Oh, you know," I said. "The plan where you enlist the coroner and cremator to help falsify Lloyd's death so he can disappear in a cloud of smoke. Remember? The plan that failed because Lloyd was actually dead—stabbed—by the time the coroner got to him. That little plan."

"Please don't feign ignorance," Mr. O'Nelligan said calmly. "Felix Emmitt has already implicated you. It's best that you reveal all you know."

Kemple's face twisted in a look almost of pain. "I knew it would go badly! I knew it! I told him it was just too complicated, but Trexler said it would all run smooth as silk. That's how he put it—'smooth as Chinese silk.'"

"Silk, alas, can rend," my partner philosophized. "Now, why did Mr. Lloyd wish to vanish from the world?"

"He told me he was tired of all the fame," Kemple said. "He wanted to become someone else, someone nobody knew. He wanted to create a new life for himself."

"But not just any life," Mr. O'Nelligan observed. "Not, for example, the life of a penniless wanderer, eh?"

"No, he still wanted his money. And he still wanted his beautiful Spanish girl. But there was something even more important that he didn't want to give up."

"Which was . . . ?"

"His legacy. He told me he needed his legacy to continue. And that was supposed to be my part." A smile of pride now touched Kemple's lips.

"Your part?" I gave a quick review of the facts. "From what Emmitt told us, your part, besides recruiting him and Johnson, was to produce the cremation document after Lloyd's fake death, and then, later, to secretly whisk him away from the crematorium.

Then, at some point, Lloyd would fly out for Spain—on a private flight, I'm guessing, so it couldn't be traced."

"Yes, I was to do all that. But there was something even more important. I was to keep his legacy going. Through the Spectricator, understand?"

"No," I answered truthfully.

"Of course you don't." Kemple was pleased. "Not much of a detective, are you?"

"Just tell it," I snapped. I was aware enough of my professional limitations without this malicious little clown needing to remind me.

"Trexler and I came up with the idea." Kemple was warming to his tale. "The Spectricator would look very complicated and technological, but it wouldn't really work. It would have two purposes, though. One, it would be the way we'd fake his death, and, two, it's how we would maintain his legacy. The plan was that soon after everyone thought Trexler was dead, I would do a special exhibition of the Spectricator. I'd rent a huge hall and invite hundreds of people—dignitaries and reporters—and, of course, they'd all come to see the famous machine that had killed the great Trexler Lloyd. I'd say, 'Look, everyone, the Spectricator really does work! The dead can speak through it!' Then I'd use the tape."

"The tape!" Now I got it. "That was the recording I heard in your room. The one with Lloyd pretending to speak from the dead."

Kemple deflated. "That was just a practice one. It was full of mistakes, completely unusable. He promised to record a better one before he left for Spain, but, well . . ."

Mr. O'Nelligan hmmmed. "And you say the purpose of the tape was to perpetuate Trexler Lloyd's legacy?"

"And my own. Trexler would be remembered for his creation of the Spectricator and for the fact that he himself was able to communicate from the death dimension with it. And I would be acclaimed as the coinventor and the one who had mastered its use."

"Wouldn't someone eventually figure out it was all a ruse?" I asked.

Kemple smiled unpleasantly. "No one would ever get a chance to inspect the Spectricator. There was to be a terrible fire right after my exhibition, and the machine would be tragically destroyed. But the legend would live on."

"Quite the complicated plot," Mr. O'Nelligan said. "One might even call it convoluted. But, in the end, it all came to naught, didn't it? For someone has undermined the scheme by actually murdering Mr. Lloyd. What were your thoughts, Dr. Kemple, when you saw the blood and realized that the game was no longer a game?"

"What was I supposed to have thought? I was in over my head. Emmitt and I decided we'd better just go through with the cremation."

Mr. O'Nelligan began firing questions. "And at the crematorium, you informed Mr. Johnson of this alteration in plans?"

"I just told him that Trexler had actually died. I didn't mention how."

"Did you and Mr. Johnson quarrel over the matter?"

"Just for a minute. He was confused about the change, but in the end he did it."

"Burned the body?"

"Yes."

"Bloodstained cloak and all?"

"Yes."

Mr. O'Nelligan pursed his lips. "You know, of course, that in keeping mum on Mr. Lloyd's slaying—not to mention incinerating his corpse—you were removing any chance for the police to investigate his murder. How curious that such a consideration didn't cross your mind."

When Kemple finally responded, his voice was subdued. "No, I guess I didn't think of that. I was very confused by everything that was happening. First, Trexler tells me the plan is off. Then, apparently, it's back on. Then, in the end, someone stabs him to death."

"Hold on." He'd just lost me. "When did Lloyd tell you the plan was off?"

"Just that night. About forty-five minutes before the demonstration was to start, Trowbridge came and told me that Trexler wanted to see me in the Portal Room."

Mr. O'Nelligan interrupted. "Was Trowbridge in on the plan?"

"No, he wasn't. Anyway, when I went in, Trexler was livid about something, but he wouldn't tell me what it was. Sometimes he could be very scornful, even to me. All he would say was that the plan was off and that he was going to cancel the demonstration. I was very disappointed. I'd been expecting that good things would come my way because of the Spectricator. I tried to convince him to reconsider, but he wouldn't even discuss it. So I left."

I was struggling to follow this. "But then the demonstration *did* happen."

"Yes, it did," Kemple said. "That's why I was so confused. Less than a half hour after he told me everything was off, Trexler sent the Miller woman to fetch me. She said he wanted to start leveling to prepare for the night's events. So, suddenly, the plan was back on. I figured he'd had a change of heart, so I went and leveled with him and the others."

"Did you ask Lloyd why he'd changed his mind about canceling?"

"I never had a chance to. After the leveling, the clients came right in and I had to get things started."

"You, not Lloyd?" I asked.

"We'd decided beforehand that Trexler would remain in his trance while I made a brief introduction and hooked him up to the Spectricator."

Mr. O'Nelligan summed it up. "And then, to your astonishment, he was dead."

"Yes. Though how someone could have managed it in plain sight, I've no idea." Kemple hung his head and added glumly, "And he hasn't even made contact with me."

"How frightfully rude of the guy." I just couldn't let up.

Kemple exploded. "You ignoramus! You know nothing about the universe! Nothing about the nine dimensions! Nothing at all!"

Mr. O'Nelligan tried to play peacemaker. "Please, compose yourself, Dr. Kemple. My companion was only—"

"Stupid people! Stupid, stupid people! None of you understand a man like me! None of you! Only Trexler . . ."

The small, angry man turned on his heel and hurried toward his car. The last thing I heard him say was "Only Trexler was my friend."

CHAPTER SEVENTEEN

WE WERE EN ROUTE TO OUR rendezvous with Trowbridge.

"You didn't need to push Dr. Kemple quite so far," Mr. O'Nelligan admonished.

I tried to bluff. "What if I told you it was my strategy?"

"I know the difference between strategy and enmity when I see it. You let your passions get the better of you back there."

"Maybe you're right. Something about Kemple seems to bring out a mean streak in me."

"Perhaps it's the recent memory of his pistol pointed at your head."

"Yeah, that could do it. I find it interesting that he isn't more concerned that Lloyd's killer be brought to justice. After all, he called Lloyd his friend."

"His friend . . ." Mr. O'Nelligan lingered on that for a moment. "Did you read yet the part of Lloyd's book where he describes himself as a light drawing human moths?"

"Just this morning, matter of fact. One of his more nauseating, egotistical passages. Wait a minute—what am I saying? The whole damned book is like that."

"Inarguably, but there was a point he made that may ring true. He noted that some people came to believe that they shared a special bond with him, that he was their staunchest friend. We've seen this with various members of his circle—Dr. Kemple, Sassafras Miller, perhaps even Miss Chauncey and Martin Rast. Apparently, he did bring out something in people."

"Neediness, maybe."

"Possibly. But perhaps something more than that."

"Doris and Rast only said that Lloyd was something special, not that he was their best buddy ever. And then there are others—Trowbridge, for instance—who seem completely immune to the Trexler charm."

"Yes, Trow . . . bridge." Mr. O'Nelligan stretched out the name. Clearly, the English butler was to him what Kemple was to me: He Who Rankles. "It's time we reckoned with that man."

"That's what we're going to do right now, isn't it? Maybe he's ready to come clean about what he knows."

"Everything seems to come back to that few minutes when Trowbridge was alone with Lloyd. Prior to that, Lloyd was in good spirits looking forward to the night's events."

"Which, originally, included his make-believe electrocution," I clarified.

"Yes. But then, after seeing Trowbridge, Lloyd decides to rewrite his will, cancel the Spectricator demonstration, and drop his scheme to fake death."

"Though, if we believe Kemple, Lloyd then flip-flops and goes back to the original plan. As if things weren't confusing enough."

"One fair question, of course, is whether we *should* believe Kemple. Or Emmitt or Trowbridge, or any of them, for that matter."

"That's what I depend on you for. To separate the truth from the balderdash."

"Well, thus far, Felix Emmitt's information, at least, seems to be ringing true. And, presently, we'll see about the butler."

"Does it disappoint you that Trowbridge wasn't involved in the scheme?"

My colleague sniffed. "I bear no ill will toward the innocent. But, in this overwrought case of ours, being innocent of one crime does not necessarily make one innocent of another. Trowbridge may yet have sins to be revealed."

"Such as plunging a knife into his employer?"

"Yes. Such as that."

IF EVER THERE was a business more wrongly named than Dapper Dan's, I've yet to see it.

As Mr. O'Nelligan put it to me upon our entry, "Grim, gray, and grimy. This place is a veritable jackpot of alliteration."

I'd complain that the barroom was underlit, if not for the fact that the poor lighting obscured the semibroken furniture, the elaborately stained carpet, and the smoke-blackened, peeling wallpaper. The dearth of lightbulbs was a mercy, really. As for Dapper Dan, I guess he could have been the unshaven, T-shirted guy behind the bar; but, if so, he must have lost his dapperness in some backroom poker game. The bar stools were filled with a half-dozen sullen male patrons, none of them our butler. Moving deeper into the room, we found him alone in a booth.

"Ah! Familiar faces!" Dressed in an unbutlerlike sports coat, he had three empty beer bottles beside him and was working on a fourth. "I came early to secure the best seating for us. The other booths look as if they'd had an ax taken to them, so I think I've made the right choice. Do join me."

I wouldn't exactly say he was drunk, but I wouldn't call him stone sober, either. We slid in across from him, and he pushed the empties to one side. The perfect host.

"We didn't see the hearse in the parking lot," Mr. O'Nelligan said. "We feared you might not make our meeting."

"I drove a less conspicuous car here. But why would you ever think I'd forsake you? I'm a man of my word. I said I'd meet you, and, by God, I have." Trowbridge took a deep draw from his bottle. "Can I treat you gentlemen to some potables? It's all swill here, of course, but it does the trick."

"No, thanks," I said.

"Then how about you, Mr. O'Nelligan? Surely an Irishman never declines an offer of drink, even at three in the afternoon. *Especially* at three in the afternoon."

My friend didn't ruffle. "For your knowledge, sir, I seldom drink. Once in a great while a glass of whiskey, but only on special occasions."

"Well, then I'll buy you a whiskey."

"This is not one of those occasions."

The Englishman laughed roughly. "Such iron-clad abstinence! Are you positive you're really Irish?"

"Most assuredly, I am," said Mr. O'Nelligan. "Now, why are we here?"

Trowbridge studied his bottle as if the answer were printed on the label.

"Well, sir?" my colleague prodded.

"I've been torn," the butler said at last. "Warring allegiances, you might call it. On the one side, there's my loyalty to Mr. Lloyd, and on the other side . . . well, maybe he's on the other side, too."

Mr. O'Nelligan sighed deeply. "Can you make this any more bewildering?"

"Not without a few more beers, old chap." Trowbridge managed a half-grin, but he was clearly growing more somber. "Alright then, here's how it all played out. For a month or so now, I've had my eye on a particular situation. Not that it was something I was entirely certain of. Nothing beyond a shadow of a doubt, you understand, because then I would have said something straight off. But, as it was, I had my suspicions, you see."

"About Mr. Lloyd?" I asked.

"What? No, no. About *Mrs.* Lloyd."

I wasn't expecting that. "Constanza?"

Trowbridge frowned at me. "My, aren't we familiar. Yes, Constanza Lloyd. It pains me to say this, but I suspected that she was having an affair."

I tried to digest this. "So, in the middle of everything else—"

Mr. O'Nelligan cut in. "Let him continue." He was no doubt concerned that I'd blurt out more than I should.

Trowbridge went on. "I believe it started around Halloween, when Mr. Lloyd was off doing his Otherworld's Fair. Once or twice a week, Mrs. Lloyd would ask me to drive her alone into town, saying she wanted to do a little shopping. This was unusual because customarily Miss Chauncey would accompany her on her jaunts, or sometimes Miss Miller. Now she insisted on going alone. I'd drop her off at a certain spot, then pick her up there at a prearranged time, usually about two hours later. The odd thing was that she rarely returned with any purchases. Then one afternoon, when I went to retrieve her at the pickup spot, I saw a young man standing across the road watching her. He'd sort of half-hidden himself in a storefront. Just as Mrs. Lloyd was climbing into the back of my car, she gave the fellow a quick little wave, and he returned it. I believe she thought I was looking the other way, but I caught her in the rearview mirror."

"That doesn't seem all that indicting," I said. "A simple wave."

"There's more," Trowbridge insisted. "The next time I dropped Mrs. Lloyd in town, about two weeks ago, I decided to check on her a bit, just to make sure everything was on the up-and-up. I followed her on foot, far enough behind so as not to be detected, but close enough to keep track of her. A butler, if nothing else, is a master of stealth. I watched as she walked down one of the side roads and climbed into a waiting automobile. As the car turned the corner, I got a good look at the driver—it was the same young man she had waved to. What's more, I returned to that area later and saw him drop her back off. They exchanged a kiss before parting, rather a robust one."

"That does give one pause," Mr. O'Nelligan said. "What did you do with this information?"

"I sat on it." Trowbridge took another drink of beer. "At least for several days. I wasn't sure I wanted to get caught in the middle of some big distasteful drama. Although I did feel torn. After all, I'd been with Mr. Lloyd for over three years, even before he married Mrs. Lloyd and we moved to Braywick. I felt I owed him my loyalty."

"That's understandable," Mr. O'Nelligan said. "So you decided to approach him with your concerns?"

"Well, it was something I overheard that finally pushed me

to act. The morning before Mr. Lloyd died, I inadvertently caught a snippet of conversation between him and his wife. Apparently, they were planning an extended trip abroad that, for some reason, no one was supposed to know about. He was promising her that they'd travel all across the world, and that he'd treat her to all sorts of adventures. After hearing this, I decided I could no longer withhold my information. It just didn't seem right for them to be heading off on some grand journey without Mr. Lloyd knowing of his wife's infidelity. I may as well confess, I had a wife myself once who betrayed me, so . . ." He trailed off.

"So you were highly sympathetic to the man's situation," Mr. O'Nelligan said.

"Yes, I was," Trowbridge agreed. "For the rest of the day I looked for an opportunity to take him aside, but it was difficult. Dr. Kemple came early on, and he and Mr. Lloyd were very occupied with their Spectricator. Then that odious sculpture arrived, and Rast and I had to drag it in the house, smashing a window on our first attempt, which got Mr. Lloyd nicely raging. Then the Gallagher girls showed up and complained that we were short on butter and flour, so I had to make a run to the grocery. It was one thing after another, and it wasn't until after dinner that I had a chance to speak alone to him."

I remembered my notes. "A little after seven in the Portal Room."

"Correct. I told him then about his wife's antics, and, of course, he didn't take it too splendidly. All but threatened to brain me, which I was half-expecting—shoot the messenger and all that. He didn't exactly combust, but he certainly steamed quite fiercely."

"He was very possessive of Mrs. Lloyd?" Mr. O'Nelligan asked.

"Oh, I would say so. His Spanish treasure, he'd call her. Without question, she's quite the beauty, and I think Mr. Lloyd prided himself on landing her."

"Which wouldn't necessarily be hard to do with a fortune as the bait." I called it as I saw it.

"Yes, my young friend, that would be the base interpretation, but life is not always as obvious as it might appear. I'd say that their marriage was not without affection."

"So, Mr. Lloyd believed your account?" my partner asked.

"Oh, yes, there was no doubt of that," Trowbridge said. "Certainly, he didn't *want* to believe it, but he had no reason to question my veracity. He fumed on for a bit, then told me to leave and send in Dr. Kemple, which I did."

"Do you know why he wanted Kemple?" I asked.

"No, I don't, but after that, Mr. Lloyd summoned his secretary. While I was taking a second shot at moving the sculpture, I heard her in her office calling the lawyer on Mr. Lloyd's behalf—something about changing the will. I presumed this was Mr. Lloyd's response to learning of his wife's infidelity."

"Have you spoken to anyone about any of this?" Mr. O'Nelligan asked. "About Mrs. Lloyd's activities or your conversation with Mr. Lloyd?"

"Not a soul. You two are the first."

"I see. And what motivates you now to come forth?"

The butler took his time to answer. "It's as I was saying before—I have conflicting allegiances, and both are to Trexler Lloyd. On the one side, there's his dignity and privacy. On the other, there's the justice he deserves if, indeed, he was murdered. I ruminated hard on it all last night. I came to the conclusion that if it truly was homicide, then my knowledge of Mrs. Lloyd's dalliance might very well figure in solving the crime. It was either go to the police or to you chaps. And since you two already seem to have the ball rolling, well, here I am."

I tried to sum it all up. "Are you saying that you suspect—"

Trowbridge shook his head warningly. "Oh no you don't. I refuse to speculate on who did what. That's your job, gentlemen. I'm beyond all that."

"You told us you were once a constable," Mr. O'Nelligan said.

"I was," Trowbridge confirmed. "But that was more than thirty-five years ago."

"Still, in your day, you guarded the streets of England against wrongdoers."

"No, sir, I served in Ireland."

"Ireland? In what capacity?'

"As a member of the Constabulary Reserve Force."

"The Black and Tans?" Mr. O'Nelligan's voice tightened. "You were part of that mob?"

In one swallow, Trowbridge drained his bottle and set it forcefully down on the tabletop. "I was a twenty-two-year-old sergeant, there at the pleasure of Lord French the Viceroy to keep you natives in order. Yes, I was a Black and Tan."

"What are Black and Tans?" I needed to ask.

Mr. O'Nelligan explained. "A rough mix of British ex-soldiers and riffraff recruited to enter my country and put the screws to us. Named after a pack of hunting hounds, they were as vicious a crew of invaders as you're likely to meet. The crown called them constables, but they were no such thing. They were killers of civilians, burners of towns . . ."

Trowbridge leaned forward. "You were out there, weren't you, O'Nelligan? Out there in the streets and the fields flinging your deadly mischief at us. Don't deny it. You're the right age, and you've got the right look in your eye."

My friend didn't answer that. "You said you were drummed out of the constabulary. What happened?"

"I rifle butted two of my own men." Trowbridge said quietly. "Did them some damage. They'd just shot a fifteen-year-old boy, and I'd had enough. Enough of the lack of discipline. Enough of the brutality. Enough of it all. You're right—some of the Tans could be a vicious lot. I wasn't like them. I wasn't a bloody indiscriminate gunman. And, when it got down to it, I wasn't all that keen on stifling a rebellion."

Mr. O'Nelligan let go a quote. "Those that I fight I do not hate, those that I guard I do not love."

Trowbridge smiled thinly. "Yeats, isn't it? Well, yes, that puts it rather squarely. But I prefer to lean on my own countrymen for my verse. Are you up on Thomas Hardy?"

"Enough to admire him," Mr. O'Nelligan said.

"Do you know 'The Man He Killed'?"

"Passingly."

Trowbridge drew his head back, closed his eyes and began reciting.

"Had he and I but met by some old ancient inn,
We should have set us down to wet right many a nipperkin!
But ranged as infantry, and staring face to face,
I shot at him as he at me, and killed him in his place.
I shot him dead because—because he was my foe,
Just so: my foe of course he was; that's clear enough; although
He thought he'd 'list, perhaps, off-hand like—just as I—
Was out of work—had sold his traps—no other reason why.

Yes; quaint and curious war is! You shoot a fellow down
You'd treat, if met where any bar is, or help to half a crown."

Trowbridge reopened his eyes. "And there you have it."

"Yes," said Mr. O'Nelligan.

"One more thing." The Englishman leaned forward again. "Would you like to confront Mrs. Lloyd's local Romeo?"

"You know where to find him?" I asked.

"I do. Earlier this week I stopped in at Spangler's, the hardware store at the bottom of Braywick's main street, and recognized him behind the counter. Has blond hair and a cleft chin, a pleasant enough looking youth. It's the first time I've noticed him there. I heard him answer to the name Ben."

"Ben," I echoed. "Has Mrs. Lloyd asked to go into town since her husband died?"

"No, not alone, at least. Thankfully, she seems to be assuming the proper demeanor of a widow. She's due to fly out to Spain this coming Wednesday, so perhaps she's decided to make a clean break from her paramour."

"Thank you for your information," Mr. O'Nelligan said as we got up to leave. "We'll see where it all leads. Now, we surely must abandon this den of dapperness before the musk of the place overpowers us."

Trowbridge returned to the offensive. "Really, sir? I would think the smell of stale liquor and burnt potatoes would be perfume to a true Irishman's nose."

Mr. O'Nelligan parried the thrust. "A common misconception, sir. In truth, it's the scent of shamrocks and gunpowder that most entices our senses."

The two old warriors exchanged nods, and we made our exit.

CHAPTER EIGHTEEN

E WERE BACK IN BABY
Blue, continuing the quest, and
I was not delighted. "Did we
really need a whole new twist at this point?"

"Well, we don't wish to become bored, do we?" Mr. O'Nelligan
responded. "After all, an unchallenged mind is a sluggish mind."

Who was feeling unchallenged? *I* sure wasn't. What with the
fake death plots, impossible stabbings, and ghostly under-
currents, I'd say my mind was being pretty well exercised without throwing in an illicit affair.

"Do you think Trowbridge is giving us the straight scoop?" I
asked.

"We'll find out soon enough, won't we? I presume you're aiming us toward young Ben the Deceiver."

"Yep, you presume right."

We reached Spangler's Hardware within minutes. The person we found behind the counter didn't quite meet our needs,

though. While his chin did sport a deep dimple, his hair was only vaguely blond—more grayish and thinning—and he didn't strike me as the womanizing type.

"We're looking for Ben," I said.

The man gave me a choice. "You want Ben Grabowski or Ben Spangler? We've got a run on Bens these days."

I wasn't prepared to have to sort through multiple philanderers. "This one's a blond fellow."

"That would be my nephew, Ben Spangler. You're in luck, 'cause Ben Grabowski's home with a busted ankle."

Mr. O'Nelligan handled the smiles. "We see, but Ben Spangler's ankle is unimpaired, we trust?"

"Oh, yeah. That Ben's ankle is fine. He's in the back of the store unpacking pitchforks."

Though I wasn't one for confronting a guy with a pitchfork—or any sharpened object, for that matter—I did my duty and led us down the aisle. In the recesses of the store, we found our man rummaging through a crate of the implements. Just into his twenties, he was adequately blond and dimpled.

He looked us over. "Hi. Can I help you?"

"A bit late in the year for garden tools, isn't it?" Mr. O'Nelligan asked cheerfully. "Or early, depending on one's view."

"My uncle likes to have them set to go. He claims people think ahead with their gardening."

I waited till his hands were pitchfork-free. "We've come to talk to you about Constanza Lloyd. We're investigators."

My statement hit Ben Spangler like a crate of tools, and the blood drained swiftly from his face. At that very moment, a woman approached him in search of snow shovels. He responded with a gaping mouth and a glazed stare. Since I had happened to notice those very items an aisle back, I took the liberty of aiming the customer toward them.

"Listen, Benjamin," Mr. O'Nelligan spoke calmly, but firmly. "We know you and Mrs. Lloyd have spent time together. We have a witness to this. You're in the middle of a very complex situation, lad, and you need to come clean with us."

Spangler looked around furtively to make sure no one was within earshot. "Let's talk low, okay? I don't want anyone to hear. Honest, we didn't even do much."

"Define *much*," I said.

Now his color returned courtesy of a blush. "We necked . . . held each other . . . We never really, you know, went total with things."

I wasn't sure I believed that. "How did you meet her?"

"She came in here a few days before Halloween with that older woman, the one who used to be an actress. Sarsaparilla or something."

"Sassafras," I corrected.

"Yeah, her. They came in to buy some Halloween decorations, and while my uncle was helping the older one, Constanza and I got to talking. I took Spanish in high school, so I tried that out a little, and she was kind of amused. Then she came back a week later on her own, and, well, y'know, she kind of seduced me."

"What? Here?" I asked. "Between the plumbing supplies and the wheelbarrows?"

"No, I've got a little apartment about fifteen minutes away. That's where we went."

I challenged him. "You take a woman to your apartment, and you say *she's* doing the seducing."

Spangler looked me straight in the eye. "I tell you, it was her idea. You've seen her, right? You know what a dish she is. Like on par with Marilyn Monroe or Jane Russell. What could I do?"

My colleague offered an answer. "You could have turned heel and avoided temptation. Did you know that she was Trexler Lloyd's wife when you first met her?"

"Yeah, I did," Spangler said quietly. "I mean, it's not like there's a ton of beautiful Spanish girls running around town. I've only been here since the fall, when I came to work for my uncle, but I'd heard all about Lloyd and his wife. They were sort of the local celebrities."

"How frequent were your assignations?" Mr. O'Nelligan asked.

Spangler was taken aback. "What? Who said I shot anybody?"

My partner's voice rose in exasperation. "Not assassination! *Assignation!* You know—a rendezvous. A tryst."

Spangler looked to me for help.

I made it simple. "How often did you fool around?"

"Not a lot," he answered. "Six, seven times tops. And, like I said, we kept it in low gear. We've never gone all out."

"We see," Mr. O'Nelligan said. "And was this admirable restraint your choice or Mrs. Lloyd's?"

"Hers, I guess. She mostly wanted just to be held, y'know? And talk. It was really her that did the talking. Mostly in Spanish. She liked to just lie in my arms and ramble on and on in kind of a slow, dreamy way."

"What did she talk about?" I asked. "You said you speak Spanish."

"I said I *took* Spanish. Two years. I think I averaged a C minus. I didn't understand more than a few words Constanza said, but she didn't seem to mind."

"What was the last time you saw her?"

"Just over a week ago. Later that night her husband died in that accident, and I haven't seen her since."

"Did she speak much about her husband?" I asked.

"No, I think she wanted to pretend that I didn't know who she was, that she wasn't married and all. But that was kind of wacky because I had called her Mrs. Lloyd that first time here in the store, so obviously she knew I knew who she was."

"So you both wrapped yourselves in a veil of denial," Mr. O'Nelligan observed. "At the end of each of your little get-togethers, did you then set up the next time and place to meet?"

"Yeah. Constanza doesn't drive, so she always had to get her butler to bring her to town. But last time she acted different. She was kind of weepy when we got together. Didn't really even want to make out. Then, when I dropped her off, she said she was going away and we wouldn't be meeting anymore."

"The end of the dance," Mr. O'Nelligan said wistfully. "How did you feel knowing that you might never see her again?"

Spangler knit his eyebrows together, searching his soul for the answer. "Sad," he finally said with a shrug. "I guess I felt sorta sad."

"That's all for now," I told him. "But in case we need to talk more later, don't stray too far from the garden tools, okay?"

"Am I going to get into trouble for this?"

"Maybe. Maybe not," I answered. "We'll let you know."

"What'll I tell my uncle if he asks why you guys came to see me?"

We were already walking away. I called over my shoulder,

"Say we were looking to buy a handkerchief folder, but they were all out of stock."

AS WE DROVE back down Main Street, Mr. O'Nelligan patted my shoulder. "Hold up a minute, Lee. Pull over here."

I complied. "What is it now? We don't need any new angles to this case."

"Not a new angle, just an old friend."

I looked down the sidewalk and saw our reason for stopping. Martin Rast was standing outside a storefront, his back to the door and his arms folded firmly before him. In this pose, coupled with the Russian fur hat that was his headwear du jour, Rast looked like a dedicated sentinel at his post. Glancing up to the overhead sign to see what he was guarding, I read the words HEAVENLY HAIRSTYLING and, below that in smaller letters, FOR LOVELY LADIES.

Leaving our car, we approached him and received a noncommittal little nod.

"Are you protecting the bouffants of Braywick?" Mr. O'Nelligan asked lightly.

Rast maintained his stance. "I am here if needed."

"Very good," my partner said. "The lovely ladies within will no doubt be relieved."

Rast let that pass. "I must do the driving here because Trowbridge is nowhere to find. Ever since Mr. Lloyd has died, Trowbridge goes and comes whenever he wishes. Sometimes he disappears for a long time. It makes things hard for everyone."

Mr. O'Nelligan clicked his tongue sympathetically. "Bad form indeed. I presume you will not be retaining his services once you take over the house."

"You mean will I have a butler?" Rast actually giggled. "Why would I ever need one? To bring me my slippers and coffee? I do not even own slippers. No, I will do fine without any butlers."

I joined in. "Of course you will. After all, you've got your ghosts, right? I'm sure with you at the helm, they'll all roll up their sleeves and chip in with the chores."

That was it for the giggles. "Not so funny," Rast said, fixing me with a cold eye. "Not so funny at all. The dead ones are never very happy to have jokes made of them. I think you are a person, Mr. Pick-it, who likes to make jokes about things he cannot understand. You are perhaps afraid of the dead ones and hide behind your jokes. Forgive me, but I must say this."

I was hoping Mr. O'Nelligan would pipe in with something like *Preposterous! Lee Plunkett is beyond all fear!* Amazingly, he didn't.

I was about to fumble out an apology when the salon's door swung open and Doris Chauncey emerged—but not just any Doris Chauncey. This one was a new and improved model, spiffy and stylish. Her strawlike hair had been cut and reformed into a pretty pile of curls that made her look as young as she actually was.

She seemed a little flustered. "Oh, Mr. Plunkett! Mr. O'Nelligan! I didn't expect you to be here."

"How could you, lass?" my colleague asked. "We happened by inadvertently, and, I must say, I'm pleased that we did. You look quite mesmerizing in your new coiffure."

Doris brightened. "Oh, why, thank you so much. I'm very happy with how it came out." Then, abruptly, a shadow of concern crossed her face. "I hope you don't think it's inappropriate."

"What do you mean?" Mr. O'Nelligan asked. "Are you referring to the style?"

The young woman shook her head. "No, I meant I hope no one thinks it's wrong for me to get a new hairdo with Mr. Lloyd only being dead for eight days."

"It's not like you're his widow," I suggested.

"No, of course I'm not," said the secretary, "but I wouldn't want people to think I was being cavalier. It's just that I felt the need to do something uplifting after all this gloom."

"A perfectly natural human response!" Mr. O'Nelligan declared. "And enhancing your hair is a grand way to do it. Why, if I had more of my own, I'd curl and coddle it as well."

That got a little laugh from her. "You're such a card, Mr. O'Nelligan. Oh, and look!" Doris thrust out her hands, and we saw that the fingernails were well trimmed and painted vividly red. "I even splurged on a manicure. That's why I got Martin to drive me. I didn't want to mess up my nails by driving myself right away."

I'd noticed that from the moment Doris had joined us, Rast hadn't taken his eyes from her. Recalling his earlier mention of her as being "such a nice girl," it suddenly occurred to me that he might actually be smitten.

Doris now turned to Rast. "What do *you* think, Martin?"

He stumbled on his reply. "Oh . . . very . . . yes, very . . . It is good to have hair."

That tickled her to no end. "Oh, Martin! You're a card, too."

I noticed something in her eyes—I guess you'd have to call it a twinkle—and I thought to myself, *Holy cow, could she be smitten, too?* I found the notion of these two awkward people being drawn to each other a little befuddling and a little touching.

"Oh, I forgot my pocketbook." Doris started to reach for the door but quickly pulled her hand back. "Darn, my nails are still wet."

"I'll get it for you, Miss Doris." Rast vanished into the salon.

"He's always very helpful," the secretary said softly.

My partner stepped in closer to her. "Miss Chauncey, may we ask you something? You are in Mrs. Lloyd's confidence, are you not?"

"Well, yes, to a degree."

"For the last month or so, she has been making trips alone to town. Have you been aware of the reason?"

"Oh, it's nothing, really. Constanza can be very solitary sometimes, that's all. She just wanted to wander aimlessly and look in shop windows like when she was a girl in Spain. What's that have to do with finding out what happened to Mr. Lloyd?"

"Perhaps little. Ah, here's your champion."

Martin Rast returned, pocketbook in hand. "I will carry it to the car for you, Miss Doris. To protect your new fingers."

We said our good-byes and watched as Rast and Miss Chauncey headed down the sidewalk, the pocketbook dangling from the man's arm.

"Think there's something there?" I asked Mr. O'Nelligan.

"Are you referring to a warm bond betwixt those two?"

"Yeah, is there any betwixting going on?"

"They would make for an unusual pair," my friend noted. "But once Cupid's arrows have arced through the air, who can truly know what mark they'll find?"

"As far as this whole case is concerned, I'm wondering if the words 'truly know' will ever grace my lips."

"Now, don't be hobbled by self-doubt. Just remember—you are Lee Plunkett."

"Right. That's exactly what I'm afraid of."

CHAPTER NINETEEN

E NEED TO GO THROUGH our facts using a fine-toothed comb," Mr. O'Nelligan said as we drove out of Braywick.

"Or better yet, with this mess, a machete."

"We could still swing by the Lloyd residence, Lee. Since Constanza has come to the forefront of things, it might be useful to—"

"Don't want to," I said like a petulant kid. "Just don't want to. And don't say it's because I'm intoxicated with her loveliness or any of that malarkey. I'm over any fascination I might or might not have had with Constanza Lloyd. Meeting her dippy boyfriend put the nail in the coffin."

"Yes, young Ben Spangler didn't really strike me as a plotting lothario so much as a—"

"Bewitched goofball."

"Are you going to let me finish *any* of my sentences?"

"Not tonight. Anyway, why would someone like Constanza waste her time on a hardware store clerk? And don't go on again about Cupid's arcing arrows."

Mr. O'Nelligan gave a little huff. "Under such constraints, I can offer no answer."

"Look, let's just head home, okay? The sun's setting, the gas gauge is dropping, and we never even ate lunch."

"You could have partaken of a Mesopotamian Meal earlier."

"Sure. Or I could have packed my stomach with cheap beer at Dapper Dan's. But I didn't. It's not like we have an expense account for this job—not that I want to revisit a sensitive subject."

"I would gladly have staked you to a Mesopotamian Meal, you know."

"Stop with the Mesopotamian Meals, already! What, has someone paid you to advertise them?"

"Not at all," my partner said. "I just enjoy rolling those words off my tongue."

"Fine, roll away. But we can wait till tomorrow for any more interviews or explorations or brainstorms. My own brain is fairly well stormed as it is, what with all the intricacies it's had to absorb. After I drop you home, I just want to burrow into my sofa and watch *Gunsmoke*."

"Is that one of those detective shows?"

"It's a Western. You know—rugged men and honest horses. And a pretty saloon girl or two just to keep things perky."

"An evening of well-earned leisure will no doubt be beneficial," Mr. O'Nelligan admitted. "Even knights on a quest deserve a warm meal and a good night's sleep. As long as we remain mindful."

"Mindful of what?"

"Of the fact that a murderer is still at large."

"Even murderers sleep."

"Yes, but for how long?"

I DECIDED TO put off my Wild Westerns momentarily and stop in on Audrey.

She met me at the door dressed in her winter coat and cap. "Oh, hi! I was just about to head out, but come in for a sec. It's cold out there."

I stepped into the hallway, noting, as I always did, how warm and welcoming it felt inside the Valish home.

"Got a date tonight?" I joked.

"As a matter of fact, yes. A daddy-daughter date. Mom left today to visit our Boston relatives, so Pop and I are on our own. We're going for dinner and a movie." She turned and called up the stairs. "Pop! Are you almost ready?"

Joe Valish's voice sailed down from the second floor. "Couple minutes. Just washing the last grease off."

Audrey sighed and turned back to me. "He's *always* washing the grease off. It's the official hobby of the professional mechanic. So, what happened today with Dr. Kemple? He didn't threaten you again, did he?"

"No, this time *we* did the threatening."

She stared at me for a long moment.

"What?" I asked.

"I'm just trying to visualize you as threatening."

I leapt to my own defense. "Well, I *can* be. Hugely threatening."

Audrey smirked. "I see."

I changed the subject. "What film are you going to?"

"The latest Hitchcock. It's called *The Man Who Knew Too Much.*"

I thought of my progress in the Lloyd case. Maybe I should star in a sequel: *The Man Who Knew Pathetically Little.*

"It's with Jimmy Stewart," Audrey continued. "Pop wanted to see the new Lana Turner movie, but I said, 'No siree! You're not going to go stare at some pretty starlet while Mom's away.' Besides, he hates romance."

Romance. The illicit one between Constanza and the Spangler kid jumped to mind. "Let me ask your womanly advice."

"Whoa. Should I sit down for this?"

I began hesitantly, not wanting to offer any names. "Let's say there's this young guy and there's this woman he's drawn to. Because she's beautiful and exotic."

"Oh? How beautiful?"

"Jaw-dropping. But this guy knows he shouldn't go down that road. Because one of them already has someone."

Audrey seemed to tense a little. "And this guy . . ."

"Probably a decent enough fellow . . ."

"Aren't they always?"

"But he's been pretty much seduced."

"Seduced?"

"Yeah, because she's so beautiful."

"You already mentioned that fact."

"And she's more worldly than he is."

"No surprise."

"So, in a way, you can't blame him."

"Oh, can't I?" Audrey folded her arms and glared at me. "Lee, what are you trying to say? Is this a confession?"

"Confession? What do you—"

"Is this one of those thinly veiled stories about what's

happened to a 'friend'? So, this man who's got a commitment—a fiancée, maybe?—is seduced by some jaw-dropping beauty—"

"No, *he* doesn't have the commitment."

"Oh, he doesn't, does he? So a two-year engagement isn't a commitment?"

"Huh? What the heck are you talking about?"

"What are *you* talking about?" Audrey demanded.

"The Lloyd case, of course."

This got a little jolt out of her. "You're talking about the case? Then why are you being so mysterious?"

I tossed up my arms in exasperation. "Because it *is* a damned mystery, and because I don't think I should be speaking too freely about who did what at this point."

Audrey now relaxed and offered a little smile. "Not even to your best girl?"

"Not even her."

"Now, back to your question . . ."

"What I was getting around to is this—why would this woman who has beauty, wealth, and position have a fling with some young buckaroo?"

"Is this buckaroo handsome?"

I shrugged. "Maybe . . . Wavy blond hair, dimpled chin, strong frame."

"Sounds handsome to me." Audrey gave an exasperated little sigh. "Well then, there's one answer right there. Do you think only men can get stupid over a pretty face?"

"No?" I said, figuring that must be the right answer.

"But more than that, just because a woman may seem beautiful and perfect to the outside world doesn't mean that's how she sees herself. Maybe all she sees are the flaws and broken parts."

"Broken parts?"

"The parts of herself that are, you know, dark and confused and hurting. Being a lofty, beautiful queen can be a lonely thing." Audrey gave a dismissive little smirk. "Not, of course, that I'd know."

I drew her close. "Hey, who told you that you weren't a beautiful queen? Tell me and I'll punch the daylights out of him."

She widened her eyes in mock delight. "Really? The daylights?"

"Or at least the dickens. I swear I'll punch *something* out."

"Wow, what a caveman . . ."

Our lips joined just as Joe Valish came pounding down the stairs.

"Hi there, Lee!" His greeting parted us like the Red Sea. "How's it going, tiger? Fair to middling?"

"Sure. Somewhere in there."

Long, lanky, and friendly, Joe gave me a warm grunt, then turned to his daughter. "You ready, girlie?"

"I've been ready since noon. Unlike someone I could mention."

Joe laughed. "All you've got to do slap on a little lipstick. Me, I've got a week's worth of garage grime to scrub off."

We stepped outside, and Joe nodded toward Baby Blue. "How's she running, Lee?"

"Like a dream."

"That's what I like to hear." He climbed into his Buick and started the engine. "That Nash Rambler is a good automobile. Solid and reliable."

Joe shut his door, and I walked with Audrey around to the passenger's side.

As we stood there, she reached over and turned my face

toward hers. "Solid and reliable. Why would anyone think different?"

We got to follow through with that interrupted kiss.

"Have fun at the movie," I told her.

"Have fun at the mystery," she countered.

"I'd trade fun for luck. A big heaping bag of luck. I'm not real sure where I'm going with this case. "

Her voice twisted itself into an extremely bad brogue. "Don't worry, me lad. After all, you're Don Quixote."

I groaned. "You make a terrible O'Nelligan. Please never do that again."

She clung to the brogue. "Aw, give us another kiss, bucko."

I held her at arm's length. "Now you're scaring me."

She giggled and returned to being Audrey. "Are you still on the clock?"

"No, I'm heading home. Done for the day."

Her father gave the horn a long toot, and Audrey opened the passenger's door.

"Hey now!" she admonished him. "Hold your horses."

Joe Valish grinned. "Let's get a move on. We don't want to miss Lana Turner."

Audrey wagged a finger. "No Lana for you, mister! Hitchcock!"

She climbed into the car and looked up at me. "Okay, Lee, you go home and just relax for tonight. No more deducting. No more daring escapades. Right?"

"Right as rain," I gladly agreed.

FIFTEEN MINUTES LATER, I entered my apartment, flicked on the light switch, and got promptly tackled. It happened so fast that I didn't see my assailant until he was standing over me.

In his midtwenties with an athlete's build, he had curly black hair and a face you would have called handsome if it hadn't been distorted by such an ugly scowl.

"Where's your gun?" he barked. "You're a private dick, aren't you? I don't see your gun."

"I don't carry one," I said from the floor.

"What kind of weak nelly crap is that? A detective without a gun? *I've* got a goddamn gun." He pulled back his jacket to reveal a shoulder holster.

"Okay," I said for lack of anything better.

"Don't piss yourself, though. I'm not going to use it. 'Cause I'm a reasonable man."

Gosh, he sure seemed like one. Taking in his red eyes and flushed cheeks, I realized now that my intruder was drunk, or at least three-quarters there.

"I'm getting up now," I said and waited for an argument. None came, so I got to my feet.

"Needed to make sure you weren't packing heat," Mr. Reasonable said. "Otherwise it could've turned into the OK Corral here. Bullets flying . . ."

"Who are you?"

"Bells. I'm Bells."

"Tommy Bells? Detective Agnelli's partner?"

"You know me? Good. 'Cause I goddamn know *you.*"

"How'd you get in here? Mrs. Titus sure didn't let you in."

"I'm a police detective, for Christ's sake. I know how to break into a place."

"Great. My tax dollars at work."

Bells took a step toward me. "Just because I said I won't shoot you doesn't mean I won't pound your face in."

"Let's take it easy here, okay? No reason to—"

"I just came from burying my partner. Know what that's like? Huh, you sunuvabitch?"

"Matter of fact I do. My father was my partner, and I buried him just over a year ago."

He didn't seem to hear that, or if he did, he didn't care. "George Agnelli was a good guy. Kinda old-fashioned, but a really good guy. Poor bastard only had three months left before retiring. Three stinking months. Where's the justice in that, huh?"

"No justice."

"Damn right there was no justice! George was looking forward to his retirement. He wanted to maybe get himself a sailboat. Just a little one. We once went out in a canoe together . . ." He trailed off, and his eyes grew even redder than they'd been.

"Why are you here?"

"I was over at George's place yesterday morning, comforting his daughter, when you called. You said your name was Lee Plunkett. I checked around about you—second-generation PI working out of Thelmont. So I tracked you down. On the phone you said you were snooping into the Lloyd case. Tell me, why the hell would you be doing that?"

"Because your partner had doubts about Lloyd's death. He asked me to look into it."

"Well, George got that wrong, okay? It was an accidental death. The coroner was convinced of it, our chief was convinced, and I was convinced. Only George thought different. He was getting to the end of his career, and maybe he was just hoping for one last big case to go out on."

"Or maybe he had a better nose for criminal activity."

"So you think the rest of us all got it wrong? Okay, four eyes, then what have *you* dug up?"

For a moment I teetered on the edge, realizing I could tell

Bells everything we'd learned so far—that the coroner was part of a foiled attempt at fraud, that Lloyd's death was unquestionably foul play, that a killer was eluding justice somewhere. All of it. Yes, here was a chance to drop the whole squirming ball of worms right in the cops' laps. It was, after all, what they got paid to do, unlike some sad-sack knights I could mention.

Bells kept at it. "Well, anything?"

I teetered on the edge but, in the end, just looked away.

He spit out a laugh. "Guess not, huh? Alright, here's the deal. George Agnelli is dead. Whatever agreement you had with him is null and void. Just walk away. I don't need you gumming up things. Get it?"

I gave him a stingy smile. "Sure, I get it. Young detective like you has a lot of potential, and you don't want anybody muddying your climb to the top. It wouldn't look right if it's found you disregarded a possible murder."

Bells took yet another step closer, close enough for me to smell the gin that could be clouding his judgment. "Maybe I'll rethink shooting you."

"Now, that would *really* hinder your career."

"Maybe I'll chance it." He jabbed a hard finger into my chest. "Just walk away."

Even though Bells was the one who walked away, right out of my apartment, it somehow didn't soothe me. And my desire to see frontier marshals slapping leather against cattle rustlers had all but fled.

CHAPTER TWENTY

SINCE MY APARTMENT SUDdenly didn't feel very homey—
probably because of the lingering
odor of death threats and gin—I hit the road again. I had dinner
at an out-of-the-way place where I figured I'd recognize the least
number of faces. I wasn't up for a lot of *Hey, how's it going?* at the
moment. I ate my ham and potatoes with minimal enthusiasm
and undertipped the waitress, just to spread the misery. Then I
drove around town for a half hour, shoving my headlights
through the darkness in search of nothing at all. Tiring of that,
I decided to head over to Mr. O'Nelligan's. I drove past the Valish residence and, three doors down, pulled up to my colleague's
house. I knocked firmly and heard him call from inside, telling
me to come in.

I entered to the sound of Elvis Presley's "Love Me Tender"
and found my friend in his book-crammed living room, seated
with his pipe before the fireplace. The lights were off, and the

high flames of the hearth gave the old Irishman a ghostly glow. On the table next to him sat the phonograph, two or three books, a Superman comic, and a cup of tea. He gestured me to pull another chair up to the fire. Close to him now, I noticed two things: the framed photo of his late wife in his free hand and the hint of tears in his eyes. We waited silently as Elvis finished his pledge to love until the end of time. When the song was done, Mr. O'Nelligan set the picture on the table and lifted the phonograph arm from the record.

"My lad from Tennessee," he said softly. "You really should acquire one of his albums, Lee."

"Maybe someday."

"So, what brings you here? It hasn't been but three hours since we parted. Surely my company isn't that compelling."

I told him about Tommy Bells, taking care not to infuse too much bravado into the account.

Mr. O'Nelligan bristled. "To have your castle breached in such a fashion—deplorable! At least the young brute didn't injure you when he hurled you down."

"No, he didn't break anything of mine that I could tell. Well, maybe my spirit."

"Never, Lee Plunkett! Never! Your spirit shall rage on against all these inequities."

"If you say so."

"I do. This incident only confirms our resolve to pursue this case independently. If Bells represents what we can expect from the local police force, then surely we're better off on our own."

"It may be hard to keep under Bells's radar. From here on out, he'll be on the lookout for anything we do involving the Lloyd household."

"Then we must be surreptitious in our actions."

"You mean sneaky, right?"

"Yes."

"Then why don't you just say sneaky?"

Mr. O'Nelligan set down his pipe and sighed. "If the compilers of the Oxford Dictionary saw fit to amass so many delightful words, then it's the least we can do to use a decent portion of them. Now, wait here while I fetch you a good cup of tea. It will settle you nicely."

I was about to decline his offer, but then realized that tea sounded just right about now. After my friend went off to the kitchen, I lifted the photograph from the table and studied it in the yellow light of the fire. I'd noticed it on earlier visits, but never really took it in. It showed a plumpish woman of around sixty dressed in a bright, floral-patterned dress. She had an open, friendly face, which at the moment was turned toward the camera in what seemed like a look of surprise. She was holding a stick of fluffy cotton candy, a Ferris wheel visible in the background.

I was still looking at the picture when Mr. O'Nelligan returned with my cup of tea. I set the photo down quickly, afraid of seeming intrusive. My friend didn't appear bothered. He settled back into his own chair and smiled gently.

"That's the last picture ever taken of my Eileen. We were at Coney Island, and it was a lovely day for us. Just lovely! I'm so grateful to have that to remember her by . . ." His voice caught slightly. "It's been over two years since she passed away, and still there are days when I half-expect her to come through the door and tell me she's been off on holiday somewhere."

"I'm sorry I never got to meet her."

"Oh, you would have liked her, Lee. She had a big heart.

Such a big heart." He cleared his throat and took up his teacup. "Ah, good, it's still warm."

We sipped our tea and stared into the fire, not saying anything for what seemed like a very long time.

Finally, Mr. O'Nelligan spoke. "A blazing log and a mug of bold tea—remember?"

"Remember what?"

"A few days back, I told you that those were the things required to put forth a proper ghost story."

"So you're making good on your promise?"

"I am," he said quietly.

Then my companion eased into a long, winding tale of a summer's night back in County Kerry when he was just seventeen. Traveling down a moonlit country lane, on their way home from a wedding, young O'Nelligan and another boy saw a man standing just up the way, sobbing pitifully to himself. He looked alarmingly like a local man who, several years before, had fallen to his death off a nearby cliff. Panicked, the boys dropped to the side of the road and buried their faces in the grass.

"I felt my heart drumming against the earth," my friend recalled, "and I began to pray to a legion of saints for our safe deliverance. At some point, I turned and saw that the lad with me had risen to his feet. He was a Tierney—a good-natured fellow who bore the nickname 'Pipes' on account of his lovely singing voice. I thought for a second that he was about to make a run for it, but instead he said, 'I'll try to calm that spirit.' And then, oddly enough, young Pipes began to sing. It was a tune I'd never heard before and have never heard since. I can't remember what it was about exactly, but I do know that it was deeply sad and lovely. Pipes Tierney sang it marvelously, and if there was any fear in him, he didn't allow even a drop of it into his voice. When he had completed his song, he stepped into the road and gazed ahead. After a moment, I got up and joined him and, don't you know, that shadowy man was gone. Simply vanished."

"So you're claiming it was a ghost on the road that night?" I asked.

"I can't truly say. But I tossed that tale about for years to come. As for Pipes, a few weeks after our adventure, he took an apprenticeship to a cobbler in Castlecove, and I didn't see him more than a couple of times after that." Mr. O'Nelligan took a long sip of tea and his voice became very soft. "Eleven years on, in the autumn of 1922, I was fully into manhood, and Ireland had descended into a bitter civil war. Those of us who had fought shoulder to shoulder against the British now found ourselves at violent odds. I had chosen my side, and one night outside a millhouse, a band of us ended up trading shots with a band of them. I fired at a corner of the building and heard a high, horrible cry. By this I knew that my shot had found its mark. The next day, our captain came to me and said, 'Good work last night. Did you hear who it was you dispatched? You probably knew the rascal, since he used to live hereabouts. It was young Dennis Tierney, the one they called—'"

"Pipes." I finished the sentence.

Mr. O'Nelligan nodded. "For all my days, whenever I bring Pipes Tierney to mind, I will always think of his voice as I heard it on two occasions. The first being that night when he sang so divinely to comfort a wayward spirit; and the second being the moment I killed him, when he screamed out in pain and outrage as his own spirit fled him. And there, Lee, is the real terror and sorrow of this tale."

His story done, Mr. O'Nelligan placed his teacup aside and

fell into silence. In the flickering light of the hearth, I took in his features—the gentle, intelligent eyes; the soft wrinkles beneath; the well-trimmed gray beard—and wondered at the ways of the world. From that good, kind face, I tried to extract the youthful rebel who had once killed an old comrade, but I couldn't quite succeed. After a long interval of quiet, I finally spoke.

"Dennis . . . You said his real name was Dennis. That's the same name that Loretta Mapes told you."

Mr. O'Nelligan looked at me. "You heard that conversation, did you?"

"Only a few words of it."

"Yes, Mrs. Mapes told me she beheld the spirit of someone named Dennis hovering about me, and that he was a man I killed."

"How could she come up with information like that? Could she have read something somewhere?"

Mr. O'Nelligan gave me a pitying smile. "Oh, Lee, dear lad, I see how you tick. You're the sort who seeks to cram the universe into a tidy little box and paint the word 'rational' in huge letters upon the lid. Only then can you be content."

"What do you mean? What's wrong with being rational? You're the most rational man I know."

"If I am, it's only because I recognize the possibility of the *ir*rational. Anyway, Mrs. Mapes said what she said. And it's true, the spirit of Dennis Tierney does hover around me. You can define it as a ghost or as conscience, but in the end it's all the same, really. It's something with the power to haunt."

"His death happened in the course of war," I said. "Bad things happen in war. You can only blame yourself so much."

"Whether I blame myself or not, there's the irrefutable fact that I still walk the earth, while the man I shot has not done so for more than three decades. I removed someone from the great pool of life. That's a thing to be profoundly acknowledged, a thing not to be forgotten. Now, in my silver years, I've been given a chance to return something to that great pool. All thanks to you, Lee Plunkett."

"Me? What have I got to do with anything?"

"Don't you know? By taking me on as your comrade, you've offered me the opportunity to seek justice for Trexler Lloyd, a man wrongfully slain. You've drawn me again into the arena of life and death, on the side of precious life."

We sat there for a little while longer and watched the logs fall apart into smoldering embers. We agreed to meet at my office in the morning to decide our next move. I thanked him for the tea and the story, then headed out the door. For a minute or two, I stood there alone on Mr. O'Nelligan's small front lawn, taking in the crisp night air and the sweep of distant stars above me. I felt tired and empty, a little melancholy, and more than ready to switch off my brain for a hundred years or so.

I HAD A dream that night. It was a crazy hodgepodge like my dreams tend to be. I think I was in a desert, only instead of sand it seemed to be snow, blowing wildly all around me. Several people came riding past on white camels. There was Mickey Mantle and Vice President Nixon and a couple of Marx Brothers. And bringing up the rear was Constanza with two women whose faces I couldn't see because of the swirling snow. In one voice, the trio called out to me, *We'll see you on the horizon.* I called back, *I'll be there!* But after they'd passed, I found myself wondering what did that even mean—meeting someone on the horizon? Then I saw Trexler Lloyd approach, his cloak fluttering behind him. He was carrying a book. He sat down on a stool that happened to be there and started reading. I asked him if it was his autobiography. Without looking up, he said, *No, it's yours.* Then I became agitated and said, *But I never wrote one! Was I supposed to write one?* Then Lloyd said, *It's alright. They wrote it for you.* With his eyes still in the book, he lifted one arm and pointed behind me. I turned around then and saw Mr. O'Nelligan with my father and another gray-haired man who looked like me, only older, standing all in a row. I said, *Thank you for my book.* Mr. O'Nelligan laughed and replied, *Oh, you would say that, wouldn't you?*

That's all I remember.

CHAPTER TWENTY-ONE

ON SUNDAY MORNING, I WAS unlocking the door to my office when someone came up behind me and grabbed my shoulder. I spun around expecting it to be Tommy Bells again. Instead, it was Betty Gallagher. Her red hair was in disarray, and her young face looked drawn and waxen.

"My cousin Katie's dead," she said, her voice trembling. "Someone killed her last night."

I stood there for a long moment, incapable of word or action, then shook off my inertia and ushered her into the office.

Betty dropped into a chair and looked imploringly at me. None of yesterday's toughness was evident in her now. She began speaking rapidly. "I waited here in your hallway half the night. Didn't even know if you'd show up. I came right from the police."

"The police? What did they—"

"I'm scared, Mr. Plunkett. I'm so very scared. Oh God, it's all because of me. Poor Katie! My poor Katie!" Then she dissolved into tears.

I tried awkwardly to offer comfort. "I'm sorry. I'm so sorry . . ."

She cried for a full minute, then wiped her eyes with the sleeve of her jacket. "I'm afraid whoever killed Katie might come looking for me. I had your card from yesterday, and I thought maybe you could find who did it. Because I don't think the police have any idea."

I pulled up a chair. "I need you to start from the beginning, Betty, and tell things in the order they happened."

She tried to bring some strength into her voice. "Alright. Katie got off work a couple hours before I did. We share one car between us, so she took it to go home. She was supposed to come back and get me at six. She never showed up. I called her, but there was no answer, and I figured she must have dozed off, because she'll do that sometimes. One of the other waitresses offered to give me a ride. We stopped for a drink first and ended up running into some guys she knew, so it wasn't until after ten that I finally got back home. When I entered the apartment . . ." Betty closed her eyes and began to tremble.

"Take a moment," I said.

Her eyes opened and grew wide and wild. "No, I have to tell it. The police made me repeat it over and over, and now I almost *want* to. Isn't that sick? What the hell's wrong with me?"

"You've had a terrible shock," I said softly. "When people have had a shock, it can really throw them."

She didn't acknowledge that she'd heard me. "Katie was lying on her side on the living room floor. I didn't even see any blood at first, and I wondered why she was sleeping down there.

It just seemed stupid. I spoke to her, but she didn't answer, so I reached down and touched her. She felt way too cold, and when I pulled my fingers back there was blood on them." Betty lifted her right hand and studied her fingertips, as if she could still see the red there. "I realized then that she'd been stabbed to death."

I caught my breath. "She was stabbed?"

"Several times," Betty said in her dazed voice.

"Did the police find the murder weapon?"

"No. But I saw that the owl box had been broken open and was lying there empty."

"Owl box?"

"It's a wooden box I have with little owls carved on the top. It's where I'd put that thing I stole from Lloyds's house."

Her words were whirling around me like buzzing bees. "You need to explain."

"Right, you wanted me to tell everything in order, but I haven't, have I?" Betty's voice softened. "It wasn't breadsticks I took the night Mr. Lloyd died. It was this . . . gold thing. I'm not sure exactly what it was, but it looked sort of like a hairpin— though the pin part was wider than you'd expect. The thing was gold plated, and it had this flat sort of top etched with pictures of the moon and stars. I just had to have it."

"So you think . . ."

She sounded angry now. "I think someone knew I took that hairpin thing and forced their way into our apartment to get it back. But I wasn't there, only Katie. Whoever it was must have found it or forced Katie to show them where it was, and then stabbed her to death with it."

This all seemed too much to me. "What makes you think she was killed with that particular object?"

"Because it was long and had a sharp point. Almost like a blade."

"Well, even if that's what was used, how do you know Katie's killer came to your apartment for the purpose of finding it? They might have been there for some other reason. Maybe there was an argument and that person grabbed the nearest thing at hand—the hairpin—and used it to attack your cousin."

Betty was growing agitated. "No! Aren't you listening? It was in the owl box, and the box had been locked. Katie's killer broke it open to get at the hairpin, understand? It wasn't just lying out in the open where someone would have impulsively grabbed it. Someone had to have been looking for it to begin with."

"Did you call the police after you found your cousin?" I asked.

"Right away. The homicide detectives came and asked me a lot of questions. It seemed to go on for hours."

"Did they bring up your connection to Trexler Lloyd?"

"Not at all."

"Really? But hadn't the police interviewed you and Katie after Lloyd's death?"

"No. Remember, we'd left the house that night before anyone called the police. I don't know that our names even came up. At least, no one ever bothered to contact us."

"Was one of the detectives last night a young man with curly hair named Bells?"

"I don't know. I don't think so."

"Did you tell them about the hairpin?"

Betty lowered her head. "No. I didn't want to get myself in trouble. How selfish is that? Katie's lying there murdered and I'm worried about getting arrested for stealing."

"So, if you omitted that part, then the police have nothing at all to go on."

"That's why I came to you, Mr. Plunkett. I'm hoping you can figure out who killed my cousin without bringing me into it. I'm going back to Delaware now. The police said to stay around, but I can't. I just can't. For all I know, whoever murdered Katie will come after me next."

Her tears returned, stronger than before. I told her that I'd be right back and went to fill a glass of water from the lavatory down the hall. On my way there, I heard footsteps and turned to see Mr. O'Nelligan coming up the stairs. I joined him and broke the news about Katie Gallagher's death.

His hand went to his heart. "Merciful God! She wasn't but twenty!" He was silent for a moment; then his face grew hard, and he swore under his breath, which I had never heard him do. "Our killer was villain enough when the victim was a man well into his fifties, but now, to steal the life of that innocent colleen . . ."

Mr. O'Nelligan headed for my office, and I went to get the water. When I returned, I found him kneeling before Betty, holding her hands.

The girl was speaking through heavy sobs. "If it had to be one of us, why Katie? I'm the one who stole, not her. I'm the one who ran around with all the boys, never Katie. She was always the good one. She went to confession every week, but what sins did she even have? Not like me. Not like my sins." She paused and a tremor ran through her body. "Oh God, oh God! I killed her! I killed Katie . . ."

"You did no such thing," Mr. O'Nelligan told her firmly. "That was done by a cruel assassin, a person of vile intent. True, you lost your way, but there's no evil in you, child. The evil is in the soul of the one who did this."

"Do you think she's in heaven now?" At this moment, Betty seemed very childlike. "I don't even know if I believe in heaven, but I want Katie to be there. I want her to forgive me."

Mr. O'Nelligan squeezed her hands. "She loved you, did she not? And you loved her. If anything is enduring, if anything is forgiving, it is love."

Betty accepted my water and managed to more or less compose herself. "I'm going now. I'm going away."

I tried to dissuade her. "We still have things to figure out. It might be better if you stayed until—"

"No, I can't. I'm sorry. I just can't."

The young woman rose abruptly and from her coat pocket extracted two things, which she handed to me. One was a scrap of paper with her Delaware phone number; the other was a heavy silver coin.

"That was Katie's lucky dollar. She forgot it at the restaurant. I don't know whether it would have protected her or not, but I never want to see it again."

Then Betty Gallagher drew in a deep, quavering breath and moved toward the door.

I suddenly thought of something I hadn't asked. "Wait, you never said where in Lloyd's house you found the hairpin."

She paused in the doorway and turned to me. "In the downstairs bathroom. It was wrapped in a towel and shoved into the tight space above the medicine cabinet. I noticed it peeking out a little and pulled it down." As she was leaving, I heard her mutter, "Seemed like an odd place to hide a thing like that."

* * *

"I MAY BE to blame for this." I'd just finished relating Betty's story to Mr. O'Nelligan, who sat brooding in his chair. "Once we knew that she had taken something from the Lloyd residence, maybe I should have brought the police in."

My friend arched his eyebrows. "And told them what? That breadsticks had been pilfered? Remember, we had no evidence to the contrary."

"But we never really believed it was just breadsticks, did we? Though, I have to admit, I was still thinking more along the lines of stolen kitchenware. When Sassafras first told us that Betty had taken something, it never even crossed my mind that it could have been the missing murder weapon. How about you?"

"Actually, I *had* entertained that notion."

"Wait a minute, you thought Betty might have a murder weapon in her possession and you never mentioned it?"

"It was never more than a fleeting speculation," Mr. O'Nelligan said. "After all, a good many things fly through my mind that I don't give voice to. If Betty Gallagher had smuggled the murder weapon out of the house, then the natural assumption would be that she—or possibly her cousin—was Lloyd's killer. After meeting the Gallaghers yesterday, I decided that neither girl was a likely candidate for that role. Then I, like you, began to think that Betty had merely stolen something like unto the gravy boat. We see now that we were wrong."

"And I'd bet the bank that this isn't the first time this 'hairpin thing' has been used to kill someone. Trexler Lloyd also died from multiple stab wounds by a sharp, slender weapon."

"An undiscovered one."

"Right. And Betty found the hairpin hidden away in a peculiar place. I'm guessing that it was used not only for Katie Gallagher's murder but for Lloyd's as well."

"I believe you're absolutely correct," Mr. O'Nelligan said. "Let's review what we know about this weapon."

I tried to fix the object in my mind's eye. "Betty said it looked like a hairpin with an ornate base, but that the pin part was flatter than normal . . . Hold on!" A forgotten image flashed across my mind. "I think I know what it was."

"Yes?"

It came pouring out of me: "When I was seventeen, I worked a summer at Selgino's Stationery. Old Man Selgino had a collection of fancy letter openers on display. They were his pride and joy, and he had me polish them every day. I remember some had ornate designs on the handle, just like the thing Betty stole. I'm guessing that's what it was—a letter opener." My gears were turning now. "And I think I know where it was before being hidden in the bathroom."

My friend stared at me intently. "Don't stop now."

"Tell me, what did Doris Chauncey say was on the table by Lloyd's chair in the Portal Room?"

"The Tibetan bell?"

"No, that was a different table. What was on the one he was sitting right next to?"

It took Mr. O'Nelligan a few seconds to respond. "Why, a stack of letters."

"Exactly. And if Lloyd had been sitting there reading letters, he might well have been using . . ."

"A letter opener! Well done, Lee. See, no life experience is without worth. A summer spent wielding a polish rag has given you a valuable insight."

In the present circumstances, I had no stomach for praise. "Even if we know what the murder weapon was, it doesn't tell us who used it to slaughter two people."

"That's true," my partner agreed, "but there are fresh concepts we can now pursue. For example, in the case of Lloyd's murder—unlike Katie's, where the letter opener was hidden in a box—it may simply have been the thing at hand that the killer happened to reach for."

I tried out another version. "Or maybe the killer knew the letter opener would be in the Portal Room and so didn't bother to bring a weapon."

"Possibly," said my partner, though I could tell he didn't buy into that one. "In any event, however the blade got into the killer's hand, we can make certain suppositions about what happened afterward. Imagine this scenario. After murdering Lloyd, the killer—for whatever reason—hides the weapon in the bathroom, planning to retrieve it later. But then Betty stumbles upon it and, per her inclination, steals it away. Later, the killer discovers the letter opener is missing. This strikes fear into that dark heart, for perhaps there are still fingerprints on the murder weapon which could identify him or her."

I tried to follow his thinking. "So, then, a couple of days ago, Sassafras remembers seeing Betty smuggle something out of the house and starts telling people. And, directly or indirectly, word gets to the killer."

"Who then goes to the Gallagher girls' apartment to reclaim the incriminating letter opener, taking poor Katie's life in the process."

"Of course, none of that explains how Lloyd's killing went unobserved in a roomful of people."

"Yes, we keep coming back to that, don't we?" Mr. O'Nelligan said. "There's a certain chaos at the core of these events. A spiral of complexities and complications that keeps spinning madly about. And now it's claimed the life of poor young Katie." He stared off and softly intoned a verse I figured was by Yeats.

"Things fall apart; the center cannot hold;
Mere anarchy is loosed upon the world,
The blood-dimmed tide is loosed, and everywhere
The ceremony of innocence is drowned."

"So what do we do now?" I asked.

"We act. Our task is nothing less than the restoration of order to the universe. Things must be set right. We know now that the murderer isn't dormant. He or she has reemerged to kill again, and perhaps not for the last time. We must act, but first we must ponder. I'm going to take a stroll."

While Mr. O'Nelligan's sudden urge to promenade might have struck the casual observer as a sign of distraction, I knew differently. My friend's long walks often yielded his most productive thinking. Agreeing to meet me back at the office in an hour and a half, he patted my shoulder and headed out. I could tell that the Gallagher girl's death was weighing heavily on him. As it was on me. I sat down at my desk and picked up Katie's coin. A Morgan silver dollar from 1885, it had heft to it and felt substantial in my hand. I studied the profile of a woman's head— Liberty—and thought that it looked a little like Katie herself. I closed my fingers around it and offered up something like a prayer.

CHAPTER TWENTY-TWO

VENTUALLY, I SET ASIDE the coin, pulled out my notebook, and slapped it down on the desktop. Pressing my hands palms down on either side of the small spiral pad, I felt the wood's old dents and scars and considered the fact that, for me, this would always be my father's desk. His desk, his agency, his legacy.

When he took me into the business in the spring of '54, I think Dad was hoping it would ground me once and for all. Since my return to Thelmont several years before that, I'd had four different jobs and was tiring of my current one. My father informed me one day that he had something he wanted to run by me and that he'd treat for dinner.

"You're closing in on thirty, for God's sake," he'd told me over steaks at the Stout Butcher that night.

"I guess that's true," I said, hardly believing it myself.

Cutting into his sirloin, Dad seemed a little nervous. Finally he got it out. "I think you should come work for me."

Then it all came gushing out of him: He'd been giving it some thought for a year or more; and now the timing seemed right; and he certainly had enough experience to share, what with twenty years in the department followed by a dozen as a PI; and if a man can't share what he's learned in life with his son, then what's the point of it all anyway?

I sat there and took it all in and didn't know what to say. Dad set his knife and fork down and pinned me with his eyes. "Well, what do you think?"

There was something in his voice that I found embarrassing—a certain neediness that didn't fit with the gruff image of him that I'd long ago settled on. It occurred to me at that moment that I really didn't want my father to care too deeply about my response. I was on the verge of telling him that the gumshoe life was definitely not for me, or possibly deferring the matter indefinitely with an evasive *let me think about it*. Or maybe even laughing it off.

Instead, I said, "Sure, Dad."

"Sure? Really? You'll join me?" He looked actually happy. Shocked, but happy.

I found it a little painful to see him so vulnerable in his pleasure. He gave me a wink and ordered us a couple of beers to celebrate the birth of Plunkett and Son Investigators.

Honestly, I'm still not sure why I said yes. Maybe I saw it as an opportunity to structure my life or show my worth to my father or make myself a more fitting mate for Audrey. It could have been any, all, or none of those reasons. When I told Audrey later that night, she was stunned. Heck, I was stunned.

The first thing she asked was "Are you going to carry a gun?"

"No, I'm not."

"Good. Because I just know you'd shoot your kneecap off."

"You're probably right."

"Do you really think you can work with your father?"

"We'll see, won't we?"

At first Dad was eager to tutor me in the fine points of his profession, but before long, seeing that I had no real aptitude for the work, his enthusiasm dropped off. My one saving grace was that I had a talent for taking notes and organizing information. Because of this, I don't think he considered me a total wash. As it turned out, the sixteen months of partnership that we shared weren't exactly chock-filled with activity. The jobs came in sporadically, just enough to make me feel that I was indeed employed. We had to track down a few misplaced people, pursue some misappropriated funds, and corner some unfaithful spouses. The latter were my least favorite cases—they always struck me as a bit seedy—but Dad somehow got a kick out of them.

Still, the thing of it was, we were working together. Yes, mostly it was him doing the talking and the deciding, but I played my part, though certainly a less rugged one—Buster packed a pistol, I packed a pencil. I wouldn't say his heart swelled with pride to have me at his side, but I think he took a certain comfort in it. Now and then, he'd slip me an extra twenty, saying, "Maybe you can put a little something aside and marry that girl of yours." Over those last few years, he'd actually grown to like Audrey (though he never did extend that affection to her father, Joe). After every time he'd see her, Dad would pull me aside and say, "She's good for you, Lee. Don't screw it up." I'd promise him I wouldn't.

Then one autumn evening, I got a call from one of Dad's cronies saying he had just died over a bowl of beef stew. The crony, who went by the sobriquet Muleface, let me know that just before the heart attack claimed him, Buster had praised his meal, saying it was the best goddamned stew he'd ever tasted.

So the business fell into my lap. Audrey wasn't sure why I kept it on, and, once again, I couldn't discern my own motives. I fully realized that it was a foolish thing to do, seeing as I lacked the natural skills for the job, but I did it anyway. I wasn't sure if my father would have been pleased or appalled. I never did remove the words "Plunkett and Son" from the office door. It just didn't seem right to do it.

I PUSHED OLD memories aside and vigorously attacked my notes. I rewrote them and categorized them and rewrote them again, hopeful that, in doing so, I would yield up something vital and revealing. I ended up flinging my pen across the room.

On one page I had written:

Constanza's infidelity → Trowbridge → Trexler Lloyd = angry Trexler

Followed by:

Angry Trexler → disappointed Kemple = Cancelled plan
+
Angry Trexler → confused Kemple = Plan back on
+
Angry Trexler → Doris Chauncey → Call to Lawyer Foster → Change will

The next equation ran:

Trexler talking → *Trexler leveling* → *Trexler &*
Clients → *Trexler dead*

That one was followed by a small army of question marks.

I had a number of other notations, which dealt with the Gallaghers, the letter opener, Kemple's surliness, and various other aspects of the case. I'd even thrown in the Tibetan temple bell for good measure. After reviewing my materials for the umpteenth time, I was still in a fog as to who did what. I decided to go for a drive. If Mr. O'Nelligan could take a stroll to gather his thoughts, then I could certainly take a spin in the Nash to see what that dislodged from my brain. As I headed out, I scooped up the silver dollar and dropped it in my pocket.

I drove around town for twenty minutes before realizing that no lightbulbs were going to pop on over my head concerning this case. I had just decided to turn back toward the office when I spotted Audrey standing on the sidewalk outside her church. The spruced-up crowd milling about suggested that the service had just let out. I pulled over across the street and watched as my fiancée, pretty in plaid, stood chatting animatedly with several people including her sister Clare. Lulu, Clare's daughter—now nine, and no longer given to bouts of room-quaking wailing—was running up and down the sidewalk in a giggling race with another girl. It was like watching a little play—a pleasingly uneventful one—being put on for my enjoyment alone.

For a little while I felt calm, content, spared briefly from all thoughts of crime and death. I just wanted to sit there forever, burrowed into Baby Blue on this mild December morning, watching the churchgoers smile and shake each other's hands as if all were unfalteringly right with the world. After a few minutes, I saw Audrey look in my direction, give a little jolt of recognition, and cross the street toward me. She opened the passenger's door and slid in.

"How long were you going to sit there just watching?" she demanded playfully. "You haven't been hired to stake me out, have you? Was it Mrs. Jerome? Does she want to make sure I'm not frequenting another five-and-dime on my day off?"

"Nothing like that." In no mood for company, I could hear the hollowness in my tone. "Just out for a drive."

"You're still on the Lloyd case, I presume. Or did you solve it overnight?"

"No."

"And you're still not getting shot at, right?"

"Right."

"Or beat up."

Thinking of Bells, I almost said, *Just a little,* but opted for "No."

"And no catapults hurling boulders at you?"

"Not that I've noticed," I said flatly.

"Good. I know how you hate medieval weapons."

I barely looked at her. "I really need to go."

Audrey studied me for a long, concerned moment. "Tell me what's going on, Lee. Is it something with the case?"

I clenched my jaw, holding back the black wave of despair that was rising in me.

"Come on, what's wrong?"

"Nothing," I said, by which I meant *everything.*

Everything in the whole sick, rotten world was wrong. Murdered geniuses and red-stained blades and faceless killers. Nice young girls barely out of their teens, dead before their time. Wrong, wrong, wrong. As for my pretension in labeling myself as someone who could solve the bleak mysteries of the world . . . well, maybe that was the most unforgivable wrong of all. Clearly, I was Buster's boy in name only.

"Listen, you're not your father."

"What?" For a weird, disconnected moment, I thought I might have just heard my own brain speaking aloud.

But no, it was Audrey. When the hell did she become a mind reader? "Lee, you're not your father."

"I know, Madam Freud," I grumbled. "Don't you think I'm very aware of that fact?"

Right then and there, Audrey could have lapsed into offended silence. She didn't. "I don't mean that as an accusation, you know. I mean you're your own man."

"For all the good that does."

She tried to extract a smile from me. "Hey, watch it, fiancé! Remember, *your* own man is *my* own man."

"Yeah, well, we might want to reconsider that. I'm sure you can do better."

That stopped her cold. She sat there silently, staring forward for a painfully long minute before telling me, "You don't mean what you just said."

I sighed so deeply it almost hurt. "Probably not."

"*Definitely* not. Absolutely, positively, don't-even-joke-about-it not. Listen, Lee, here's a little story."

What I wanted to say was *For God's sake, no more stories. In the last twenty-four hours, I've heard more than my share. Trowbridge's tale of the unfaithful widow. O'Nelligan's saga of ghosts and slain young men. Betty Gallagher's bloody account of her murdered cousin. Way too many ugly narratives.* Instead, I said, "I've heard all your stories, haven't I?"

Audrey gave a little shrug. "Well, not long ago you said you'd never heard the one about my grandmother's spirit, so maybe I've still got a few up my sleeve. You remember Dale?"

"Your sailor beau. My predecessor and everybody's pal."

"Yes, that's Dale. A nice guy by all accounts."

"But in reality . . . ?"

"In reality, he was a *very* nice guy. Not only that, but his whole family—mother, father, three sisters, four brothers—all very, very nice. You could scour all forty-eight states and not find a better bunch. They always seemed to be crammed around the dining table, joking happily and offering each other the lion's share of the mashed potatoes."

"Sweetest people in captivity," I intoned.

"They were! You just had to love them."

"And did you?" I asked. "Or, more specifically, did you love Sailor Dale?"

Audrey didn't offer as rapid a "no" as I would have preferred. Instead, she seemed to ponder the question before replying. "I think I loved the *idea* of Sailor Dale."

I frowned. "If this tale is supposed to uplift me, it's sure missing its mark."

"What I mean is that I was really taken with the notion of this big, bustling, wonderful family. Everybody seemed to smile morn to midnight, like no shadow had ever crossed their doorway. And each member was exactly who you'd want them to be—the doting mom, the handsome navy son, the sweet-tempered little sister. And, believe me, it wasn't a facade—they were all genuinely charming. Charmed, too. One time, Dale was on his battleship when a Japanese plane burst out of the clouds and strafed the deck. He was standing in a cluster of seven men, just come up for a work detail, and he was the only one of them who wasn't killed or wounded."

"*That* must have cast a shadow or two across his smile."

"Not really. Whenever he talked about it, he'd always grin and say, 'Golly, I am one lucky fellow!' I'm sure he felt bad for the men who died, but it was just his nature to find the bright spot in things."

"So why didn't you stay with him?"

"That's the reason I'm bringing this all up," Audrey said. "I'd started to compare myself with Dale and his family, and I just didn't seem to be up to their caliber of cheeriness and goodwill. I began to look down on myself, especially when I thought of possibly marrying Dale and trying to fit into that big merry mob. I just knew I'd come up short."

"Why? You're one of the most positive people I know."

"Sure, I'm generally an upbeat gal, and I know I come from a good family myself, but I definitely don't ooze sunshine the way Dale's people did. Then something occurred to me—kind of a revelation, actually. I suddenly understood that I didn't want to."

"Didn't want to what?"

"Ooze sunshine. I realized that, when it comes down to it, I like a little shadow mingled with my light. For me, a nonstop, beaming grin would just kill my cheekbones."

It took some effort not to smile at that, but I still wasn't ready to give up my gloom. "So what's the point of telling me all this? To show why my murky nature suits you better than Dale's gleaming one?"

"No! It's to let you know that you don't need to keep comparing yourself to your father."

"Are you saying that Buster was another version of Smiley the Sailor? Because, believe me, he wasn't."

"I'm not saying that at all. My point is this—once I'd figured out that I didn't have to model myself on someone else, I was able to better accept who I was, not the sunshiny girl I thought I was supposed to be. Then I was able to wish Dale well and send him off toward the open sea. And after I'd given up trying to be somebody I wasn't, a really great thing happened."

"What's that?"

She looked me in the eyes and said it softly. "I fell in love with Lee Plunkett."

At that moment, held in her gaze, I think I was on the verge of reaching out for her. But then the insistent rapping started.

"Aunt Audrey! Hey, Aunt Audrey!" Lulu had come up alongside the car and was knocking on the passenger window.

Audrey opened her door, and Lulu gave me a windmill of a wave. "Hi there, Mr. Plunkett! You can't have Aunt Audrey right now. No smooching for you two!"

I laughed despite myself. Lulu was a cheeky little fireball, but I liked her.

"And why's that?" I asked.

" 'Cause Aunt Audrey said she was treating Mommy and me to ice cream sundaes."

"December's a lousy time for eating ice cream, isn't it?" I reasoned.

Lulu narrowed her eyes in a look of severe pity. "Not when it's a Sunday, Mr. Plunkett. Geeze, don't you get it?"

"Oh right. Sundaes on Sunday."

"Let's go!" The girl began tugging at Audrey's arm. "Time's a-wasting!"

Audrey giggled, then turned to me. "Come and join us, okay?"

For a moment, I thought about saying yes. No doubt it would have been nice to hunch over unseasonable sundaes for a half hour or so. Warm butterscotch on vanilla ice cream. Idle chitchat about whether or not the church choir had stayed on key. Wild guesses as to what new films were coming to the Bijou. But I knew that anything I said or did would be a lie of sorts, a denial of what was really going on in my heart and head. The moment's pleasantries would be drowned by the dark tide of violence that I felt so near at hand. In the end, I told Audrey to go on without me and drove off, leaving her to the brightness of her day.

WHEN I GOT back to the office, I realized that I was somewhat on the late side for meeting up with Mr. O'Nelligan. My colleague wasn't there, but he apparently had come and gone while I was away. He'd left a note.

Dear Lee,

I strolled, ruminated, and returned. I believe I have come up with a plan which may lead us to a desirable outcome. As I arrived back earlier than you, I took the liberty of making a number of phone calls. My intention is to facilitate a gathering tonight at the Lloyd residence. Since I did not reach every intended party, I borrowed the contact list so that I might continue calling at my leisure. I notice that you are in the process of aligning your notes. If you could continue in that endeavor, it would be quite helpful. Perhaps you might switch to prose, as opposed to the quasi-mathematical formulas which you have thus far favored. Clarity is always appreciated. I go now

to further ramble and reflect. Let us meet tonight back here at
7 pm to make the journey to Braywick.

Yours, O'N

I had no idea what Mr. O'Nelligan's grand plan was, but I
was happy to comply with it, seeing as I had none of my own to
offer. I retrieved my pen from the floor and commenced to redo
my notes in the prose that my partner requested.

After completing my assignment, I drove home—entering
my apartment cautiously, lest Tommy Bells should have planned
a return visit—and fixed myself a late lunch. Afterward I decided to try to relax in preparation for whatever the evening
might bring. I sprawled on the couch and scooped up a copy of
Pulverizing Tales. Three pages into a hard-boiled detective story,
I thought, *What the hell am I doing?* and tossed the magazine
aside. One thing I didn't need right now was to follow somebody
else's "Torrid Trail of Mayhem." I had my own to pursue. I next
turned to the Sunday funny pages. If the elevated mind of Mr.
O'Nelligan could find contentment in Batman's Robot Twin,
then Little Orphan Annie and Prince Valiant would do me just
fine. That filled about five minutes tops. I eventually found myself drawn once again to *Myself and No Other*, like one of those
damned moths sucked into Trexler Lloyd's blinding light. The
passage I landed on concerned the inventor's interest in life after
death.

It strikes me as bizarre that an energy as kinetic and dynamic as,
let us say, my own should simply be severed from the world by the loss of
the corporal body. The first law of thermodynamics states that while
energy can be transformed from one form to another, it can neither be
created nor destroyed. Nor destroyed! So, I ask, if the energy of a human

250 }   **MICHAEL NETHERCOTT**

life cannot be destroyed upon death, what then can it be transformed into? Why, perhaps the very thing that countless legends have risen around—the Ghost, the Specter, the Prowling Wraith! Have you not seen them, these unsleeping dead? Have you not heard their cries from beyond the dark curtain? Seek not false comfort in the belief that these spirits exist only in the fireside tale or the titillating radio show. No, they are among us. Shakespeare's Hamlet labeled death as "the undiscovered country, from whose bourn no traveler returns." But I must disagree with the bleak-souled prince—some travelers do, indeed, return.

My eyes grew heavy, and I began to doze off over Trexler's words.

These travelers are made of mist. Their hearts beat like the tide on a faraway shore. They return and whisper to us in the blackest realms of the night . . .

CHAPTER TWENTY-THREE

WAS JOLTED OUT OF MY NAP by loud insistent ringing. I jumped up and grabbed the phone. It was Audrey.

"Hey, Lee. I just wanted to check how you—"

"What time is it?" I was in a daze.

"About six thirty."

"In the evening?"

"Uh, yeah. You were napping, weren't you? You know how groggy you get when you nap late in the day."

"Six thirty. Holy smoke." I'd been out for two hours and had to meet Mr. O'Nelligan in thirty minutes. "I've got to go."

"Lee, are you okay?"

"Sure. Bye, Audrey."

It's unlikely that my abrupt hangup put her at ease.

* * *

I DROVE THROUGH the darkness, and Mr. O'Nelligan told me his plan. Sort of.

"With your permission, I'll say a few words to the assemblage tonight."

By "a few words," he meant that he would play maestro and conduct the proceedings. Which was just dandy with me.

"Permission granted," I said. "What assemblage are we talking about?"

"I've arranged for everyone who was at the house the night of Trexler Lloyd's death to meet us there at eight o'clock."

"Everyone?"

"Well, not Betty Gallagher, but the rest of the lot. All members of the household will be there, as well as Dr. Kemple, the Greers, and Mrs. Mapes. I also placed a call to the Vermont State Police to ask them to visit Felix Emmitt's cabin with a message for him to join us."

I was impressed. "How did you ever get everyone to agree to come?"

"Each person required a different style of coaxing. I like to think that I have a certain competency in that field. In another matter, I asked Miss Chauncey about the whereabouts of the household last night. I posed my question without mentioning Katie Gallagher, and Miss Chauncey said nothing about her, either. I don't believe word is out yet about the girl's death. Anyway, it seems that, for much of the evening, everyone was on their own, scattered in various directions."

"So anyone could have gone out during the time when Katie was killed."

"Correct, and a car would not necessarily have been required. Remember, the Gallaghers' apartment is only a mile from the

Lloyd residence. A brisk walk to and fro would have taken little more than a half hour to complete."

"Or it could have been someone from outside the household."

"Yes. Now, please forgive me, for I must reflect." Mr. O'Nelligan flicked on my flashlight (which I'd prudently refilled with fresh batteries) and began looking over my newly arranged notes.

After several minutes, I said, "You're not going to let me in on what you've figured out, are you?"

"I'm not prepared to aver any postulations just yet."

"Mind rewording that so a Plunkett can grasp it?"

"I mean that I'm still pondering," my friend said distractedly.

"But you think you're onto the solution, yes?"

"That remains to be seen."

"Well, fine, then. Just let me know if I'm supposed to flee from anybody, okay? You know, like if the murderer's about to make a lunge at me? You'd give me the heads-up for that, I assume."

That got Mr. O'Nelligan's attention. "I would never put you in harm's way. You know that, lad. If I'm being elusive, it's only because things are still settling in my mind."

I knew he was being honest. It wasn't that my Irishman was trying to exclude me from his deliberations, but rather that he needed to sink into his own intellect to sort things out. At such times, I'd learned it was best to let the man withdraw and reflect. I drove on, played with the radio dial, and left my colleague to his musings.

THE GATES HAD been left open in anticipation of tonight's guests. As we slid through the dragons, I wondered if this would be our last time seeing the twin terrors or if we were destined to return here time and time again. When we reached the house, we noted several cars lined up in the driveway. Just as we were getting out, another automobile pulled up beside us. The occupants climbed out, and, by the light from the porch, I saw that it was the Greers.

Herb Greer approached us. "Alright, we're here. Against my better judgment, I might add. But you talked Adelle into it." He nodded toward my comrade. "You with your smooth brogue."

Adelle came up close to me. "You lied, Mr. Plunkett." There was a barely controlled anger in her voice. "You lied about you and the spirits. Mr. O'Nelligan told me it was all made up."

I tried for a reply. "Well . . . You see . . . Sorry . . . It's just that—"

She waved off my stammering. "I realize you had your reasons."

"Yes, and I never—"

"Listen to me. It doesn't matter what you believe or don't believe. Because *I* believe, do you understand? I've seen my Andy, and it doesn't matter what you or anyone else thinks about that."

Herb rested a hand on his wife's shoulder. "C'mon, Adelle. Don't get yourself all churned up, now."

Adelle kept on. "This world's just too full of people telling other people what they should feel, what they should know. Well, I believe there are more things in this life than we can even imagine. Amazing, mysterious things. And Mr. Lloyd said he believed that, too. That's why I'm here tonight. Out of respect for Mr. Lloyd."

Then she moved past us toward the porch, followed by her husband, who shot us a look of undefined warning. With Mr.

O'Nelligan, I brought up the rear. This time we were met at the door by both Doris Chauncey and Trowbridge.

"The congregation still gathers," the butler declared. "Come this way, please."

Mr. O'Nelligan hung his jacket on the coat rack. "Mr. Plunkett and I will be along shortly."

As Trowbridge led the Greers away, my partner turned to Doris, whose new curls looked a touch less bouncy today. "Has everyone arrived, then, Miss Chauncey?"

"Everyone but Mr. Emmitt," she answered.

"Well, he had that long journey from Vermont to make. Hopefully, he will not disappoint us."

"I'm putting everyone in the living room. Oh, have you heard about Katie Gallagher?"

"Yes, we have," said Mr. O'Nelligan quietly.

"It's so upsetting! We just caught it on the radio a couple of hours ago. It seems that it was some terrible accident."

"An accident?" I looked at her squarely. "That's what they said on the radio?"

"Yes, but they were vague about what exactly happened."

Apparently, the police were playing their cards close to the vest. As were we. I glanced over at Mr. O'Nelligan and received one of his *say nothing* looks.

"Such a terrible loss." This didn't come from the secretary but from a voice behind us. Turning, I found myself face-to-face with a heavyset woman in an apron. It took me a few seconds to recognize Mrs. Perris, the cook, whom I'd only seen at night lit up by headlights.

"That poor young girl," she said. "Sometimes you have to wonder why certain things happen in life. I've been praying for her ever since I heard."

Mr. O'Nelligan nodded. "I, too. Are you here tonight, Mrs. Perris, in your professional capacity?"

"You mean cooking? Yes, I'm done now, but I thought I might stay a bit longer to hear what you had to say. Doris says it has something to do with Mr. Lloyd's death. I've felt badly that I wasn't here the night he died, so, seeing as my Jack's feeling much better now, I thought perhaps I could stay. That is, if you gentlemen are alright with that."

"Of course," Mr. O'Nelligan said. "As a member of the house-hold, it's fitting you should join us. We'll begin shortly."

The two women left us to see to various tasks. Alone now in the foyer, my partner and I faced each other.

"What do you make of this 'accident' stuff on the radio?" I asked. "I assumed the police would have let people know that a murderer was on the loose."

"Hopefully, after tonight they won't need to."

"What? Then you do know who—" I stopped myself as foot-steps approached.

Trowbridge had returned. "So, we meet again." His voice was low, conspiratorial. "What exactly is the purpose of tonight's little get-together?"

"The revelation of truth," Mr. O'Nelligan replied.

"Ah, but of course—truth itself. The Irish are always so grandiose in their intentions. But more specifically, will you be driving a murderer out into the open?"

"We shall see."

The butler smiled mildly. "I am giddy with anticipation. By the way, I've said nothing to Mrs. Lloyd of our conversation yester-day. She's still unaware that anyone knows of her indiscretions."

"That's probably for the best," my partner said. "All things in their time."

"A sound philosophy, indeed." Trowbridge gave a little bow and exited.

Hearing a creak on the stairwell, I turned and saw Constanza Lloyd standing partway down the steps. Had she overheard the butler's remarks about her? The blank look on her lovely face betrayed nothing.

"Ah, Mrs. Lloyd," Mr. O'Nelligan said. "Good evening to you."

"Good evening," the young widow replied without emotion. "You will talk to us now?"

"Very soon," I answered. "If you'd like to join the guests in the living room, we'll be right there."

"I will do that." She descended the stairs and walked past us without meeting our eyes.

I turned to speak to my colleague, but he had already started off, not toward the living room but down the side hallway. He stopped before the closet there, and as I joined him, he pulled open the door. Once again, we found ourselves gazing upon the hideous giant eyeball. Manhole cover, lightning bolts, corkscrews, propellers—it was all still there.

"As gorgeous as ever," I noted. "Did you think someone would have snatched it?"

"Not at all. Its unwieldy bulk, coupled with its unsettling appearance, will, I trust, forever spare it from the grasp of robbers."

He closed the closet door, and we continued down the hall. Coming to the bathroom, he reached for the knob. Just then, the door flung open, nearly slamming him in the face, and Sassafras Miller emerged.

"Whoa, Blarney!" She looked taken aback. "Never sneak up on a gal when she's powdering her nose. A man of the world like yourself should know that. I almost smashed in those good looks of yours."

"I beg your pardon, madam," Mr. O'Nelligan said. "I didn't mean to cause surprise."

"No harm done. So, I guess you fellas are going for broke tonight. Are you planning to hit us with all your fanciest deductions?" As usual, Sassafras didn't wait for a reply. "Why, sure you are!"

"We'll see," I answered. "I don't know how much fanciness we're capable of."

Sassafras patted my chest. "Oh, you guys are swell as hell. Don't let anybody say you're not. Hey, has Constanza come down yet?"

"Just now," Mr. O'Nelligan said. "She's joined the others. We'll be along presently."

He waited until Sassafras was out of sight, then stepped into the bathroom, leaving the door ajar. As I watched, my comrade reached into the narrow space between the medicine cabinet and the low ceiling and ran his fingers slowly back and forth. He didn't seem to be hunting for something so much as reflecting on the object that had been hidden there. After a moment, he reentered the hallway, and we headed on toward the muffled sound of voices. Passing through the small, book-filled waiting room, we paused on the threshold of the Portal Room as our eyes adjusted to the near-darkness there. Only one of the candle stands was lit, and by its low, amber glow we saw two people standing side by side talking: Martin Rast and Loretta Mapes. Fashionwise, Rast had returned to his pirate scarf look, while Mrs. Mapes wore a brown dress and pillbox hat. Not noticing our presence, they continued their earnest conversation.

"No, no, dear woman," Rast said. "You must make a mistake. He is long gone."

Mrs. Mapes tilted back her head. "Oh, I don't know about that."

"Do you see him now?"

"Not in this room. Maybe he doesn't like meandering here right where he died. Some spirits prefer to keep a respectable distance from their death rooms, you know. But I did perceive him for a moment when I first came in the house. Just a wisp. He was going up the stairs."

"I think perhaps you saw Reverend Hayes," Rast suggested. "He looks a little like Mr. Lloyd, but more skinny because of the consumption."

"No, it was definitely Mr. Lloyd. Though, come to think of it, I did hear someone reading from the Good Book a few minutes ago. Deuteronomy, I believe it was."

"Yes, the reverend always is preparing for his last sermon that he never got to give."

"And then there's some child keeps running in and out of the house."

"You mean Little Violet."

"She's a spunky one, that girl. But she's got a powerful fear of dogs."

They went on like that, so focused on dead people that they hadn't noticed the two live ones standing nearby. A clear realization came to me just then: Even though I didn't believe in haunted houses, I really hated being in one. Partway through Rast's description of a disembodied head, Mr. O'Nelligan signaled our presence with a theatrical cough.

Loretta Mapes squinted at us through the dim light. "Now, those two there aren't spirits."

"Not yet," my partner said. "I myself am hoping for another decade or two before I slip off my mortal shell."

"Oh, it's Old Irish and his friend." She stepped toward us. "I know what you mean there. As chummy as I am with the deceased, I'm in no rush to join their number. The Lord knows I'm content to stay earthbound up till the day when I feel those angel wings sprouting out of my back."

"I trust that won't be anytime soon," Mr. O'Nelligan said.

"Well, I'm trusting, too. Are things about to commence?"

"Yes, they are, madam."

Rast joined us. "That is good. Because I have my chores to do afterward."

"Even at night?" I asked

"It is now the rats!" he declared. "I must trap them. We have seen rats lately, and they scare the people. First the flies, then the rats. Always it is something here."

"So very true," Mr. O'Nelligan agreed. "Always it is something."

We exited the Portal Room as a group. While the others passed straight through the waiting room into the hallway, I hesitated for a moment. Unobserved, I bent over the vicious little stuffed raccoon and patted his head three times for luck, as Sassafras had done.

"Let's bring this case to a close, okay, boy?"

The raccoon declined to respond.

Returning to the foyer, I found Mr. O'Nelligan now standing alone, eyes closed and hands folded before him.

"Are you leveling?" I asked.

He opened his eyes and smiled lightly. "In a way."

"Do you know what you're going to say to these people tonight?"

"I believe I do. Everything has settled into place, and I feel an answer is at hand."

We heard footfalls outside on the porch. I opened the front door to find Felix Emmitt standing there, his hat and shoulders covered with white, and a brisk snowfall tumbling behind him.

"It just started to snow," he said. "Luckily the sky was clear on the way down."

"Ah, Mr. Emmitt." My partner gestured the coroner in. "You've made the long trek to join us. We do appreciate that."

Emmitt pulled off his snowy coat. "Wish I could say it was my pleasure." He looked directly into Mr. O'Nelligan's eyes. "You do what you need to do here tonight. Say what you need to say."

"Be assured I will," my colleague said solemnly.

Raised voices reached us from the direction of the living room. Loud, angry, clashing voices. And a man cried out, "I'll kill you! I swear I'll kill you!"

CHAPTER TWENTY-FOUR

URRYING INTO THE LIV-
ing room, we found all of them
on their feet—and Herb Greer
and C. R. Kemple nearly at each other's throats.

It was Greer who had bellowed the threat, and now he
offered Kemple another. "You nasty little bastard! You want
ghosts? I'll send you to them! By God, I will!"

Inches away from the large man, Kemple all but spit in his
face. "Buffoon! It's stupid lummoxes like you that keep us from
evolving to the death realm."

"You want a death realm? Fine by me!"

As Greer pressed in on Kemple, his wife cried out, "Herb,
don't! Don't!"

Kemple's right hand slipped into his jacket.

Of everyone in the room, it was Trowbridge who reacted
first. Darting forward, he wedged himself between the two com-
batants, placing a hand on each of their chests.

"That will do, I think, gentlemen."

Extending his long arms, Trowbridge pushed the two men apart. In doing so, he apparently felt something in Kemple's jacket and with a quick hand plucked out the pearl-handled revolver that I knew too well.

"That's mine!" Kemple protested.

"So we see," the butler said calmly. "But perhaps it would be best to keep it out of reach for the present, seeing as tempers are running a tad hot." He reached up and placed the weapon on the top shelf of a bookcase.

Mr. O'Nelligan stepped forward. "It is unfortunate that we should begin things with such discord."

"Yeah, well, tell *him* that." Herb Greer pointed at Dr. Kemple. "We're not here ten minutes and that little louse starts shaking down Adelle for more cash."

Kemple ran a hand over his bald dome, as if there were something to smooth down. "That thug threatened me! Look how agitated I am. I was only offering his wife an opportunity to subscribe to a series of lectures. People are always against me. Always!"

"Maybe they're just jealous of your dazzling personality." I couldn't help taking a jab at him.

Kemple glowered at me. "I don't like you at all."

"Say it ain't so," I countered. "I was hoping for a lifelong friendship."

Sassafras gave a loud guffaw. "Wow! Brawling men . . . death threats . . . pistols . . . It all brings me back to my Carefree Cabana days. Hey, Trowbridge, is there any bathtub gin kicking around? That would really get me nostalgic."

Mr. O'Nelligan cleared his throat. "I think our present situation would best be served by sobriety—in every sense of the word. Now, please, let everyone be seated."

The chairs filled up. A few individuals remained standing, most notably Kemple, who wedged himself into a corner and seethed. I took a couple of steps backward to lean myself against the wall and bumped into someone behind me. I turned around and swore. It was Tommy Bells.

"What are you doing here?" I demanded.

"Special invite from O'Nelligan." The young detective looked past me. "I assume that's you, Pops."

My partner came over and rested a hand on Bells's shoulder. "I trust you will abide by our agreement, Detective. You'll stand aside and listen until I have completed my presentation. Correct?"

"That's the deal," Bells said. "But no monkeyshines."

"I assure you, no simians will be shined in your presence."

Bells almost smiled. "Fair enough." Then, turning to me, he said, "No hard feelings, eh, Plunkett?"

I didn't answer one way or another. Taking Mr. O'Nelligan by the arm, I drew him aside and whispered in his ear, "What gives here?"

He whispered back, "My apologies, Lee. I forgot to mention that I'd contacted Bells. It's best, I believe, that we have a police representative present. I convinced the young man that it would benefit his career were he affiliated with tonight's results."

"You actually talked him into that?"

"It appears I did. Shall we commence?"

"Sure. Commence away."

Leaving Mr. O'Nelligan to center stage, I took my place against the wall and gazed out at the "assemblage," as my colleague called it. Discounting the two of us, there were a dozen parties in the room. Seated were the Greers, Mrs. Mapes, Emmitt, Sassafras, and, off to one side, Constanza Lloyd and Miss

Chauncey. Those standing numbered five: Trowbridge, Rast, Mrs. Perris, the still-steaming Dr. Kemple, and Tommy Bells, who'd placed himself near the room's exit.

As if he were about to deliver the grandest of soliloquies, Mr. O'Nelligan drew in a fortifying breath and began. "It should be acknowledged that we are here tonight because of a man named George Agnelli, now deceased, who refused to let the truth lie unrevealed. It is he who brought Plunkett and Son Investigators into the case. As the firm's de facto assistant, I will now present Lee Plunkett's findings."

I wondered how many people he was hoodwinking with that last bit of modesty. Not many, I guessed. Certainly not me.

"What exactly is being investigated here?" Adelle Greer asked.

"Wrongful death," Mr. O'Nelligan answered. "Or, more specifically, two wrongful deaths. The first, as most of you are now aware, is that of Trexler Lloyd. The second, which has not been public knowledge, is that of young Katie Gallagher. Yes, she, too, was murdered."

This drew several gasps and exclamations. Mrs. Perris cried out, "Don't say that! Who would do such a thing?"

"Who, indeed. That is the question we now seek to answer." Mr. O'Nelligan paused and shifted gears. "Back in Kerry where I hail from, there was an old woman by the name of Fiona Taggart who, shall we say, liked to follow her own tune. She was what some might label eccentric, though I always thought of her as bold and colorful. One day, while walking along the River Fertha, I came upon Fiona casting herself a line. It was unusual to behold a woman fishing, but seeing as that woman was Fiona Taggart, I was not too mightily surprised. Her success at the task was testified to by the half-dozen fish beside her. She said something to me then that I've never shaken loose—'You've got to let the river ripple back and forth to make your catch.'

"Now, to be honest, I'm not quite sure what that meant in terms of fishing, but for life in general, I've found it to be true. In the case before us, I believe we must let the narrative ripple back and forth to arrive at the right conclusion. In that vein, I will start with Katie Gallagher's death. Poor Katie was killed because her cousin stole something from this house on the night Trexler Lloyd perished. That object was a daggerlike letter opener that had been used to kill Mr. Lloyd and, afterward, was hidden in the hallway bathroom. Miss Chauncey, as his secretary, no doubt you are aware of such a tool."

Doris gave a small shudder. "Why, yes, it was very long and had stars on it. You say it was used to—"

"Stab him to death!" Sassafras groaned and sank deeper in her chair. "What a rotten way to die. Poor Trex."

Mr. O'Nelligan continued. "Soon after Mr. Lloyd's killing, the murderer would, of course, discover that the weapon had been removed from the bathroom. Last night, having learned that Betty Gallagher had stolen something from the house, the murderer went to the girls' apartment, confronted Katie, who was there alone, and retrieved the letter opener. Then, so as to leave no witness, Katie was made the next victim. The same weapon that had dispatched Mr. Lloyd was used on the girl."

"This is all too horrible," Adelle Greer protested. "Do we really need to stay and hear this?"

Bells summoned his most official voice. "Sit tight, lady. No one's going anywhere till this thing is done."

Mr. O'Nelligan turned toward the young detective. "You agreed to let me conduct this without interference."

Bells smiled smugly. "Who's interfering? I'm just backing you up here."

"I appreciate the sentiment, but, for now, I'm just fine." My colleague turned again to his main audience. "I ask your indulgence, Mrs. Greer. I ask this of all of you as we seek justice for Mr. Lloyd and the Gallagher girl."

Mrs. Perris, standing to the side, let out a low moan. "God forgive me, I'm the one who first asked Katie to work here. If I hadn't done that . . ." She was unable to finish.

"There's no need for self-recrimination here," Mr. O'Nelligan said. "Several people have made choices—some in good faith, some in bad—that may have led to dark outcomes in this case. And I do not exclude myself. But trust me, Mrs. Perris, providing a young woman with honest work is nothing to chastise yourself for. Now, let us leave poor Katie to our prayers and make our way back to the death of Trexler Lloyd. Mr. Lloyd was a complex, complicated man. In accordance with that fact, the circumstances leading to his demise are extremely complex—gnarled, we might even say. I will lay them out now for all to observe. Understand, please, that while I'll be as delicate as possible in the telling, my highest obligation here is to the truth."

"Can't go wrong with that way of thinking," Loretta Mapes offered.

Mr. O'Nelligan gave her a little smile. "One would hope not. First, I must reveal that in the course of our investigation, we've learned of an elaborate plan conceived by Mr. Lloyd to fake his own death."

"Fake?" Sassafras's eyes went big. "You mean Trexler is still—"

Mr. O'Nelligan cut back in. "No, alas, he is truly dead. The original plan involved his wife, Dr. Kemple, Mr. Emmitt, and the local cremator. The Spectricator was rigged to produce a display of sparks and smoke at a preordained time to make it appear that Lloyd had been electrocuted. Afterward, he would make his way to Spain to reunite with Constanza and claim his fortune. In this way, Trexler Lloyd would, in a sense, remove himself from the world. But in the midst of this complicated scheme, someone actually *did* remove Lloyd from the world—with several thrusts from the aforementioned weapon. Now, as if this were not a tangled enough storyline already, yet another thread weaves in here. We've discovered that Mrs. Lloyd, unbeknownst to her husband, had been paying visits to a young man in town. These visits, I'm afraid, were not of an innocent nature."

"Mr. O'Nelligan, stop!" Doris Chauncey looked shocked. "You're making things up now. Constanza, tell him he's wrong."

The Spanish woman, instead of denying the allegation, lowered her head. "It's true," she said softly.

Doris, her mouth agape, stared at her friend as if seeing her for the first time.

Mr. O'Nelligan returned to his account. "We can hold nothing back at this point. Mrs. Lloyd's actions are significant because when her husband learns of them everything begins to shift. Everything, in a strange way, begins to lead to his murder." He took a moment to study his audience before continuing. "Let us examine that pivotal moment and the events that follow. It is approximately seven o'clock on the evening of November thirtieth, and Mr. Lloyd has settled himself into the Portal Room. Letter opener at hand, he's looking over some correspondence, perhaps merely out of habit, for very soon he will have no need of correspondence. That's because he is content in the knowledge that, in just over an hour, his plan of feigned death will be enacted. Then Trowbridge, the butler, enters with news which his conscience forces him to impart. This is the moment that changes everything.

"Upon learning of his wife's dalliance, Lloyd gives way to anger. Now, according to the individuals involved, this is what next transpires. Dr. Kemple is summoned in and informed, without explanation, that the whole plan is off, including the Spectricator demonstration. Then Miss Chauncey is told by Lloyd to contact his lawyer for the purpose of changing the will—we can presume to block Constanza out of it. Then Martin Rast, in attempting to ask about moving a sculpture, finds Lloyd still in a dark mood and is booted from the room. Next Sassafras Miller enters to ask if she may ring the bell that night and if the leveling should begin. By now, Lloyd has calmed down and gives his assent to these things. With Sassafras, Miss Chauncey, and the confused Dr. Kemple, he then meditates in preparation for the Spectricator demonstration. Afterward, Sassafras rings the bell, the clients enter, and, soon thereafter, the sparks shoot out and Lloyd is discovered to be dead by Coroner Emmitt. Not falsely dead, but slain in earnest."

Herb Greer raised his hand as if we were in a classroom. "I've got a question. How the hell could somebody stab Lloyd when we were all sitting there? Everybody was looking at him."

"The ghosts!" Kemple stirred in his corner. "Don't you see? It was the beings from the death dimension that did it. Somehow the Spectricator must really have summoned them. It's the only explanation."

Herb spit out a laugh. "Right. The ghosts stabbed him. Why didn't *I* think of that?"

Rast now weighed in. "Possible, I suppose. Yes, possible. Some of the dead ones get very angry. And Gillmond did once beat someone to death with his cane."

"Ridiculous!" This came from Loretta Mapes. "What are you all talking about? The spirits don't kill people. Couldn't even if they wanted to. That's just not how it works. Some of you," she said, looking from Kemple to Rast, "claim you've got the gift, but then you spout all that crazy nonsense."

Mr. O'Nelligan squelched this paranormal debate. "Please hear me out. The great puzzle of this case has always been the question of how a man could be murdered in full view of a half-dozen people. I can now tell you, the immediate answer is very simple—he wasn't. And, contrary to some suggestions here, no ghost took his life."

"Of course not," Mrs. Mapes said with satisfaction.

My partner pressed on. "Just now I offered a brief chronicle of what we were told occurred in the Portal Room that night, as testified to by the participants. But, I must now tell you, not every part was true. That is because, during our investigation, we were presented with false assumptions and outright lies by certain individuals. At this juncture, like old Fiona Taggart, we must ripple backward to make our catch. I will now review events in reverse order to reach the actual moment when Trexler Lloyd was murdered. Mr. Emmitt, when you approached him, Mr. Lloyd was already dead, yes?"

"Without question," the coroner replied. "He'd been stabbed. That's the one thing I can say for certain."

"So you've claimed," said Mr. O'Nelligan, "and I believe you. Now, falling back several minutes, starting with when the clients first entered the Portal Room, can anyone who was present say absolutely that you heard Lloyd speak? Well?"

A few heads shook, and Sassafras shrugged.

Adelle Greer spoke up. "No. His eyes were closed, and he kept silent. Dr. Kemple did all the talking. Then the Spectricator started sparking, and Mr. Lloyd slumped over. He never spoke the whole time I was there."

"Exactly!" Mr. O'Nelligan raised a finger to accent the point. "I contend that the man was not merely silent then, but already dead."

Again a wave of exclamations passed through the room.

"But wouldn't we have noticed?" Adelle asked.

"There was no reason for anyone to presume that Lloyd was not among the living," my partner replied. "His wounds were hidden by the cloak he wore, he was propped up in his chair, and everyone believed he was merely being taciturn. Why would anyone imagine him to be dead?"

"That's it!" Mrs. Mapes called out. "Remember, Mr. O'Nelligan, when I told you I thought the spirits had a grip on Mr. Lloyd that night? Well, that's why, don't you see? It's because he was already with them."

"Indeed he was," said Mr. O'Nelligan. "Alright, now let's fall back again, this time to the fifteen-minute interval when Mr. Lloyd and three companions were leveling. Here again, we have a period in which Lloyd speaks to no one and no one speaks to him. In fact, no one speaks at all because it is a time of meditation. It has been mentioned by more than one party that when leveling, Trexler Lloyd was always beyond distraction.

"Now, Sassafras here has previously shared a little anecdote concerning a fly. It seems that this large, irksome fly was buzzing wildly about during that evening's leveling. Sassafras and Kemple found the insect annoying, and Miss Chauncey found it absolutely discombobulating. Only one of the four had no reaction at all—Mr. Lloyd. The fly actually landed on his nose for a few moments without garnering a response. This struck me as rather singular, even for a man deep in meditation. While his companions may have attributed it to his great powers of concentration, I offer another explanation. As in the previously noted time period where Mr. Lloyd's lifelessness was mistaken for mere silence, so, too, was it here."

Doris Chauncey gasped. "You're saying he was dead even while we were leveling?"

"I am," Mr. O'Nelligan said, "It was presumed that he was in a trancelike state when, in fact, he was already departed."

"Wait, now." A note of distress entered Doris's voice. "If that's all true, then the last one to see Mr. Lloyd alive was the person who was alone with him just before the leveling." She looked across the room. "That was you, Sassafras."

Sassafras stiffened in her chair. "What are you saying, Doris?"

"According to what Mr. O'Nelligan's been telling us, Mr. Lloyd was dead after you left him. When you came out of the Portal Room, you told me the leveling was about to start, and I went in immediately. There was no time for anyone else to slip in after you and kill him." She struggled to get out her next words. "My God, Sassafras, it was you!"

Sassafras jumped to her feet. "No! No! I loved Trexler! I could never harm him. I could never harm anybody. He was alive when I left him. I swear! He'd just been talking to me—"

Mr. O'Nelligan took control again. "You say Mr. Lloyd was talking to you, madam. But when you first described your conversation with him, you presented it as you posing questions and him responding. You asked about ringing the Tibetan bell and about starting the leveling, did you not?"

"Yeah, that's right," Sassafras said.

"And he answered in the affirmative."

"He sure did."

"Please, take your seat again."

Sassafras dropped back into her chair and ran a hand through her hair, disheveling it in the process. She looked on the verge of tears.

My partner offered her a gentle smile. "During our brief acquaintance, I've noted a particular characteristic of yours, Sassafras. One that is significant to our present discussion. You have a great tendency to pose a question and not bother to wait for a reply."

"Right!" Suddenly, I guessed where he was going with this. "Instead, she'll blurt out something like 'why, sure you do' as if the listener had agreed to whatever she just asked—when, in reality, he hasn't responded at all."

Mr. O'Nelligan nodded appreciatively at me. "Precisely. And I suggest that this is what happened in those minutes when Sassafras was alone with Mr. Lloyd. She so wanted to hear affirmative replies to her questions that she honestly believed she had received them. Yes, Trexler Lloyd was propped up there in his chair, his face burrowed in his cowl, but, as we have seen in the other scenarios, he was not alive. When we add up these various time periods, we see that Lloyd was dead for approximately a half hour before Mr. Emmitt beheld the stab wounds. It was merely a chain of assumptions that prevented anyone from discovering that fact."

Tommy Bells forgot his vow of silence. "How far are you going to go back with this, O'Nelligan? A day? A week? Christmas 1930? How long was Lloyd sitting there dead without anyone noticing?"

"It's as I've just stated," my partner answered. "Roughly a half hour. Prior to that, Trexler Lloyd was indeed alive. Several minutes before Sassafras went in to ask about the bell, an agitated man—misinterpreting something he had just heard—marched into the Portal Room to confront Lloyd. During the ensuing argument, this person seized the letter opener and, in anger, plunged it several times into Lloyd's chest. I will tell you now, that man was Martin Rast."

CHAPTER TWENTY-FIVE

R. O'NELLIGAN'S STATE-
ment settled over us all like a
cold fog as everyone turned to
stare at the groundskeeper. Rast, standing near the back of the
room, remained perfectly still, neither his face nor his body responding to what had just been said. A small yelp issued from
Doris Chauncey, but besides that, no one made a sound.

My colleague continued. "As complex as this case has been,
there is a certain cause and effect to things. Had Trowbridge not
overheard the Lloyds discussing their secret travel plans, he
would not have felt compelled to tell Mr. Lloyd of his wife's infidelity. Had Lloyd not received that information, he would not
have instructed Miss Chauncey to phone his lawyer regarding a
change to the will. And had Rast not overheard that phone conversation, he would not have jumped to a certain conclusion and
ended up killing his employer."

"I think you have made a confusion here," Martin Rast said softly.

"I assure you I have not," Mr. O'Nelligan responded.

Up to this point, the Irishman had been standing more or less stationary. Now, as his narrative shifted into high gear, he began to move about—at least as much as the crowded room allowed for—his hands gliding and gesturing in emphasis of the story. Here, without question, was the master actor doing what he did best.

"Here's how it all came to pass," he said. "Let us return to that moment when Miss Chauncey, having been given instructions to phone Mr. Foster, has returned to her office and is placing the call. As she is doing so, Rast and Trowbridge are right outside in the hallway struggling to move the eye sculpture, their second attempt of the day. Rast overhears Miss Chauncey telling the lawyer that he is needed as soon as possible to make a change in Lloyd's will. The groundskeeper here makes an assumption that will prove fatal for Mr. Lloyd. When Rast hears that Lloyd wants to change his will, he leaps to the false conclusion that the purpose of that change is to remove *him* from the document."

Trowbridge now joined in. "Why ever would he think that?"

I flung out the answer. "Because of the window that you and he broke earlier—as far-fetched as that might sound. We've been told that Trexler Lloyd could be a harsh, demanding employer. What was that motto of his?"

Trowbridge provided it. "'I am exacting in all things.' Mr. Lloyd said that often."

I nodded. "Right. He was exacting—and, from what we've heard, hard-nosed and maybe ruthless at times. If he thought that someone had failed him in some way, Lloyd wasn't above cutting that person out of his life."

"That is true enough," Trowbridge agreed.

I didn't stop. "Rast might have figured that Lloyd was so angered by the breaking of that window—the damaging of Lloyd's favorite dwelling—that he'd punish those responsible by purging them from his will."

Mr. O'Nelligan looked at me like a proud papa, then took up the tale. "In Martin Rast's case, being purged from the will meant losing the house here that he had been promised, and, more to the point, losing his beloved ghosts. To Rast, the spirits that he believes inhabit this place are like unto family. He could not tolerate life without them. His great hope and dream was to outlive Lloyd, who had perhaps twenty years on him, and one day inherit this domicile.

"So then Rast, upon hearing of a change to the will, makes his rash conjecture and decides he must confront Lloyd on the matter. He offers Trowbridge the excuse that he is going to go ask about the sculpture. Barging into the Portal Room, Rast faces off against his employer. Of course, we cannot know exactly how this played out. Perhaps Rast was supplicant, perhaps he was belligerent. Quite likely, Mr. Lloyd, still smoldering at his wife's infidelity, refuses to even listen to Rast's petition. We can presume that Rast is never enlightened as to the true reason for altering the will. But there is rage and there is a sharp object at hand. In a flash, that object is in Rast's grasp, and he has murdered Trexler Lloyd."

At this point, I glanced around the room to take in the group's reaction to all this. Each man and woman seemed transfixed, some dazed, and all eyes were upon Mr. O'Nelligan. Here and there, a head would turn toward Martin Rast—who stood off by himself—before quickly turning away. Doris Chauncey alone seemed unable to stop staring at the groundskeeper. Her face looked frozen and bloodless, and I really felt for her. As for Rast himself, he remained as motionless as a statue, his arms hanging stiffly at his side and his expression unreadable.

Mr. O'Nelligan pushed on. "Rast has the presence of mind to wipe the blood off the blade, perhaps with the interior of Lloyd's cloak, and conceal the weapon on his own person. He leaves Lloyd's lifeless body still seated in the chair and exits the room. We can only guess at Rast's thoughts at this point. After all, he must know that someone will eventually enter the Portal Room and discover the slain man. Then it would surely come to light that Rast was the last person in his company. Still, he does not attempt to flee, which would seem to be the natural course of action. What he does do is enter the hallway bathroom, wrap the letter opener in a towel, and hide it above the medicine cabinet. Then Rast returns to Trowbridge and Miss Chauncey. Since he had made the excuse of going to ask about the sculpture, Rast must now fashion a lie concerning it."

I was getting this. "So he tells them that Lloyd, in a bad temper, has given instructions for the eye to be placed in the hall closet for the time being."

"Quite so," agreed my partner. "Accordingly, Rast and Trowbridge complete this task. Now, we are unsure of Rast's actions for the next half hour. For whatever reason, he does not retrieve the murder weapon. At some point, the clients begin to arrive, so perhaps it is inopportune for him to reenter the bathroom. Perhaps he communes with his spirits during this time, asking for their guidance. We cannot know. What Rast must be becoming aware of is the fact that there has been no hue and cry concerning the murdered man. Rast has no doubt seen that people have been entering the Portal Room since the killing, and yet, apparently, no one has discovered the death. I have already explained to you all how this phenomenon was possible, but, at the time, he surely is confounded by it.

"Later, as Rast stands in the foyer with other members of the household, Sassafras runs in screaming that Lloyd has been electrocuted. Hastening to the Portal Room with the others, Rast finds, to his amazement, that Lloyd's death is being declared an accident. Throughout the rest of the evening—in fact, throughout the rest of the week—the groundskeeper becomes convinced that his actions are somehow beyond the realms of normal men. He has killed, and yet, miraculously, the universe has stepped in and covered up his deed. Even the fact that the letter opener is gone may add to this view. For who could have made it vanish like that? Why, poltergeists! Martin Rast comes to believe that he is much like his spectral companions—existing in two worlds simultaneously. More than once, Rast told Lee Plunkett and me how blessed he was. Blessed. I think that, in his reality, he felt that fate had spared him from all consequences."

I added my two cents. "But then things start to change. Rast discovers that we're actually investigators and that we suspect foul play in Lloyd's death."

"Yes, and he has also heard Sassafras's assertion that Betty Gallagher stole something from the house. Rast begins to think that perhaps it wasn't the poltergeists after all who took the letter opener. He begins to feel desperate. The truth of Lloyd's murder might be revealed. The murder weapon, perhaps still bearing fingerprints, might be discovered. He has to act. He has to kill again." Mr. O'Nelligan now took a great, cleansing breath. "And that, we believe, is how it all occurred."

No one said anything for a long moment.

Then Martin Rast began to laugh. Loudly and wildly.

"Yes, yes, yes!" he cried out, his voice high and trembling. "You are so right! So very, very right! What a clever man you are!"

"Oh, God," Doris Chauncey seemed about to fall out of her chair. "How could you, Martin? You killed them! Mr. Lloyd and that girl . . ."

A pained look intruded on Rast's mania. "I am sorry, Miss Doris. I never meant to disappoint you."

At that moment, Constanza Lloyd, who had been silent throughout the proceedings, leapt to her feet. "My husband! He was a great man, and you murdered him! You are nothing! Nothing!" Then, unleashing a fierce torrent of Spanish, she lunged at her husband's killer.

It all happened swiftly. As Constanza clawed at his face, Rast shoved her forcibly backward. Trowbridge rushed forward to break the woman's fall, and, in doing so, ended up toppling with her to the floor. To my side, I saw Bells reaching into his jacket for his revolver, but Rast had already bounded to the bookshelf and had Kemple's pistol in hand. The groundskeeper fired, someone screamed, and Bells fell to his knees, clutching his side. Rast pushed past several people and raced out of the room. I heard the front door being flung open, and then, to my own great surprise, I found myself sprinting madly after a gun-wielding murderer.

A MONTH OR two before my father died, I joined him in a foot chase down a series of long, dark streets and alleys. The object of our pursuit was a young, long-legged burglar who favored black leather jackets and crowbars. A few days earlier, this fine youth had used one of the latter to knock out a housewife before absconding with her jewelry and a set of bowling trophies. At sixty-one, Dad really shouldn't have been doing this, but, to tell the truth, he was beating me in the race. Our quarry finally aided our efforts by running smack-dab into a fire hydrant. As the burglar lay there cursing and holding his groin, Buster clicked on the handcuffs and tried to catch his breath. I was breathing like a steamboat myself. In between huffs, my father tossed me some wisdom, "It's better to run at something than from something."

As with a lot of Dad's insights, I don't really know what that even meant. Even so, as I rushed out into the night in pursuit of Martin Rast, those words were with me. I'm not sure what I was thinking at the moment. In the grand history of smart moves, this surely wasn't one—Rast was armed; I was not. Still, something hurtled me forward. The snow was falling thickly now, and by the porch light's glow I could see fresh footprints along the side of the house. I knew the garage was out back, so I guessed Rast was going for one of the cars. Rounding the left corner of the house, I ran along the side toward the back until I saw the garage lights. As I started to veer toward them, a shadow shot out from my right and swung at me, striking my head with something very hard. Suddenly, my world turned into pain and disorientation and coldness.

As I lay crumpled in the snow, I could feel a warm, thick liquid trickling across my brow. Seconds stretched themselves to the breaking point, and, in a weird swirl of time and space, I began to hear things. First it was voices, many voices, urgent but muffled, and out of that cacophony, one of them, a little girl, began singing something about flowers and fountains. I heard distant barking, but only for a moment, and the girl said, "Don't worry, they can't reach us here." Then the voices stopped, and I thought I felt someone squeeze my arm. Somehow, it seemed like my father. I think I caught a whiff of Old Spice aftershave.

My eyes were open now, and I saw a hazy gray figure hovering nearby in the falling snow. Noticing my glasses lying just inches away, I pulled them to my face, and the gray figure suddenly became a pirate. Rast. He seemed no longer concerned with me but with Mr. O'Nelligan, who now stood several paces away from him.

"It's all over," my friend was saying. "Just lay that gun down and there'll be no more troubles tonight."

"I will kill again," Rast hissed. "It does not matter anymore."

With that, he extended his arm, aiming the pistol directly at Mr. O'Nelligan.

I had pushed myself up to a kneeling position and now, half dazed, began raking my hands through the snow in search of something to use as a weapon. A stone, a heavy stick, anything . . . My fingers closed around something round and flat. It was Katie's silver dollar, fallen from my pocket. It had some weight to it, so I drew my arm back and hurled it at Rast's head. My aim was remarkably good. The coin struck him on the bridge of his nose, causing him to stagger and fire wide. Then, from around the back of the house, Trowbridge appeared and pressed a revolver to Rast's temple.

"That's it, then," the butler said firmly. "Drop it or I fire."

After a moment's hesitation, Rast let the gun slip from his hand.

"Nicely done, Trowbridge." Mr. O'Nelligan walked forward, snatched up the weapon, and came over to crouch beside me.

"And you, too, lad. Oh, you're bleeding a touch. How do you fare?"

"Can't complain."

"Well, aren't you the tough fellow. But what will I tell Audrey, letting you get all mussed up like this?"

I never had a chance to reply due to the high, maniacal scream that tore through the air.

Rast was crying out, reaching his arms to the snow-filled night. "Reverend Hayes! Miss Winifred! Help me! Violet! Ezekiel! Someone help me!"

"Forget it, Rast," Trowbridge said, still leveling his gun. "No one's coming. Even your bloody ghosts won't have you."

CHAPTER TWENTY-SIX

IT WOULD TAKE A COUPLE OF days for my head to stop swimming. I really wouldn't recommend getting slugged with a pistol butt to anybody. I thought of lying about it all to Audrey to spare her from anxiety, but, of course, she dragged the whole story out of me that next morning. We were sitting at my kitchen table, sipping coffee and sifting through all the dire details of the case, which it seemed, at last, I was ready to share with her.

After she'd heard everything, Audrey said, "You're very brave and very foolish. When I told you not to get yourself shot, I should have added not to get bludgeoned, either."

"You'll have to be more specific next time."

"Apparently." She reached over and squeezed my hand. "You know, you don't have to keep doing this kind of work, Lee. Certainly not for my sake. And not for your own. You've more than proven yourself."

I squeezed back. "The strange thing is, now that I'm on the other side of this case, I'm thinking maybe this isn't such a bad job for me after all. Having Mr. O'Nelligan to help steer me has made a big difference. Of course, as sleuths go, I'm no Buster."

Audrey affected a schoolmarm's singsong tone. "Now, now, Leander. What did we say about comparisons?"

I faked a look of confusion. "That we shouldn't want to be sailors because they're too damned happy?"

She laughed. "I think you misunderstood yesterday's instructive tale."

"Yeah, well, I always was a slow learner."

She reached over, gently drew me in, and planted a kiss on my lips.

"Your father would be proud of you. You know that, right?"

"Would he? I'd like to think so."

"I'm sure he would, Lee."

I hadn't said anything to her about sensing Dad's presence as I lay in the snow. Maybe I would eventually, but, for now, I was trying to chalk the moment up to a mild concussion.

Audrey pressed on. "I'm proud of you, too, you know. Proud and fretful. Chasing an armed killer like that! Would it do any good for me to insist that you never ever pull anything like that again?"

"Maybe," I answered. "I wouldn't mind if you kept trying. Maybe it would eventually sink in."

"I'll never stop trying," she said softly.

At that moment, I had a major revelation as to what a first-class knothead I was. If I didn't marry this woman very soon, I should be taken out and, well, slugged repeatedly with numerous pearl-handled pistol butts.

*   *   *

THREE DAYS AFTER Rast's arrest, I was sitting in my office with Mr. O'Nelligan, reviewing the case.

"How did you put everything together?" I asked. "It was all very O'Nelligan-ish of you."

"As these things go, it was a combination of facts and feelings," my colleague said. "The impossibility of Lloyd being murdered in a roomful of people demanded that some other explanation present itself. Once I'd accepted that the killing had to have taken place earlier, it was merely a matter of retracing events until they converged with a likely culprit."

"When did you decide that Rast was our man?"

"Not until late in the game. At one point or another, I had considered everybody—the wife, the secretary, the butler, even the lad from the hardware store."

"The whole smorgasbord of possible perpetrators," I managed to say.

"If you must put it culinarily, then yes. The whole smorgasbord. With each new discovery—Lloyd's plot to falsify death, Constanza's unfaithfulness, Betty's thievery—a different set of suspects would rise to the foreground. Throughout it all, Martin Rast always struck me as someone to seriously consider. The man exhibited a marked twitchiness of character, a certain detachment from the earthly plane."

"An otherworldliness?"

"In fact, yes. I came to believe that murder was something he might indeed be capable of. I kept coming back to the grotesque eye, the broken window, and Rast's obsession with the spirits of the house. In the end, those things did factor into the resolution."

"I never figured it out," I admitted. "I guess my private eye-ing is so private it's barely noticeable. Lucky for me, I can at least handle a notebook."

"Don't underestimate those notes of yours, Lee Plunkett. Their precision most certainly helped guide us to the solution. That and your dogged questioning."

"Guide *you* to the solution, you mean."

"Talents vary, lad. And don't forget that you yourself were able to add several pieces to the puzzle. Most impressively, it was you who blazed out into the night in pursuit of a desperate killer."

"Yeah, but who came blazing after me?"

Mr. O'Nelligan gave a little shrug. "Well, what was I to do? You had thrust yourself into harm's way. What manner of assis-tant would I be if I had held back?"

"A sane one?"

"Perhaps. Now, since you were in recovery over the last few days, I took the liberty of following up on some matters."

"Such as?"

"I checked in with young Detective Bells. He seems to be healing nicely from his wound and was actually grateful to have been included in Sunday night's denouement. His department will be contacting us soon to further plumb our knowledge of events. I also communicated with Loretta Mapes and strongly urged her to reach out to the Greers."

"For what purpose?" I asked.

"To perhaps aid them in the matter of their son. If Adelle Greer has indeed beheld her boy's spirit, I know of no better person than Loretta Mapes to consult with. Of all the person-ages we encountered in our investigation, Mrs. Mapes seemed to have the most authentic connection with the hereafter."

"Maybe." I remembered her statement about my father stopping by to check on me from time to time. "Maybe she does. Who knows?"

"In another matter, I've discovered that Felix Emmitt has voluntarily stepped down from the position of coroner."

"Will he be facing prosecution?"

"Perhaps, perhaps not. Ultimately, since Lloyd's plan never went through, it may be hard to assess legal wrongdoing. Lastly, I phoned Betty Gallagher in Delaware to say that her cousin's killer was in custody. That seemed to give her some solace, though the lass has a long road ahead in terms of forgiving herself. Oh, I'd almost forgotten. Here's something else." Mr. O'Nelligan extracted a folded newspaper from his coat pocket, opened it and read aloud. "Noted medium Dr. C. R. Kemple will be delivering a lecture next Saturday entitled 'How I Solved the Murder of Trexler Lloyd with the Assistance of Zexalla from the Death Dimension.'"

My jaw dropped, and something between a laugh and a curse spilled out. "You've got to be kidding me."

"Do you really put it past the man to do such a thing?"

"Not at all. Although I sure don't recall seeing Zexalla in the room when you solved the case."

My friend chuckled. "Nor I. But, after all, he does abide in another dimension."

"Maybe we should show up at Kemple's little talk and offer an alternate view of things."

"That would undoubtedly be amusing. To us, at least, if not to Dr. Kemple."

The phone rang. I picked up and found myself talking to Lewis Trowbridge.

"Ah, I've actually found you at your fort," the butler said.

"I'm at a phone booth just outside Thelmont, and I have with me a carful of ladies who would like to see you."

"That sounds intriguing."

"Is O'Nelligan with you, by chance?"

"He is."

"Splendid. Can you meet us somewhere on the street? Our stop must be a brief one, as we're rather pressed for time."

I suggested a meeting spot. Trowbridge said he'd see us there shortly and hung up. I repeated the conversation to my partner, and we headed down into the street. It was a cool, clear afternoon; wintery, but not oppressive. Within minutes, a certain familiar hearse pulled up. Trowbridge was at the wheel with Sassafras next to him. Behind them a backseat had been installed, and in it sat Doris and Constanza. The space in the far back was crammed to the top with luggage.

As the group emerged from the vehicle, Sassafras, not surprisingly, got in the first word. "Hey, Blarney! Hey, Lee! Guess what? We three gals are going to travel the world together. Can you believe it? What a helluva team we'll make. The three amigos!"

"*Amigas*," Constanza corrected. "Amigos are male."

"Well, males we don't need," Sassafras declared. "This trip is strictly for the dames. That is, unless we happen to run into some luscious conquistador. Then all bets are off."

"Sassafras, please!" Doris Chauncey rolled her eyes, then turned them toward Mr. O'Nelligan and me. "Constanza has generously invited us to fly back to Spain with her and take an extended trip through Europe."

"All on her dime," Sassafras added. "Swell, huh?"

I wondered if, in Sassafras's case, the invite had been offered or extracted. I didn't bother to ask. "Sure. Very swell."

Constanza took a step closer to us. "I must thank you gentlemen for bringing us the truth of my husband's death. And even my own truth, which I regret." She cast her eyes down, and I guessed she was thinking of her hardware honey. "I have no family back home. I have much money now, but I have no family. I do have friends, though." She gestured toward the two other women. "We will journey together."

Trowbridge cut in with a cough. "We really must be off, Mrs. Lloyd, if we're to make it to the airport on time."

"Bless you both." Constanza gave us a little nod, then climbed back into the car. Sassafras followed her.

Doris Chauncey paused to shake our hands. "I want to thank you as well. As hard as it's been to believe that Martin could do such horrid things, I think it's best to know the truth."

"Always," said Mr. O'Nelligan. "Always it is best to know." He gave her a dose of what I guessed was Yeats.

"Come away, O human child!
To the waters and the wild
With a fairy, hand in hand,
For the world's more full of weeping
Than you can understand.

He took her hand again for a moment. "You're a young lass, Miss Chauncey. Leave old darkness behind you, and go discover the better side of this world of ours."

"I will, Mr. O'Nelligan. I promise." Then Doris went to join her companions.

Trowbridge gave me a parting nod before turning to my colleague. "Well, it's been somewhat illuminating. I never put much stock in Irish deduction before."

"And now you do?" my friend asked.

"I don't know that I'd go that far," the butler said dryly. "However, you didn't give too despicable an account of yourself, I'll concede that."

"I believe I'll accept that as a compliment."

"If you're so inclined, O'Nelligan."

"Oh, I am, Trowbridge."

The Englishman and the Irishman exchanged moderate bows. I think I might have glimpsed a flicker of a smile on each of their lips. Trowbridge took his place back behind the wheel and started up the engine.

As the hearse began to pull away, Sassafras rolled down her window and bellowed, "Watch the newspapers, boys! We're sure to make a splash!" Then they were gone.

"Those three women should make interesting traveling companions," I noted.

"Indeed. Sometimes the most oddly matched individuals forge the best alliances." My comrade favored me with a smile.

"Well, that pretty much ties things up, doesn't it?"

"So it seems. We attended the Otherworld's Fair just over a month ago—on the night of Samhain, when the dead are supposed to be closest to our earthly realm. In a way, that was the beginning of everything. Fittingly, in the end, this case was truly all about spirits. After all, Rast killed to maintain his connection to the ghosts he believed inhabited that old house. As for you and me, hopefully we've done justice to the three spirits that have risen from this case."

"You mean Lloyd, Agnelli, and Katie Gallagher?"

"I do," Mr. O'Nelligan said. "Those three—a lauded, complicated genius; an aging detective who toiled in obscurity; and a poor young girl who never had a chance to make her mark in the world. We, who still live, can but hope they find peace. As Foster, the lawyer, put it, that's really no more than anyone deserves."

Responding to a sudden, brisk wind, I slipped my hands deep into my coat pockets. At once, my right hand found the Morgan silver dollar and closed around it instinctively. The coin seemed to generate its own warmth, giving me the sense that I was holding something almost alive, something enduring. Side by side, Mr. O'Nelligan and I began to walk back down the street, each content in his own silence.